He was not thinking, he had no will!

His body was animated by some external force of great energy.

His hands went out and they seemed to belong to someone else. He watched them impersonally.

Linda awoke instantly.

Her lids flew up and her eyes glared. And then her hands darted to her throat and gripped his and began to pull.

Her mouth was wide open now and her breath whistled as her cheeks changed color from red to gray-violet and her eyes filmed over . . .

The Murderer Is a Fox

Ellery Queen

BALLANTINE BOOKS • NEW YORK

SBN 345-24364-1-125

First Printing: February, 1975

Printed in the United States of America

BALLANTINE BOOKS
A Division of Random House, Inc.
201 East 50th Street, New York, N.Y. 10022
Simultaneously published by
Ballantine Books, Ltd., Toronto Canada

CONTENTS

PART ONE

PART TWO

PART THREE

PART FOUR

CAST OF CHARACTERS

PART ONE

PART ONE

1. The Fox Cubs

"WHAT TIME IS it now, Talbot?" Emily Fox asked her husband. As if she had never asked the question before.

"Now Emily," sighed Talbot Fox. "The Atlantic States doesn't pull in for a good ten minutes yet."

Linda sat squeezed between her foster-parents in the special touring car the Wrightsville Committee on Welcomes had provided for the occasion. The small bloodless oval of her face wore a formidable smile, like the daguerreotype of Daddy Talbot's maternal great-grandmother on the baby grand in the Fox parlor. But Linda did not feel formidable; she felt weak inside, as if she were waiting for an operation.

As perhaps in a way she was.

The sun—co-operative star!—tickled the limbs of the throng heaving in and about the squatty, venerable Wrightsville Station . . . Lin's whole plain little world, all packaged for this moment. Mother Emily tormenting her corsage of baby orchids, a gift from Andy Biroba-tyan of the Wrightsville Florist Shop, who had contributed all the floral decorations for the Official Reception Lunch which was to be held later in the Grand Ballroom of the Hollis Hotel, in the Square. Daddy Tal trying not to steal glances at his wristwatch. The slicked-up Select-men chattering politics, crops, and conversion. The American Legion Band milling around in their newly drycleaned uniforms, tossing the sun from their silver helmets like the prize bulls at the Slocum State Fair. One-toothed Gabby Warrum yelling from the doorway of the stationmaster's office at the swarm of yah-yahing

1

kids with dusty feet shoving one another about on the handtrucks. Mrs. Bradford, *née* Patricia Wright, Chairman of the Committee on Events, hurrying down the platform, flinging retorts right and left, on her way to confer with some official or other about a last-minute change in the line of march. Miss Dolores Aikin, Chief Librarian of the Carnegie Library and unofficial genealogist of Wrightsville's first families, standing on tiptoe on the edge of the platform, pen and foolscap in hand, anxiously scanning the country toward Wrightsville Junction, whence the hero's train should soon appear. Emmeline DuPré, who earned her livelihood by giving Dancing and Dramatic Lessons to the youth of the Wrightsville gentry, darting from group to group having a field day. Miss Gladys Hemmingworth, Society Editor of Frank Lloyd's *Record*, waggling her perpetual pencil decorously aloft to catch the eye of the Chairman of the Committee on Welcomes, Hermione Wright, wife of John F. Wright, whose great-great-great-great-something Jezreel had founded Wrightsville in 1702.

Old Soak Anderson tottered to the doorway of Phil's Diner next to the Station, waving two little American flags.

All for Davy.

Directly above Linda's head hung a long banner which stretched from the Station eaves across the tracks to the water tower.

WELCOME HOME CAPTAIN DAVY FOX!!!!
WRIGHTSVILLE IS PROUD OF YOU!

Are you?
How times changed.

Davy Fox hadn't always been a hero. Davy Fox hadn't always been "just" a Wrightsville boy, such as you could find on any street corner in Low Village, or in any big house on the Hill. They hadn't formed committees for Davy *then* . . . at least, not welcoming committees.

Something memorializing and fixative about the scene

around her turned Linda's thoughts backwards.

Davy Fox hadn't lived in the Talbot Fox house . . . then. Davy had lived in that house next door. It was only later—on that never-forgotten day when Mother Emily locked herself in her bedroom and Daddy Tal stumbled about the house with a hunted look and Linda wasn't allowed to leave the playroom—it was only later that Davy came to live with his aunt and uncle and the little girl they had taken from the Slocum Orphanage five years before.

That coming across two lawns, his hand in his uncle's, a small boy of ten in torn knickers marched from one house to another while Wrightsville stared in hostile silence from the unkempt sidewalk of the Hill—it had been a journey from the moon. The boy had been tight-mouthed to keep the tears from spilling out, afraid and suspicious—too obedient and too quiet and too all-inside-himself—until, inside his uncle's house, out of sight of those accusing eyes, he was broken down by his Aunt Emily's embrace and gave way to his fear. Davy used to say scornfully that he'd really wanted to stamp and kick and break things that day, but Aunt Emily had treacherously made him cry instead by putting her arms around him.

Gabby Warrum roared from the stationmaster's office: "She's on time!" A sizzzz! ran through the crowd, and then the American Legion Band burst into a nervous tootling.

It had been forbidden to talk about the thing that had happened. Nevertheless, Davy and Linda sometimes braved the tabu, whispering about it through the transom between their childhood bedrooms while Emily and Talbot Fox slumbered in the big room down the hall. But not too often. It was too huge, and it was too terrible—too big with big people's secrets—to be bandied about and become commonplace and so, in time, be forgotten. And if there were times when it might almost be forgotten, there was always the house next door—a deserted dinginess growing more silent by the year. Linda was scared to death of that aging reproach. It housed

great eyeless threats. And Davy would never go near it.
He avoided even looking at it.

*"Hi, Linda!" The Wrightsville High delegation was
struggling to form a hollow square at one end of the
platform. They were waving placards nailed to broom-
handles.* YOU MADE THEM REMEMBER KUNMING,
DAVY!!!—YOU SURE LAID A MESS OF EGGS, YOU
FLYING FOX!!!—WRIGHTSVILLE HIGH'S MOST-LIKELY-
TO-SUCCEED . . . AND HOW!!! *Linda smiled and waved
back.*

How Davy had loathed them, the jeering kids. Because *they* had known; the whole town knew. The kids
and the shopkeepers in High Village and the Country
Club crowd and the scrubskinned farmers who drove in
on Saturdays to load up—even the Hunks and Canucks
who worked in the Low Village mills. Especially the
shop hands of Bayard & Talbot Fox Company, Machinists' Tools, who merely jeered the more after "Bayard
&" one day vanished from the side of the factory, leaving a whitewashed gap, like a bandage over a fresh
wound. That was another part of his native Wrightsville
that Davy shunned.

He had hated the grownups even more than the kids,
because he could jump in on the kids with his fists or
otherwise intimidate them by playing the role Wrightsville had assigned to him—which was, simply, to be the
son of his father. There were whole years of licking kids,
and being licked. And now other kids were brandishing
placards and getting ready to give their alumnus the
rackety-rax with nine locomotives, usually reserved for
football victories over Slocum High.

"What time is it now, Talbot?" asked Emily Fox.

"Now Emily," said Talbot Fox irritably. "There's still
seven minutes."

*The crowd was staring along the twin dazzle of the
rails towards Wrightsville Junction, three miles up the
line, as if they would bend light and see beyond curves
and past culverts and woods.*

Wrightsville's 10,000-odd . . . Other times, other
scandals. That Polish family—with all the j's and z's—

they turned on the gas in their two-room warren in Low Village and they were all found dead, the whole family —father and mother and eight dirty children—and no one ever found out why. The Jim Haight case involving the noble Wrights—and today Patricia Wright Bradford was married to the man who had prosecuted her sister's husband for murder and only a few, like Emmy DuPré, ever recalled it. And Lola Wright's running off with that Major, and fat Billy Ketcham, the insurance man, being arrested when he crossed the state line with the youngest Graycee girl, "the bad one." The world of Wrightsville moved on, on and away from Davy Fox and the shadow under which he had grown to manhood. Linda smiled from the car, nodding at people she had known since she was four. They had forgotten. Or seemed to have.

"Five minutes, Emily," announced Talbot Fox nervously.

"I wish that darned old train would pull in," fretted his wife. "So we could get all this over with and take Davy off by ourselves and—I don't know. I've had a premonition."

"About Davy? Why, Emily," laughed Talbot. But he seemed uneasy.

"Premonition, Mother?" Linda frowned slightly. "What do you mean?"

"Oh, I don't know, Linny."

"But he's all right, isn't he? I mean—they said except for the exhaustion and exposure and . . . Mother, you know something about Davy you've kept from me!"

"No, dear, no. Really," said Emily Fox hurriedly.

"Emily, you talk too blamed much," growled her husband. "Premonitions! Didn't we all talk to Davy on the phone when they set him down in Florida?"

Linda was appeased. But she couldn't help wondering why Daddy Talbot's voice sounded so funny.

"Imagine," sighed Emily. "All this for Davy."

"And for his little wife! Eh, sweetheart?" Talbot Fox patted Linda's hand.

"Linda, your nose," said Emily, smiling down at

snubnosed Mrs. Donald Mackenzie (Wrightsville Personal Finance Corp.). "It's shiny."

His wife, thought Linda as she fumbled for her compact. That day, on his last furlough before . . . They had gone to Pine Grove on a picnic, the nephew of Talbot and Emily Fox and their adopted daughter. And somehow, after the mayonnaise spilled on his tunic, and she was wiping it off his wings, it happened. She had always known it would happen, although not quite so absurdly. Their tie had always been stronger than mere blood—it was the tie of waifs, woven out of secrets, a mysterious dear bond. She was in his arms, and Davy was kissing her with a passion that frightened her, it told so much. He was asking her, without a word—as if he were afraid to use words. Words came only later, as they lay side by side in the grass of the Grove clasping hands and dreaming up into the pines. And even then they were sober words.

"What about Uncle Tal and Aunt Emily?" Davy had asked. "They won't go for this, Linny."

"Won't—Why, Davy, they *love* you, darling!"

"Oh, sure. But you're their only child, and—you know what I am."

"You're my Davy." Then Linda realized what he had meant and sat up crossly. "See here, Davy Fox. In the first place, I'm a Fox by adoption. You're one by blood—"

"Blood," said Davy with a crooked little smile. "You said it, honey chile."

"In the second place, what happened when you were a little boy—why, Davy, anyone would think *you* were to blame eleven years ago! A child shouldn't be made to suffer for what his parents do. Look at me. I don't even know who my real father and mother are. If they're alive, or *anything.*"

"That's different. That's negative. My parents' past is what you might call on the positive side."

Linda had grown angry—because she was scared. "Davy Fox, if you're going to start off our life together by feeling sorry for yourself and letting . . . it . . .

stand in our way, you can darned well do it all by your lonesome!"

"Now Linda—" Davy had said miserably, the way Talbot said "Now Emily—"

"Davy, here's what we're going to do. We're going to tell Mother and Daddy right now. If they approve— fine; it will make everything a lot easier and all of us happier. But if they get sticky about it—"

"You'd marry me anyway?"

It was the first time Davy had used the word.

Linda had kissed his hand to hide the fear in her eyes. And after a long time she pushed away from him and sat up, gasping. "Davy. Dearest. Let's go tell them. There's not . . . very much time, is there?"

She had always been afraid. She was afraid that day, and she was afraid now—with the long bright banner over her head and all of Wrightsville in their Sunday best at the Station to welcome Davy home.

"Tomorrow?" said Talbot Fox slowly. *"Tomorrow,* did you say?"

"We'd do it today, Daddy," said Linda, "only I suppose it takes a little time to get a license and make arrangements with Dr. Doolittle at the First Methodist and all—"

"Married," repeated Emily Fox. She glanced apprehensively at her husband, tall and gray, standing near the piano a little turned away from them. Linda knew what her vaguely smiling, chubby foster-mother was thinking. Emily was thinking of how strong Talbot always looked, and how weak he could be.

"You're against it, Uncle," said Davy belligerently.

"Well, Davy, it's sort of complicated, isn't it?"

"Linny, I told you—"

"Now Davy, wait. Don't be mad." Talbot seemed to be having difficulty choosing his words. "Davy . . . you're both so young. Twenty-one and twenty. That's pretty young, son."

"You and Mother were even younger," retorted Linda.

"That's right, Talbot," said Emily Fox anxiously. "We were."

"Besides, times have changed," Linda went on. "We're living kind of quickly these days, aren't we? Davy isn't too young to be a fighter pilot, and I don't think, Daddy, you'd call a girl of twenty a child exactly."

"Linda," Davy said. And something in his voice made Linda stop, chilled. "Uncle, that's just an excuse, and you know it. Why don't you come out with what you're really thinking?"

"What do you mean, young man?" growled Talbot Fox.

"Let's face it, Uncle Tal," said Davy. "You know what I mean."

"All right." Talbot set his handsome jaw. "You won't be able to let the past alone, Davy."

"I knew it!" shouted Davy.

Linda jabbed him in the ribs, hard.

But Davy rushed on: "You're scared of the talk—the scandal!"

"If I'd been scared of the scandal, Davy, do you suppose I'd have taken you into my home eleven years ago —brought you up as if you were my own son?"

"That's not so very fair to your uncle or me, Davy, now is it?" Emily added in a trembly voice.

Davy looked ashamed. "I'm sorry, Aunt Emily, but—"

"It's not only Linda I'm thinking of, Davy," Talbot went on quietly enough. "It's you, too. I've studied you, boy. You were always a sensitive kid, and what happened at that time naturally left its mark. A bad one."

Linda saw her foster-mother's eyes widen, looking at the tall man by the piano as if, after so many years of marriage, she could still be surprised by him.

"You won't be able to let it alone, Davy. You never have. Another boy might have forgotten it, or licked it. But you've let it get under your skin. And I'm afraid it would crop out again if you and Linny got married. That's the only reason I'm hesitating, Davy—absolutely the only reason."

As if it weren't enough of a reason.

Davy stuck his stubborn chin 'way out. "If you're scared of what the old cackleberries in Wrightsville'll say, Lin and I will go away after the War. We'll set the crate down somewhere else. They can't touch us outside this town!"

"I know you, Davy. You wouldn't find it easier to lick in Chicago or New York or, for that matter, the Fiji Islands. I wish to God you would."

Time to get in on this, Linda had thought.

"Daddy," she said calmly, "you're overlooking one thing." But oh, she had wanted to shut her eyes to the past!

"What, sweetheart?"

"In three days leaves."

"In three days Davy leaves?" Emily said faintly.

"Yes," said Davy with a bitter kind of satisfaction. "And maybe I'll never get back."

"Davy," his aunt moaned. "Don't *say* awful things like that!"

"Wait a minute," Talbot said. "Suppose Davy's right. Suppose he *doesn't* come back, Linny?"

Linda hated the big gray man in that moment. It was a mean thing to have said. Even meaner, because it was so true.

"And if he doesn't, sweetheart, wouldn't it be fairer to you if—"

"Fairer my eye!" Linda had burst out. "We may as well tell you just how we feel. We want Mother's and your consent. But if you won't give it, Davy and I are going to have Dr. Doolittle marry us tomorrow, anyway." Her chin wobbled. "You can't cheat us out of two whole days. Maybe the only two days we'll ever . . ."

She put her arms suddenly around Davy.

"That's it, Uncle," Davy grinned over her head.

"Well," Talbot Fox grinned back. "It doesn't look as if we have much to say about it. Mother, what do you think?"

Emily flushed, as she usually did when she became the star of a moment. But her voice was quite steady. "Davy dearest, I'd rather it didn't happen. I agree with your uncle. Somehow—somewhere—that . . . thing is going to come back, interfere with your happiness. That's selfish of us. We don't want to see Linda's life spoiled—or yours, Davy—before we . . ." But then Emily had shaken her head, helplessly. "It's all mixed up, and I love you both so much. Children, if you really believe your happiness lies in marrying, God bless you."

"I wonder how he *looks*," said Emily Fox with a frown.

On the other side of Linda, Talbot Fox stirred. "Well, now, Emily," he mumbled, "it's been a whole year and the boy's gone through a lot of flying over there in China. Don't expect miracles."

Something in her foster-father's voice jerked Linda out of her reverie. She began to ask a question—

"Now Linny," said Talbot almost in a shout, "don't *you* start in on me, too, darn it all!"

Linda went white. And Emily Fox stared at her husband with a terrible anxiety.

"But you've been assuring us how fine Davy is." Linda sounded miles away to herself.

"I guess I'm no great shakes as an actor," muttered Talbot. "I should have told you and Mother weeks ago, sweetheart. Maybe stopped this Reception—"

"Talbot Fox," said his wife in a deadly tone, "what are you trying to say?"

"I spoke to some Army doctor at the St. Petersburg Convalescent Center over the phone," said Talbot miserably, "when we first got word Davy'd been flown there from the hospital in India. It seems he's not . . . well . . . just *exactly* the same as when he went away. I mean—"

Linda said stiffly: "He's—not—whole."

"No, no, no!" cried her foster-father. "He's all in one piece! Of all the fool notions . . . See here. Davy's cracked a bit. His nerves, the doctor said—they're sort of shot. Oh, it's nothing serious. Nothing that a few months of his home town and wife and aunty's cooking won't fix up fine!" Talbot Fox assured the two women with a great heartiness.

He took off his executive-type glasses and, a little red, wiped one lens vigorously.

As from a great distance, Linda heard a tiny thunder of voices. And the imperious whistle of the Atlantic State Express.

It seemed to her that this was all dream—that the reality lay in a sunken-gabled, disheveled house, with a little boy in torn knickers emerging through the doorway of a mystery . . . a confused little boy who would burst into tears as soon as he reached the warmth of loving arms.

2. The Flying Fox

You GET ON his tail and let him have it. You get on his tail and let him have it. You get on his—

"Mighty smart country, huh, Captain?"

Davy Fox turned from his examination of the familiar flowing countryside with a smile. His neighbor in the club car, a stout man in a wrinkled seersucker suit, was beaming at him.

"Uh-huh," said Davy.

He turned back to the window. You get on his tail—

"Noticed you admirin' on it," said the stout man. "Peaceful, huh? I saw that smile on your face."

Fine. Now dry up.

"China-Burma-India theater, huh? I know that patch. Fourteenth Air Force, or 10th? How many Nips did you bag? You're sportin' a lot of ribbon, son! Say, I bet you'll have some real thrills to tell your folks about . . ."

Such as being caught on the ground with Zeros twisting and tumbling all over the sky and falling flat on your face in the stinky guck of a Chinese rice field, or pulling Myers out of his cockpit with his stomach lying on his knees after he brought his old P-40 down only God knew how. Such as the mysterious disappearance of dead Jap pilots when you shot them down among the hungry yellow folk near Kunming. Such as the flies that bit you and the stench that rose from everything and the brassy Chinese sun that cooked you and the shivering curs that fled from empty Chinese soup pots. Such as having your coffee grinder conk in the middle of a swarm of bandits and belly-landing in scrub on the knife-edged hills—seeing Lew Binks's coffin drop like lead aflame, and Binks hitting the silk, trustful guy, and then the hornet Japs zipping around him with their spiteful tracers hemstitching the sky. Such as lugging Binks on your back a hundred and sixty-seven miles through Jap-held country with a Thompson submachine gun under the other arm and the two cartridge drums hooked to your belt . . . and Binks's legs dangling, all chewed up. Such as being holed up in the gray rocks over Binks's gray face, listening to him cough his life up and wondering which of them would be luckier when the little Sons of Heaven closed in . . . Yes, there were a lot of thrills, friend.

"How long you been away, Captain?"

"Year. I don't know."

"Haven't seen your family all that time? Boy, I can imagine how you feel! Married?"

"Yes." Yes.

"Say, that's all right. You on your way home and the little gal waitin' for you. Son, I envy you."

Listen, you—

She shouldn't have. I'm nothing to wait for. She'll naturally expect the same moony kid not dry behind the ears, nuzzling for pap. And she's getting back the big hero, the Flying Fox, the killer they gave medals to.

I'll have to tell her, Davy thought dully as the stout

man gabbled on. She's got to know what she's getting back.

He kept smiling out the window.

It was bad enough before I went away. How can I make her understand that flying a P-38 over Southern China didn't make it better, but worse? You shot, and you killed, and it didn't get anything out of your system. It put more in.

"Home, sweet home. That's the stuff, huh, Captain?"

Maybe for a lot of them. The uncomplicated guys. The ones that love their wives or girls and don't also have a cancer eating away at them inside.

"Now that we're reconvertin' for the peace—"

That time he had set his riddled crate down on the brown-gray Kunming field after getting one Zero and another probable . . . He had walked stiff-legged, with the taste of death still on his tongue, into the Alert Shack to find six long-overdue letters from home. Out of one envelope, postmarked Wrightsville, had tumbled some newspaper clippings. Just clippings, without a scribbled word to indicate their sender. He had recognized the source: the *Wrightsville Record*. One clipping was from the Gossip Column—he knew that typographic setup:—

Seen at the Chamber of Commerce Red Cross Rally: Mr. and Mrs. Donald Mackenzie, Mr. and Mrs. Hallan Luck, Mr. and Mrs. John F. Wright, Senator and Mrs. Carter Bradford, Dr. Milo Willoughby, Judge and Mrs. Eli Martin, Mrs. Davy Fox on the arm of Mr. Alvin Cain, Miss Nancy Logan escorted by Technical Sergeant Morton F. Danzig . . .

The words "on the arm of" had been heavily underscored in red crayon.

Hands shaking, Davy had searched through the other clippings: "What young war bride well known in Hill society was seen at The Hot Spot on Route 16 Saturday night with what forty-one-year-old pharmacist?"—"Second prize at the War Bond Dance at Danceland in the Grove: Linda Fox and Alvin Cain, for the Rumba." There were two or three others.

The itchy shakes had come over Davy's hands then for fair, so that the Operations Officer glanced at him sharply and Davy had had to turn away. After all Linny had promised! And that smug, oily, wisecracking—Cain! He'd always chased Lin, from the time she was a soph at Wrightsville High. Why, that night at graduation . . . Now that I'm in China being a bloody hero, forty-one-year-old Pharmacist Cain makes hay. And Linda lets him. Sure. How does she know? Maybe I'll never come back . . .

Seething, Davy had picked another letter open. From Linda. *Dearest . . . miss you so . . . we've had no word . . . is there malaria there? . . . Alvin Cain . . .* The name had jarred Davy's vision into focus again.

The funniest thing, darling. You remember Alvin Cain? How I used to detest him? Well, Alvin's a changed man—really he is, dear—you wouldn't know him. I bumped into him at a Red Cross dingbat some time ago and he was so nice, so different from the old Alvin that I didn't think there'd be any harm letting him take me to a movie in a crowd that included Patty and Cart Bradford, Carmel Pettigrew and some Navy boy—Carmel's latest!—etcetera. I didn't think you'd mind, lover. After all, husband mine, I haven't been *out* since you "deserted" me!!!!

So we all went—it was the following Saturday night—and afterward we dropped into the Hot Spot for some beer and we had to split up at separate tables and all Alvin and I talked about was you, Davy dear—Alvin's very proud of you, really he is—and I've seen him a couple of times since. Oh, yes, Mother and Daddy and I went to a War Bond Dance at Pine Grove (admission by War Bond only) and of course Alvin was there—everybody was—and he came up to Mother and asked if she'd object if I was his partner in one of the dance contests, and poor Mother

looked worried—you know what a prude *she* is—
but Daddy ahemmed and charrrrrumphed and said he
couldn't see any harm in it and . . . well, Davy, the
stupid thing is—"they've" started talking and I've
had to cut it out. I suppose it *was* unwise—you know
Wrightsville!!!!

There's been a dirty crack or two in the gossip column of the *Record,* and of course town-crier Emmy
DuPré has been waggling *her* sinewy tongue. . . . I
feel like buying ad space in the *Record* and announcing: "Dear Wrightsville: It ain't true." Ever hear
anything so *inane?* Alvin Cain, of all people on this
earth. I'm sure the poor fashion-plate is kuh-rushed.
He's phoned me a few times—of course I haven't
hurt his feelings—for all his mannerisms he's rather
lonely, I think, and it's pathetic he wants to be friends
with us so badly—but naturally I'm putting him off.
Oh, my own Davy, you don't know how my heart
stops every time the phone rings or a wire comes or
something—oh darling darling darling I love you.
Finish the War quick and come back to your own
Wife LINDA.

And I love you, Linny. I love you, but you don't know
me any more. What's happened to my mind. I love you,
and I was a skunk to doubt you, but it's no good, it's no
good. . . .

The blind rage had come over him in a resurgent tide,
and he had scanned the envelope and bits of newspaper
again and again, vainly, for a clue. In the end he decided the sender had been Emmeline Dupré—the whole
thing reeked of the old bat's technique!—and his anger
had drained away, leaving his hands . . . as
always . . . itching and shaking.

"Captain Fox."

The conductor.

"We've just passed Wrightsville Junction, Captain.
You've got about two minutes."

"Oh! Thanks."

Davy got out of his chair to reach for a bag.

The stout man's jaw had dropped. "Say! You the Flyin' Fox I been readin' about? The Wrightsville hero that knocked all those Japs out of the sky and killed that raft of 'em on the ground with a tommy gun when they holed you and Binks up, before the Chink army got to you? They're givin' you the Congressional Medal of Honor, I hear. Well, well—" The stout man looked worried suddenly. "What's the trouble, Captain? Don't you feel good? Your hands are shakin'. Here, lemme help you with those bags. No, no, it's no trouble. Mighty proud to do it—"

Davy braced himself against the rocketing of the train and looked down at his hands. They *were*. Shaking. Again. Accompanied by that itching feeling. Like a million irregularly dancing needles. Or as if the fizz in club soda were shooting through them and erupting through the skin. "It's all in your mind, Captain Fox," the Army doctor had said. "A nervous reaction to what you went through on that walking tour of yours through the Jap army." And Davy's Flight Surgeon at Kunming had said the same thing. But he'd never told the Flight Surgeon, or that doctor in Karachi, or any of the other doctors, that the itchy shakes appeared chiefly when his thoughts flashed back to the Wrightsville of a dozen years before . . . and the thing that had happened there to a small boy in torn knickers.

The stout man was already wrestling with the bags.

Aloud, Davy said: "Roger," never losing the sweet surface smile that had disturbed the Army doctors so.

As the Atlantic Stater edged into Wrightsville Station to let him off, Davy saw without surprise or even interest a wild jam of laughing people waving flags, a band with an army of glittery instruments being puffed on by red-faced men, cars and banners and placards and prancing kids, everybody in his Sunday best even though Davy was pretty sure it was a week-day, and he wondered if he hadn't mistaken the date; could it be Fourth of July? They certainly were making a lot of noise.

Then the train stopped and he glimpsed the mammoth banner across the tracks with his name on it.

The next moment he saw Linda.

"Linny, Linny—"

"Don't talk, lover. Just let me hold you close."

Miss Aikin, librarian and genealogist, leaned over the car door, her purple hat a little askew, and screamed: "Captain! Captain Fox! Sign here, please? Please, Captain?"

She was holding out a sheet of heavy paper, and a trembling fountain pen.

"It's Miss Aikin, dear," said Emily Fox, nibbling her handkerchief.

"Your collection, Miss Aikin?" boomed Talbot Fox. "Now you're made in this man's town for fair, Davy. Go ahead—it won't bite you. Sign it."

"What?" There was so much noise Davy was confused; and then he couldn't see well for some reason.

"Miss Aikin wants your autograph for her collection of Famous Wrightsvillians, darling," explained Linda in his ear. "You know—the one she's been collecting for years?"

"Please, Captain?" screamed Miss Aikin again.

"But gosh, I'm not—"

"But you *must!*"

"Please, dear," said Linda.

Davy took the pen from Miss Aikin's bony hand. Nothing seemed real. He wrote, very carefully: "Davy Fox, Captain U.S.A.A.F."

The cavalcade rolled in chesty triumph past the crackerbarrel houses of Low Village, all festooned with crepe paper and hung with flags. People were leaning out of windows throwing confetti. The Legion band swung smartly before the hero's car, blowing hard. Davy stood in the open car, smiling and waving.

Linda's fingers clutched his left leg, digging into the wasted muscle. The pain was acute, and he felt grateful.

Dead Myers was grinning up at him from the red dust of the Kunming field and jeering: *You hot pilot, you. Medals and celebrations yet.*

Blow a kiss to my mother, said Binks's bitter gray lips from the Karachi hospital bed. *She lives in Canton, Ohio, you bloody hero.*

Okay, Binks, okay. For God's sake.

Corner of Slocum and Washington. Turn . . .

Logan's Market. "FINE DRESSED MEATS. FRESH-KILLED POULTRY." There was blood on Mr. Logan's butcher apron; he was standing spraddle-legged in his doorway, waving.

Old Bloody Logan. Just the same. Not a thing changed.

It's impossible.

You bloody hero.

Okay, Binks. Take it easy.

It'll soon be over, and they'll forget me. I hope. I hope!

"I can't, Lin. I just can't!" Davy writhed in her arms on the bed in the suite at the Hollis Hotel which the Committee on Welcomes had reserved for Captain and Mrs. Davy Fox's use before the Official Luncheon.

"You've got to, dearest," crooned Linda.

"But—a luncheon! Speeches!"

"The Governor will be there, Davy."

"I can't make a speech!"

"Say just as little as you feel like saying, Davy dearest."

"If I said what's on my mind, they'd—they'd put me in jail! Linny, Binks didn't want to be saved! Binks didn't want me to lug him across half of Southern China! He wanted to die where the Japs shot him down—"

"Davy—"

"He'd done his job and he knew he was finished and he didn't want to be 'saved' to come home, Linny! Binks was scared to death of what the War had made him learn about himself. I guess we . . . all are—"

"Yes, Davy. Now don't talk—"

"Binks was sore at me for saving him. We were in beds next to each other after they flew us from Kunming to the hospital in Karachi. He reared up in bed, Linny, just before he died, and he called me . . . names. He was right! A man's got a right to die when he's all chewed up and no use any more and he's scared of coming back—"

She kissed him as he rushed on, black with the spurt of words, kissed him over and over. She hardly knew what he was saying.

"Didn't you hear me, Linny? I'm scared!"

"There's nothing to be scared of, Davy, any more."

"Any more! Why, it's just beginning! Linny, don't you understand? I'm not the same guy you married. I've got red hands. I know what it is to kill. I . . ." But then he stopped, so abruptly Linda was shaken out of herself.

"Yes Davy?"

"Oh, Linny, I've missed you like hell."

"I've missed you, Davy."

But that wasn't what he had started to say. Fearfully, Linda held him away from her, examining him. But he was smiling now, a vague sort of smile, a sweet smile. She had noticed that same smile on his lips as he had stood on the bottom step of the train, shaking the clamoring hands.

She pulled him to her breast and after a while, suddenly, he fell asleep.

Linda held him lightly, not daring to move.

Oh, Davy, Davy, there's hardly anything left of you. You're just a sack of bones. Your skin is all dried out and brown and crackly like that horrible old leather chair Daddy put out to pasture on the back porch. And your eyes, that used to flash so deep-water blue, they're riddled with sick little reddish streaks. They've fallen into your head like an old man's.

And your hair. That glossy black tangle of yesterday. All spoiled with gray.

He's twenty-two, thought Linda. Twenty-two!

It can't be just what he's been through. It's something else. It's something . . . old.

But then Linda shut her mind, instantly.

3. The Sick Fox

LINDA'S ORIGINAL PLAN had called for setting up housekeeping in one of the newer sections of Wrightsville, a plan formed as soon as she learned that Davy was probably through with the War. There would be a spick-and-span little New England cottage surrounded by flower beds and set among flowering bushes, cherry and apple trees, a rose arbor and a grape arbor, an herb and vegetable garden. In Linda's mind she had furnished the little house from top to bottom, even to the nursery. The nursery had been a particular trial. There were so many things you couldn't get! There had been a queer, sweet satisfaction in being resentful over the things you couldn't get for the nursery in the house that didn't even exist, and a mysterious baby that was very, very far away. A baby that might never be, for all Linda had known.

But this was all before Davy came home . . . before Linda discovered for certain that in a few months Captain Davy Fox was to be honorably discharged from the United States Army Air Forces as a "neuro-psychiatric casualty."

If the destruction of her imaginary house left her empty and sick inside, Linda gave no sign of it.

"Of course that was a stupid idea," Linda brightly told Emily the very night of the day Davy returned. "We've got to give Davy a chance to get used to things again. To . . . to get entirely well first."

"Yes, dear, of course," said Emily, frowning the least bit. "I'll talk to your father tonight."

The next morning, at breakfast, Emily announced cheerfully: "Well, children, it's all arranged. Talbot and I decided last night. Didn't we, Talbot?"

"What's all arranged?" Davy asked slowly.

"You and Linda are going to have a real good time first, Davy. I mean, you're not to worry about a blessed thing. Is he, Talbot?"

Talbot beamed. "I should say not. We'd no idea you'd be home so soon, Davy, or you'd have found things all ready for you. Linny, you and this fine young hero of yours are to have the entire top floor to yourselves. Effective immediately. Who seconds the motion?"

"Oh, Daddy," cried Linda. "Davy, did you hear that? Won't that be grand?"

"Sure. Swell," mumbled Davy.

"If you want to set up housekeeping, Linny," Talbot went on, "why, I'll see if I can't rustle some kitchen fixtures and things out of Clint Fosdick. That north spare room upstairs could easily be converted into a kitchen—"

"No, Talbot," said Emily firmly. "I *won't* have Linda slaving over a hot stove and fussing with meals right off. They're going to pretend they're at a hotel or something, that's what. A real honeymoon! For just as long as you want it that way, children. Isn't that so, Talbot?"

"Sure as shootin'," said Talbot heartily. "Uh . . . Davy. Given any thought to what you're going to do?"

"Do?" Davy looked up from his plate.

"I mean, do you want to finish your engineering course, or will you go right into the plant with me?"

"Oh." Davy toyed with his hotcakes, thinking. Finally, he said: "If you don't mind, Uncle Tal—neither."

"Daddy, what's the matter with you?" Linda put in swiftly. "Of course Davy doesn't know yet what he wants to do! There's loads of time for that decision—"

"I should say," sniffed Emily, glaring at her husband.

"Oh, sure, sure," said Talbot Fox, bewildered but snatching his cue. "I didn't mean right off, Davy. I mean when you're good and ready. Naturally."

"Thanks, Uncle Tal." Davy looked up again. "But I can't just live off you, like a bum."

"Davy Fox, what a *horrible* thing to say!" cried his aunt.

"Now Emily," said Talbot, on surer ground. "Of course Davy feels that way. But you've forgotten, son. You passed your minority while you were in training. That trust fund I've been administering for you—your father's fund—it's yours now, Davy."

Davy's fork dropped and made an unpleasant little clatter.

"Oh, yes," he said in a choked voice. "It is, isn't it?" And he sat dejectedly. Then he said: "Linny—what do *you* think?" His sunken eyes begged.

"Whatever you say, darling. Whatever you want."

"Well, I don't feel much like . . . anything just yet, Lin. If we stayed here we could pay Uncle Tal and Aunt Emily rent out of my fund—"

"Rent!" Emily began to cry.

"Now Emily," glared her husband. "Turning on the waterworks just because Davy's a man and has a man's gumption! I understand, Davy. You work it out your own way. I'll arrange to have the fund turned right over to you—"

Davy shrank. "You keep taking care of it for me, Uncle. I don't know anything about money."

"A fine business partner *you're* going to make," growled Talbot Fox; and that made Davy grin, so Linda and Emily and Talbot laughed and laughed, and they finished their breakfast in a kind of intoxicated gaiety.

And Linda's dream-house became four rooms on the top floor of the huge old house she had lived in ever since that dusty ride in Daddy Tal's old Dodge station-wagon from the Slocum Orphanage, when she was four, in Mother Emily's arms.

Davy was a sick boy. No doubt of that. What made it so hard for Linda and her foster-parents was that the sickness wasn't something old Dr. Willoughby could write a prescription for, or see in X-ray pictures, or send in a sealed bottle to the Wrightsville General for laboratory analysis. In fact, under the softly pressing attentions of Linda and a ceaseless, inexorable procession of "things Davy liked" from his aunt's kitchen, Davy began to look very well indeed.

No, whatever ailed Davy was not physical.

Nor was it mental, as Wrightsville rated such things. A "mental case" was Estrellita Aikin, for instance—the Carnegie chief librarian's elderly spinster sister, who one day in her late forties was found dancing in a luncheon cloth among the tombstones in Twin Hill Cemetery and who wound up in the "dilapidated" ward at Slocum State Hospital. But Davy was perfectly lucid. If anything, he was too lucid. He seemed since his return to see things with an apocalyptic clarity, as if his year in China had been a sojourn in the Messianic kingdom; he had developed the antisocial faculty of stripping every subject down to its bare bones. It was difficult to engage him in small talk, or to discuss the large and simple verities of the *Record* editorial page. Either Davy sat in that sweet-smiling silence and refused to be enticed, or unaccountably he lost his temper and lashed out at the bewildered family.

It was maddening. One day he would be interested, energetic, co-operative, even cheerful. But the next would find him sunk in deepest melancholy, out of which it was impossible for even Linda to draw him back. At such times he exhibited a chilling preference for being alone. He would wander all day in the woods behind the Fox property, hands plunged in his pockets, indifferent to the weather; or Linda might find him sprawled in the tall crab-grass near the lake at Pine Grove, asleep under the sun. She would watch him from behind a tree, like a spy; and when he stirred and woke she would follow his almost imperceptibly unsteady progress through the cool Grove with eyes full of tears. Then she would blot them and powder her nose and hurry off at a tangent to "run across" him from a different direction.

"What have you been doing, darling?"

"Nothing."

"You've got grass stains on your pants."

"Oh. Yeah. I pounded my ear a while near the lake."

"No wonder," Linda would laugh. "You slept hardly a wink last night."

"Why . . . how did you know that? You were in dreamland."

"Women in love with their husbands, Davy Fox, know a—a whole lot."

Davy would give her a queer look, and then they would walk home arm in arm, in silence.

Linda had long since decided not to question him. But once, when they were toiling up the Hill on their way back from the Grove, in the customary silence, a tide gushed up into her throat and to her horror she heard herself cry:—

"Davy, for God's sake, what's wrong?"

She felt him stiffen; and she could have wept, she was so angry with herself.

"Wrong?" Davy's lips shaped that sweet smile she had come to fear and hate so.

Something drove her. She couldn't keep it back any longer.

"What is it? *Davy, don't you love me now?*"

She couldn't help it. It had to come out. She had to know whether it was that . . . or something else.

"Love you, Linny? Hell, yes. I guess I always will."

"Oh, Davy!"

"I don't know why you put up with me, Lin. I'm no good to you. I tried to tell you the day I got home—I'm not the same as when I left. Or maybe I'm the same, only more so. What's the use? I only worry the life out of you."

"Now Davy," said Linda desperately. "Davy, wait for me! Davy, you mustn't say such things. You mustn't *think* them. Dearest, why not confide in me? What's a wife for? I can help you, Davy! What is it?"

"Nothing. My nerves. My nerves are shot."

"Yes, but . . . isn't there something else, Davy? Don't try to keep it from me. Tell me about it, dear.

Maybe it's . . . just in your mind. Maybe if you shared your thoughts with me . . . everything would be all right."

Davy walked on in silence. For a moment Linda thought he hadn't been listening. But then he mumbled: "I'll be all right, Linny."

That was all she could get out of him, and she did not bring the subject up again. They slipped back into the deepening rut . . . her tracking him to some lonely spot, their "casual" encounters, their strolls home in the bursting silence, the strain and the heartbreak in their rooms afterward. On these walks Linda might take his hand and swing it, if he were not too remote. He would be visibly grateful, and Linda's step might lighten.

On such crumbs Linda Fox subsisted for three months.

One night, in desperation, Linda suggested the movies.

"Let's all go," she said. "Davy, wouldn't you enjoy a movie for a change?"

"You want to go, don't you, Linny?" He was listless.

"Oh, no," said Linda quickly. "Not if you don't, dear."

"What's playing?"

"A revival of *Suspicion,* with Cary Grant and—"

"No!" Davy shouted it. They all stared at him, a little frightened. Then he flushed and mumbled: "I mean, I don't think I could sit still that long. Linny, you go with Aunt Emily and Uncle Tal."

"Leave you here alone? I will not," said Linda, blinking. "But Mother and Dad, you haven't been out of the house at night for months. Go ahead."

"Would you like to, Talbot?" Emily asked her husband rather plaintively. It was true; Davy's return, his inexplicable behavior, had tied them all down.

"Well, I bumped into Louie Cahan in the Square this noon," said Talbot sheepishly, "and Louie tells me he booked a swell Disney cartoon starting today . . ."

In the end, Emily and Talbot went to the Bijou.

"Davy," said Linda quietly when they were alone, "why didn't you want to see *Suspicion?*"

"I saw it. In China, or India, or some place—I forget now."

"That's not the reason, Davy."

"It is so the reason!"

"All right, Davy, all right."

They sat in the parlor without conversation, Linda mending some of Davy's socks, Davy flipping the pages of an old copy of *Life.* He flipped too quickly.

Linda wondered as she sat there wielding her needle and biting off snips of thread how long she could hold up under the pressures of their compressed and lidded relationship. Something would happen; something would give. And then . . . But Linda tried not to think of what might happen then. For weeks her intensest efforts had been to keep from thinking.

The front-door bell rang.

Davy jumped, the magazine falling from his lap.

"Goodness, Davy," laughed Linda. "You're as nervous as old man Hunker's Bessie."

"Who is it, who is it?" muttered Davy.

"How should I know? Maybe it's Daddy back—he may have forgotten his wallet or something. Answer the door, Davy."

"It's some snoop. I don't want to see anybody, Lin!"

"Now that's childish," said Linda calmly. "Seeing and talking to people again will do you good. We've been hermits ever since you got back. You answer that door, Davy."

Davy nodded, his feet dragging.

Linda stopped sewing to listen. Perhaps it was Patty Bradford and Cart. That would be nice. Patty had phoned several times, and Linda had put her off each time. She must think it was very queer. Maybe she'd dragged Cart out to see for herself what trouble Linda was in. That would be like Pat . . . Very queer. Yes. Yes!

Linda bent over her sewing again, fighting tears.

Then she heard voices from the hall, and when Davy appeared between the portiéres she was smiling.

Davy was smiling, too. Linda glanced quickly beyond him.

It was Emmeline DuPré and Miss Aikin.

"Why, how nice!" Linda exclaimed, jumping up. Trouble. Where Emmeline DuPré slithered, there was blood and mess.

"Yes, isn't it?" smiled Davy. "Real neighborly, Lin. Sit down, Miss DuPré. Right here, in this nice comfortable armchair." He paid no attention to Miss Aikin, who looked a little scared.

"How fit you're looking, Captain. Your aunt's cooking, I'm sure," said Emmeline DuPré. Her bright little eyes swept over Linda's trim figure. "And you, Linda. Aren't you putting on weight? Around the middle?"

"If you mean," retorted Linda, "am I going to have a baby, Miss DuPré, the answer is—not yet. Sorry!"

The ladies tittered. Red spots had appeared in Linda's cheeks. She bit her lip; she must control her temper. Keep cool, Linda; she hasn't fired her big gun yet.

"Miss Aikin and I happened to be passing—" began Miss DuPré.

Miss Aikin nodded nervously.

"Oh, don't apologize. I'm glad you dropped in, Miss DuPré," said Davy to the angular woman with the bright, quick eyes. "You don't happen to have some odd newspaper clippings around you, do you?"

"Newspaper clippings?" Miss DuPré paused. "Now, whatever do you mean, Captain?"

Davy said brutally: "I never thanked you for that batch you mailed to me in Kunming, China."

The woman's dry gray skin did not change color. Only her eyes betrayed her—a snaky flicker, and then a curtain of secretive lid.

"I can't imagine what you mean, Davy Fox. *I* mailed you newspaper clippings?"

"Oh, nuts," said Davy. His interest had flickered out. He said to the librarian: "Would you excuse me, Miss Aikin? I was reading an important article," and he trudged over to the other side of the room, picked up the magazine, and sat over it round-shoulderedly.

Miss DuPré glanced at Miss Aikin. Her glance said: You see? I told you he's acting queer.

"Davy," said Linda. He tossed a smile at her, but he remained where he was. Linda turned to the two ladies. "I'm sure it was kind of you both to drop in, but Davy's still not entirely recovered from his experiences in China—"

"We know," said Miss Aikin hurriedly. "We wouldn't have dropped in at all, Linda, if not for the fact—"

"What Miss Aikin means, my dear," said Emmy DuPré, "is that we dropped in with a *purpose*."

I'll bet, Linda thought grimly.

"You see, Linda, Miss Aikin needs your assistance." Miss DuPré rarely used a short word when a long one would do.

"Me?" Linda frowned.

"It's about my collection," said the librarian eagerly, "and Emmy thought—"

"Let me tell it, Dolores," said Emmy. "Linda, you know Miss Aikin's collection of the autographs of Famous Wrightsvillians, of course." Linda nodded, growing more puzzled by the moment. "Well, in her collection she has an autograph of every member of the Wright family beginning with Jezreel Wright in the early 1700's—"

"It's really the heart of my collection," Miss Aikin said in a reverent voice.

"Anyway, Miss Aikin's collection in the Wright Family section is complete except for one autograph." Miss DuPré's ophidian face thrust forward, extending her skinny neck alarmingly. "*Shockley Wright's signature is missing,*" she hissed.

So that's what it was all about! Linda felt like laughing, she was so relieved. Miss Aikin's efforts to procure a genuine Shockley Wright signature for her tiresome collection were almost legendary in Wrightsville. For years she had been searching for one, and for years she had been unsuccessful. John F. and Hermione Wright

The Sick Fox   29

had been not too helpful. Shockley Wright, John F.'s uncle, had been a playbox, a pixy, and a sort of painter. During his long tenure in the town of his illustrious fore-bears Uncle Shockley had wielded the red paint-brush recklessly, and his departure on the rods of a fast freight in the dead of a winter's night, when he was well past sixty, had been shrewdly calculated to keep a County Sheriff from doing his sworn duty. Nothing had ever been heard of Uncle Shockley again, much to the relief of the Wright clan.

It was Miss Aikin's misfortune that apparently Shock-ley Wright had not bothered to learn the art of penman-ship until late in his life, having had no time in his youth for such frivolities; and what specimens of his handwrit-ing existed had been burned by Hermy Wright on the heels of Uncle Shockley's judicious departure.

But then, in her darkest hour, Miss Aikin miraculous-ly ran across the trail of a specimen.

It was two years before. Miss Aikin, having exhaust-ed all the obvious sources, was down to canvassing the older tradespeople of Wrightsville. Eventually she had queried Myron Garback, proprietor of the High Village Pharmacy in the Square. And Myron Garback had one! He recalled that many years before, Shockley Wright had come in to renew a prescription, and because the medicine contained a powerful soporific, the pharmacist had had Shockley sign for the renewal in a ledger—"my record book," Garback had called it. Miss Aikin had come very close to fainting. But she had managed to keep her head. Could she have it? She would pay any-thing—anything! Myron Garback had smiled. The sig-nature was of no use to him, and Miss Aikin might have it with his compliments. However, it would take a deal of searching—he could not remember the exact year of the entry, and the record book covered similar entries for a period of more than two decades—he would take the ledger home that very week end, find Shockley Wright's signature, cut it neatly out, and present it to Miss Aikin on the Monday following.

But on the preceding Saturday Myron Garback

dropped dead in the Prescription Department of his pharmacy.

Miss Aikin had been beside herself. It was out of the question to disturb the widow in her grief, even for such an important purpose. Miss Aikin with difficulty waited a decent interval. When she returned eagerly to negotiate with Mrs. Garback for the precious autograph, it was to find that the pharmacist's widow had sold the store to her late husband's clerk, Alvin Cain, and had moved to California.

"That man," said Miss Aikin to Linda through her teeth, which clicked. "That Alvin Cain!"

"Imagine. He would *not* give it to Miss Aikin," said Emmeline DuPré. "He utterly *refused*."

Linda felt a chilly premonition. She stole a glance at Davy. He had scarcely listened to the dreary tale, but at mention of the name "Alvin Cain" he had sat up straight.

"But I'm afraid I don't quite see—" said Linda. "I mean, where *I*—"

"Well, you see, I tried for a long time to make Alvin Cain change his mind," said Miss Aikin hastily. "He's just been mean about it, that's all! With his fine talk about 'professional trust' and all that—that booshwah! So finally I asked Emmy DuPré if *she* wouldn't try, you see, and—"

"I couldn't resist such an appeal," said Miss DuPré with dignity. "There's a good deal at stake here, Linda, as you must see. That Wright collection *must* be completed. Well, I must say Alvin Cain, despite my best efforts, hasn't seen fit to be even *polite* to me. The other day he virtually *ordered* me from his drugstore. But then I had an idea." She glanced slyly at Davy. "I said to Miss Aikin: "If there's one person in this town who can get *anything* out of Alvin Cain, I mean just *anything*, it's Linda Fox—"

Davy said, choked up: "Get out."

He was on his feet. His hands were shaking.

"Oh, my," said Miss Aikin faintly. She rose, clutching her purse. "I think, Emmy, perhaps we'd better—"

"Well, I never," snapped Emmeline DuPré. "War hero or no war hero, this is just about the *last*—"

"Get out, you old bat!"

"You'd better go," said Linda in a low voice.

"Oh, we shall," said Miss DuPré, tossing her head. "But you know the saying: A guilty conscience—"

"Did you hear me?" Davy asked very quietly.

The two ladies fled.

"Davy."

He was red. "Well, what the devil did that damned old witch mean by that crack? I don't like it, Linny—I don't like that kind of talk!"

"You're jealous," said Linda with a little laugh.

"You bet. All the time I was in China—"

"Now Davy," Linda said calmly, "if you're going to start harping on that foolishness, I'm going to bed."

Davy stood there, his jaws rippling. Finally he muttered, "I'm sorry, Linny."

But when Linda kissed him she found his lips hard and cold against hers.

And then, the very next evening, while Linda and Davy and Emily and Talbot Fox were sitting on the front porch, enjoying the dew-cooled breeze that swept down the Hill after a hot day, Alvin Cain himself came striding briskly up the walk.

Linda recognized him first, and her heart began to beat faster. She did not quite know why. Surely Davy could not seriously think . . . Still her heart beat faster, and she felt her cheeks heat up and she was absurdly grateful for the dusk that was almost darkness.

Then Davy spied him, and Lin's eyes closed against the spectacle of her husband's rigid rage.

But she opened them quickly and said, "Hello, Alvin," trying hard to sound casual.

"Well, of all people." Emily Fox put her knitting in her lap and glanced at her nephew with anxiety.

"Hello, hello, hello," said Alvin Cain.

He was a swarthy, broad man—broad head, broad shoulders, broad hips—and so squat he looked foreshortened. Yet his features were not unattractive; although his eyes were small and shrewd and his curly black hair was thinning on top, he had splendid teeth and a good nose, and when he grinned a dimple showed in his thick chin.

Cain was elegantly attired—"the best dresser in town," as Sol Gowdy of the Men's Shop, Wrightsville's *arbiter elegantiarum,* liked to say; the pharmacist was his best customer. And indeed no one had ever seen Alvin without a perfectly knotted tie, or minus his jacket, or with unpolished shoes.

"Well, well, Davy. Or should I say Captain? I never did get a chance to tell you how darned proud we all are. I'm tickled to see you looking so fit. They treating you right, boy?" Cain revealed his dimple as he took Linda's hand. "And little Linny. It's a cinch having hubby back is doing *you* good!" He nodded at Emily and Talbot. "Mrs. Fox. Mr. Fox . . ."

Emily murmured nervously and Talbot grunted something, going over to the porch radio and pointedly putting his ear to the loud-speaker.

"Came over to see what had happened to you folksies," Cain went on, shedding his beams impartially. "Wrightsville's saying you've all crawled into a hole and died."

"Well, you know," said Linda. "It's . . . Oh, I'm sorry, Alvin. Won't you sit down?"

"Thanks, I just dropped by for a second," said Alvin, carefully spreading his breast-pocket handkerchief on the top step of the porch and easing himself down. "Hotting up, isn't it? Most as torrid as that night last September at the Grove, Lin, when you and I showed the yokels how to dance the rumba and practically had to do a striptease afterwards to get dry. . . . Well, well, Davy boy. It's mighty wonderful having the big hero back amongst us."

"I know all about that rumba contest," said Davy.

Linda said quickly: "I wrote Davy about it, Alvin."

"You did?" Cain's handsome nose seemed displeased by the odor of that intelligence. But he laughed. "The faithful frau. Say, how about you two stick-in-the-muds taking a spin with me? Get some air. What d'ye say? I've got plenty of gas." He winked.

"I've got all the air I want right here," said Davy.

"Oh, still the hero hiding from the rubes, hey?" Cain now winked at Davy exclusively. Then he dismissed Davy and looked at Linda. "How's by you, Lin? I promise I won't take my hands off the wheel."

"Thanks, Alvin. But I really don't—"

"Oh, I'm harmless," said Alvin Cain, winking at Davy again. "Ask any doll in town. Ask all of 'em."

Davy rose.

"Okay, Cain," he said.

"I'm sure we must all be thirsty," said Emily, jumping up. "Linda, run in and get that grape-juice punch out of the refrigerator—"

"Cain, didn't you hear me?" said Davy. "Take off."

Cain gawped at him.

"You'd better go, Alvin," said Linda in a smothered voice. "Davy isn't well enough yet to receive company—"

"But he . . . told me to . . ." Alvin was spluttering, and his swarthy skin was purple. Then he said thickly, "Say, d'ye know what I'd like to do?"

"What?" said Davy, taking a step toward the pharmacist. But then he stopped, looking at his hands.

They were shaking like the leaves on the syringa bush below the porch.

Even Talbot Fox had straightened up.

Alvin Cain looked wildly at Captain Davy Fox.

With a grimace of fury almost Italian in its intensity, he ran down the walk toward his car.

"Davy. Dearest," begged Linda.

Davy went into the house.

"Wait a minute, Linda," said Emily in a tight tone. "Talbot, turn that radio off."

Talbot did so without the usual protest.

"It's time we all faced this," continued Emily quietly. "It's no use making believe there's nothing wrong. What are we going to do about Davy?"

Linda put her arms about the porch pillar and stared blindly out over the moonwashed lawn to the old apple tree she and Davy used to tell secrets in when they were children.

"He's a sick Fox, all right," said Talbot, shaking his head. "I thought he'd snap out of it, but it appears to me he's getting worse. I don't know, Emily."

"I get the feeling Davy's . . . oh, *hiding* something," Emily replied with a frown.

Her husband stared at her. "I'll bet that's it!"

Linda whirled. "What's it?"

"The old trouble. Just occurred to me. Sweetheart, it's what I always said. Since Davy's got home I've caught him time and again staring at Bayard's house. Sort of brooding on it."

"Bayard's . . . house?" Emily glanced with swift apprehension at the house next door . . . the empty house, from which Talbot had led the boy Davy twelve years before.

"I always said it was a mistake for Lin and Davy to get married," Talbot went on heavily. "I knew Davy wouldn't be able to lick the past—"

"That's not true!" cried Linda. She was pale as the grass.

"Then what else—" Talbot blinked.

"Talbot, Talbot," moaned Emily.

"I won't even discuss it!" Linda flew into the house.

4. Fox-Sleep

HE WAS SWIMMING in a river that was thick and red, like tomato juice, swimming fast with powerful strokes and joy in his throat and then it was anger because she danced ever out of fingers' reach no matter how fast he swam and he opened his mouth wide to shout at her and swallowed some of the river and it was not tomato juice but something salty and strong and acrid and hot.

And then Lew Binks was coughing between Davy's feet and down there in the brush were millions of Japs with machine guns, all shooting, all the fire converging on the rock, a sheet of living metal raising stone splinters and whining off, and Davy suddenly saw a Jap get up and walk toward the rock, smiling and bowing cheerfully and shooting from the hip as he came, and Davy rose and threw a stone at him and the stone went right through his body but he kept coming and as he came Davy saw that the Jap's face was Alvin Cain's face and Cain came closer and closer, smiling and scraping and shooting, and Davy's hands began to itch and shake and . . .

Davy opened his eyes.

He was in prison. Bars of silver hung over him.

He sat up in his bed, rubbing the sleep away. A puff of sticky wind came in past the Venetian blinds, shaking them, and the silver bars on the ceiling wavered and became rigid again.

He could not control his hands. They were trembling violently. Full of the fizz.

He sat crouched in bed feeling the hot sheet sticking to him and the sweat inching down his cheeks and chest and back.

He peered at his hands.

After a moment he thrust them beneath his thighs, savagely.

But the shakes simply traveled up his arms. His biceps were seized and shaken, too.

Davy wet his lips, trying to think. But his brain felt soggy. You got on his tail—

A moan brought his head around in a flash.

Linda.

In the other twin bed.

Moonlight on her throat.

She lay on her back, arms and legs flung helter-skelter in the heat, her eyes shut.

Her throat.

It was silver and tender-looking and alive in the moonlight with a helpless little beat of its own.

Blood and Binks and the rock and the whine and the Jap and the face of Alvin Cain.

Beat in her throat.

His legs prickled and his hands came free.

He found himself suddenly standing on the strip of washy-colored hooked rug between their beds looking down at the moon-flooded flesh.

The fizz in his hands impelled them forward and they shook their way toward her, shaking but with purpose. They moved to the flesh to touch it and feel it and bury their shakes in it and so destroy shakes and fizz and soggy skull-pain.

Linda's eyes opened.

"Davy?"

Davy straightened. He felt cold, tight, clear.

"What's the matter, dear?" She yawned.

The yawn revealed her teeth and the curve of her throat so tender and blameless and without defenses.

"Nothing, Linny," muttered Davy. "I couldn't sleep. I came over to kiss you."

She smiled, snuggling into her pillow.

"You angel."

Davy stooped, touched her lips with his. "Go back to sleep, hon."

"I love you, Davy."

Linda sighed and smiled again and closed her eyes, snuggling a little longer.

Davy stood there looking down at his sleeping wife.

The bell in the Roman church in Low Village came in on a gust through the blinds, beating the time of the world.

All at once he began to shiver. He shivered and shivered. His whole body seemed encased in ice.

He jumped into his own bed and drew the sheet tight about his own throat, shivering and praying for endless, empty darkness.

5. Fox Paws

WHAT DAVY CALLED upon himself to do in the nights that followed was to fox the thing that prickled and shook and moved his hands.

It always began the same way: the graphic dream of blood, pursuit, death, and danger, the awakening in a sweat to find night smothering him, his hands trembling, and Linda sprawled in summer sleep on the next bed.

Then the game would begin.

To stay in his bed.

To stay in his bed so that he would not go over to the other bed and obey the prickling of his thumbs and other fingers.

He fought without sound, so that Linda might not know.

At such times there seemed to be empty spaces in his brain through which enormous gales howled silently. Through this inaudible tempest he could not think in formal images. Linda was not so much a woman as a hateful idea, and in itself this was horrible, for the quieter chambers of his mind held Linda as she was—the pert and tangible, the faithful, the loved and loving Linda. But those chambers were buried deep, as in sea-caverns. On the surface raged the storm that shook him like a wave-tossed derelict—shook him all over, but especially his fingers.

Alvin Cain was not a true character in the drama. Davy recognized this as through a glass darkly; the picture was confused, but a sort of primitive intelligence beat down the confusion and penetrated to that fact, at least. Alvin Cain was an excuse. No, the true hatred was for Linda; and because this was so hysterically unreasonable Davy found the will to give it battle. He would fight, crumpled within himself, night after night after interminable night. While Linda slept on, or turned and exposed her throat. Sleep would come only with exhaustion. More often than not the room was cold and oyster-gray with dawn when Davy sagged into unconsciousness, another battle won.

But through all the long struggles and limp victories, Davy knew an even deeper terror: Sooner or later his will would give way, battered down by contention. Sooner or later he would lose the struggle to stop himself from creeping out of his bed and over to the other.

The evening had been a dead weight; under it nothing stirred. The least exertion brought a leaping sweat. The nervous system crackled.

They sat on the porch, panting.

"Going to rain," gasped Talbot, wiping his neck. "A noisy one, too. Hey, pilot?"

"Yes," Davy scanned the skies, dully. Disorderly clouds were rushing by.

Linda moaned: "My head feels as if it's being squeezed by iron bands. Davy, let's go on up."

"I'm not sleepy, Lin. You go."

"Not without you, boy friend."

It's going to be a bad one, Davy thought. I'd better not chance it. I'll stay up all night. She'll never know the difference.

He got up from the slide-swing and shuffled toward her.

"Now don't be a stubborn wench."

Her face looked up at him in the quarterlight, naked. There were great violet cusps under her eyes. *She knows,* something said to him suddenly. *But she can't!*

"There's no sense in both of us losing sleep. You go on up, Linny. Go on, now." That's it. Casual.

"Not without you."

"Damn it, Linny—"

"Now children," groaned Emily. "Goodness, how heavy the air is! I can hardly breathe."

"Davy needs the rest," said Linda stubbornly. "Look at him, Mother. He's losing weight again. He looks like the devil after a bad Sunday."

Davy jeered. "You're googly, Linda Fox-Fox."

Linda rose. "And don't think you're going to kid me out of it, Foxy, because you're not. You're coming up to bed with me this second."

I'll fool her, Davy thought desperately as they plodded upstairs with their arms about each other. I must. Get out of that bedroom. And stay out. Especially tonight.

"Mind if I read a while, Lin?" he asked carelessly as he fumbled with a shoelace.

Linda kept undressing. "You oughtn't to, darling."

"I tell you I'm not sleepy." Control your voice.

"All right, then," said Linda. "Read aloud to me."

They had done a great deal of that in the early weeks after his home-coming. It had given Davy something useful to do, and Linda loved to lie in bed darning his socks or sewing buttons on his shirts and listening to his clear, deep voice.

"We haven't done any community reading for weeks," Linda continued. "I think that's a swell idea, Davy."

"All right." He rose. Hopeless.

"But why did you stop taking your shoes off?" she demanded. "Get undressed, General!"

He nodded, in silence.

When he came out of the bathroom Linda was lying in his bed.

Oh, no, he thought. No.

He yawned. "Where's the book we were reading?"

"Right under your silly nose," murmured Linda. She was on her back, gazing with a secret smile at the ceiling. Her cheeks were pink and her eyes livelier than they had been for days. She had bound her green-gold hair with a chartreuse ribbon, to match her chiffon nightie. "On your night table, darling."

"Sure!" Davy laughed nervously. He picked up the reprint of *the lives & times of archy and mehitabel*, removed the frayed snapshot of him and Linda in the apple tree which marked their place, and began to read aloud rapidly, shuffling up and down the bedroom.

"But Davy," cried Linda, popping up in his bed, "you're not going to read walking *around*?"

Davy's hands began to shake. He looked foolish.

"Well . . . all right."

He went over to the Cape Cod rocker near one of the windows and continued to read about mehitabel and the coyote in a dreary mumble.

Linda stared at him.

"Toujours gai is my motto toujours gai."

Suddenly she scrambled out of his bed, her small features pinched and pallid, and climbed into her own.

"Never mind, Davy. I . . . think I want to go to sleep."

Davy stopped reading.

So that's what she's been thinking.

Linda put her hands over her face and burrowed into the pillow. He saw that her hands were shaking. He looked slowly at his own. They were shaking, too.

He thrust them into the pockets of his robe, quickly.

When Linda had cried herself to sleep, Davy rose from the rocker. He passed her bed as if it were not there. Very carefully, he sat down on the edge of his. His hands were still buried in his robe. He did not withdraw them. Even when he swung his legs up and fell back on his bed.

The light.

It's still on.

But he dared not make an extra movement.

He lay there listening to Linda's heavy breathing, listening to the wind which had risen and the slap and snap of the curtains being whipped against the bedroom screens—hearing and not hearing.

And the long night began.

It was two-eleven by the tiny chrysoprase clock on Linda's vanity when the storm broke.

Davy lay spent by his struggle and heard the first whisper of the rain. At first it carried no meaning to him. Then a sequence of quick flashes, like heavy artillery touched off across night distances, and the grumble and crack of deep thunder brought him to a sitting position in bed.

As he sat up the rain increased. Lightning, thunder, rain tumbled and clasped.

Linda moaned. The springs rasped as she tossed herself over in bed. Davy turned cautiously to look at her. The cheek she now exposed was anger-red and the green-gold hair at her temple was damp and untidy.

He willed himself to tear his glance away. Each thunderclap re-echoed in his brain. Each lightning stroke struck fire there.

The curtains flapped crazily.

Raining in.

Davy heard the splatter.

Right on the rug Aunt Emily's mother had hand-hooked in 1893. Emily had given it to Linda, and Linda treasured it.

It was getting soaked.

Well, get up. Get out of bed and go to the windows and shut them.

Simple enough.

Oh, but it's too simple.

It's a trick, Davy thought with contempt. It's a damned trick and I see through it. He was laughing deep inside. Pretty smart, aren't you? But I see through *that* one.

He did not move.

But Linny will be furious. Maybe the thing shrinks. Funny if she wakes up in the morning and it's shrunk to the size of a postage stamp. The thought made him laugh deep inside again and the laugh turned into a snarl which got him out of bed an a bound and then he was stooping over his wife with crooked fingers.

He was not thinking.

He had no will.

His body was animated by some external force of great energy.

His hands went out and they seemed to belong to someone else. He watched them impersonally

Linda awoke instantly.

Her lids flew up and her eyes glared. And then her hands darted to her throat and gripped his and began to pull.

The curtain flap-flapped and the rain hissed in and Linda's body thrashed about as she tore at his hands.

Her mouth was wide-open now and her breath whistled as her cheeks changed color from red to gray-violet and her eyes filmed over.

Gradually the whistling turned to gurgling.

Her nostrils trembled like a brittle leaf.

Her hands plucked feebly now. Her body merely twitched, or arched like rubber.

Out of deepest darkness and the suspension of life, light came. It did not assail the sense of sight alone; it was a light that Davy felt as well as saw, a light with the power to move mountains.

It moved him.

There was an odor of ozone in the room.

Davy tried to think. His hands were hanging loose.

Then he saw Linda. She was lying on her bed still, her hands on her throat still; she was still looking at him. Although her breath came in gasps, her eyes were untouched. She was not afraid, but resigned.

She expected to die.

Remembrance smashed at him and he staggered over to his bed to drop onto it and stare incredulously at his wife.

Linda's lips parted. She started to say something, but only a broken sound came out and she swallowed her saliva, wincing.

After a moment she was able to say: "You tried to kill me, Davy."

Her voice was unrecognizable.

Davy stared at her.

"Davy."

He wet his lips.

"You were going to kill me."

"I guess so."

He shook his head, a meaningless movement. And when he had started shaking it, he could not stop. He sat there shaking his head. To his surprise he felt two cold hands on his cheeks. She was on her knees before him, disheveled and compassionate. He throat was swollen and purple. He uttered a sick, groveling sound and tried to pull his head away. But her hands held firm.

"Davy—"

Linda sprang to her feet. Someone had knocked at their bedroom door.

She swallowed several times, rapidly.

"Yes?" she called. She swallowed again.

"Are you and Davy all right in there?" Talbot Fox sounded anxious.

"Yes, Daddy."

"Thank the Lord. That flash of lightning hit the chimney. Linny, you're sure you're both all right?"

"Oh, yes, Daddy. It gave us a scare, but we're fine now."

"Far as I can make out, it didn't do any damage except knock a few bricks loose. We're lucky pups. Mother was scared stiff. Say, sweetheart, what's the matter with your voice?"

"Not a thing, Daddy. I'm a little hoarse—may have caught cold or something. That rain washed in. Don't worry about Davy and me." Have to wear a scarf in the morning over the welts—say it's a sore throat. "Good night, dear."

"Good night, kids."

They heard his heavy tread going down the stairs.

"Davy."

"Why didn't you tell him?"

"Why did you do that?"

"I don't know. Why didn't you tell Uncle Tal?"

"You don't know!"

"I don't expect you to believe me." Each word was a

wrench. There was no color in what he said; it was all flat and mechanical.

Linda shook his face, hard. "Davy, look at me! You must know. Do you hate me that much?"

"I love you."

"But then——"

"I've been fighting the desire every night for . . . I don't know how long, Linny. It's in my hands, my fingers. It comes over me and I battle it. It's all mixed up. I don't understand any of it. Tonight the heat, the storm . . . All of a sudden it licked me. Linny . . ." Davy looked at her then with red-rimmed, spilling eyes. "You can't believe I'd want to do a thing like that."

"Then, Davy, how could you?"

"I don't know. I was sick all the time it was happening. But I couldn't stop myself. . . . Don't look at me that way! It's the way Lew Binks looked at me in Karachi!" He tried to pull away. But Linda put her arms about him.

"I'm not looking at you any way, my darling. I'm simply trying to—to look at *it*. Davy, don't fight me any more. Let's talk this out. Please, dear. Let me help you——"

Davy was staring at her stupidly. "You mean—even *now* . . ."

"But I love you, Davy. Maybe I'm a fool, but . . . I don't believe you really wanted to, either."

He shook his head.

She stroked it and stopped the shaking.

"It's the old trouble," she said gently, "isn't it?"

She saw the answer in his eyes before he spoke. But now he spoke in a tempest of release, like a bewildered boy in his mother's arms. "I thought it was dead and buried, Linny! But in China it came back. It's all mixed up, I tell you! The last few weeks—the War has something to do with it, I guess—and—I don't know, but my brain's been spinning with it—and with Binks and bloody dreams and that bastard Cain and—My God, Linny, do you suppose I'm insane?"

He succeeded in breaking her grip then, touched off as if by a fear of contaminating her.

"Davy, if you were that, the Army psychiatrists would have found it out."

"That's right, isn't it!" He began to stride up and down. "They told me I wasn't batty. They said something about an 'anxiety neurosis'—"

"There you are." Linda dragged to her feet and put her arms around him again. "So at least we know the cause."

"What good is knowing the cause?" he cried. "Those psychiatrists tried to fill me full of hop—dig 'way down —I told them all to go to hell!"

"Davy. Knowing the cause is the way to a cure in itself."

"Not in my case, Lin! At first I tried to co-operate with them. They gave me all sorts of 'therapy'—they even had me knitting. Knitting! For my nerves, they said. Oh, I can knit and purl and drop stitches with the best of the femmes," he said bitterly, "but it didn't help. Nothing helped. It's like a curse. A curse I've carried around with me since I was a kid, and my father—" Davy stopped. Then he said quietly: "Linny, I've got to get away from you. I should have done it long ago. I can't stand another night fighting. Maybe the next time there won't be lightning handy to stop me."

Linda's arms drooped. She was shivering in the chill that had set in; she hugged herself as she sat down on the edge of her bed.

"Well," said Davy fiercely, "why don't you say something? What are you thinking about?"

" 'Toujours gai,' Davy, 'toujours gai.' "

"Huh?"

"I'm thinking, Davy," she said, looking up at him, "that we need outside help. And right away, too."

"Oh. A magician, maybe!"

"Now Davy," said Linda calmly. "Dramatizing yourself won't do either of us any good. I think you can be helped—I think I know exactly how. It's been buzzing around in my mind for days now. I felt funny about mentioning it before. But now that this has happened . . ."

Something hungry came into his eyes; a starveling hope, perhaps. But he muttered: "No one can help *me.*"

"I think I know someone who can, Davy."

"I won't go to any doctor!"

"He's not a doctor."

"He's not?" Davy looked suspicious. "Then who—"

"Do you remember the trouble in Patty Bradford's family a few years ago, Davy?"

"The John F. Wrights? You mean Jim Haight—and Pat's older sister Nora?"

"That's it."

"That writer!" Davy stared.

"He's more than a writer, Davy. He's a detective."

"So *what*, Linny?"

"He came to Wrightsville once before and tried to help the Wrights when they were in trouble.* He's always helping people, I understand. Maybe he can help us."

"But how could a detective do anything for me, Linny?" cried Davy. "Twelve years ago he might have been of some use. But now?"

"Don't shake your head, Davy. I have an idea how he can help," said Linda resolutely. "Maybe it's wild— maybe it's childish. But I've racked my brains and it's the only thing I can think of that hasn't been tried. We're going to write to Ellery Queen for an appointment, Davy Fox."

* *Calamity Town,* by Ellery Queen (Little, Brown and Company, 1942).

6. Tale of the Fox

ELLERY SEATED THEM in the Queen living room, poured a glass of Bristol Cream for Linda, and mixed a Scotch-and-soda for Davy and one for himself.

"Of course," he said, "it's a great pleasure seeing someone from Wrightsville again. I grew very fond of your town. How's Patricia Wright? I mean, Bradford?"

"Oh, swell," said Linda. "Same old Patty. She and Cart are terribly happy. Terribly, Mr. Queen."

Davy just sat there with his hands on his knees, like an awkward boy, looking about the room. Ellery paid no attention to him.

"And Pat's baby?"

"Oh, little Nor's a great big girl now. Patty has two, you know. A wonderfully beautiful little boy was born last year."

"I can imagine how Daddy's acting," chuckled Ellery. "I got a letter from Pat, by the way. It came in the same mail as yours, Mrs. Fox. She speaks very highly of you and your husband."

"Patty would. I . . . phoned her before we wrote you. She's been awfully sweet to Davy and me. She told me she'd drop you a note."

"Sweet," said Davy. "She hasn't been near us."

"She's phoned and phoned," said Linda quietly. "It's not her fault, Davy."

Her husband flushed.

"Does Pat—or Cart—know about this trouble you're in?"

"Oh, no, Mr. Queen!" Linda said it quickly. "No one

does. We haven't even told Mother and Daddy . . . I mean, about what happened that night during the storm. We didn't think they'd . . . well, understand."

"You'll have to tell them eventually," said Ellery with a frown. "Well, now, Captain," he said suddenly, "you're sitting here feeling quite sorry for yourself, aren't you?" Davy started. "I must tell you, before we go on, that I don't ordinarily waste my time and sympathy on husbands who try to strangle their wives. What have you to say for yourself?"

Davy had turned scarlet.

"You don't understand, Mr. Queen," Linda put in with an anxious glance at Davy. "It's not Davy's fault, really it's not. It's something so much stronger than he is —than anybody would be—"

"I'd rather your husband spoke for himself, Mrs. Fox," remarked Ellery, studying Davy with his silver eyes. "Well, Captain? Why did you try to kill your wife?"

Davy glared at him. But then his glance fell, and he seized his glass and gulped.

"*Because,*" he said in the most hopeless of voices, "*my father killed his.*"

Ellery nodded, as if this explained everything. "Your father murdered your mother."

"Yes!"

"Here, let me refill your glass." As Ellery busied himself with the ice and soda, he went on in a matter-of-fact way: "Of course, I've looked over those newspaper clippings you enclosed in your letter, but they don't tell much. This happened twelve years ago?"

"That's right, Mr. Queen," said Linda.

Ellery warned her with a glance. "Go on, Captain," he said encouragingly. "Tell me all about it."

I was ten years old [Davy said in a listless voice], and Linda was nine.

My father, Bayard Fox, is my Uncle Talbot's brother.

They were in business together in Wrightsville—Bayard & Talbot Fox Company, Machinists' Tools.

The families lived next door to each other—Uncle Talbot and Aunt Emily and Linny in the house they still live in, and my mother and father and I in the next house. It's on Hill Drive. After the thing happened, Uncle Tal took me into his home, and my father's and mother's house was closed up—left just as it was, and locked. It's still standing there, untouched—inside or out. Nobody'd ever rent it or buy it . . . knowing. Wrightsville's a little superstitious about those things.

[Ellery nodded, remembering the bright little house of Jim and Nora Haight years before.]

My father was arrested, tried, and found guilty. The case got everybody pretty excited. The papers played it up big and called my father "The Wrightsville Fox"— they sure ran him down! He was sentenced to life imprisonment and was put away in State Penitentiary. That's where he still is. The case against him was absolutely cold—not a shadow of doubt. From the facts, my father was the only one who could possibly have poisoned my mother. At least, that's what everyone's always said.

I loved my mother. I guess every kid does, deep down. But I loved my father, too, in a different sort of way. I suppose you could say he was my hero. Dad would take me on fishing trips, or we'd go camping up in the Mahoganies week ends. He was always teaching me things—about the woods, about animal-life and bird-life, about trees and plants and mosses and insects. I don't know where he'd picked it all up, but I do remember he was a lonely sort of man, always a little sad. He'd get a quiet kick out of our trips together, just the two of us; and of course it was great stuff to me. We didn't do it often, because Mother wasn't well and couldn't be left alone too much. The only thing that made our trips possible at all was that Uncle Tal and Aunt Emily lived right next door, and they always saw to it Mother was well taken care of while we were off in the woods.

[Davy drained his second Scotch-and-soda, staring into the Queen fireplace.]

I was only ten, as I say, and when they told me my father had killed my mother, I fought and snarled like a treed cat. I didn't believe it. I couldn't. Not *my* father. But then, after the trial—I wasn't allowed to go, and I didn't know what it was all about, naturally—after Aunt Emily and Uncle Tal talked to me—why, I wanted to die myself. I was all mixed up inside. I didn't believe in anything or anybody after that. I guess it was the kind of shock no ten-year-old could stand up under without having it screw him all up.

[Ellery nodded.]

One of the things that happened to me was that I didn't want to see my father. I just couldn't. I tried to forget he'd ever been my father, or that anybody named Bayard Fox was related to me at all. And as for him— well, he signed papers making Uncle Tal my guardian and giving me his entire estate, which included his share of the plant, in trust with my uncle, till I came of age. Just as if he'd died. I guess he figured that where he was, he might just as well be dead.

[Davy smiled that sweet smile, and Linda shut her eyes.]

For a long time after the murder of my mother—her name was Jessica, Mr. Queen—I couldn't think of anything but that my father was a murderer and I was his son.

I got a queer notion in my head that it was like having blue eyes and black hair and lots of freckles—if your father had them, the chances were you'd have them, too. It's a fact I take after Dad physically; Uncle Tal says I look just like him when he was my age, though I'm bigger and more solidly built. . . .

So gradually I came to have a whopping big fear.

["A fear?" asked Ellery.]

I was afraid I'd grow up to be a murderer, too.

[Linda took Davy's hand, and Ellery glanced from Davy to Linda and back again. "Go on," he said.]

I won't go into my adolescence. It was plenty grim. I couldn't get away from the name Fox or my "past"—the kids of Wrightsville saw to that, and their parents weren't much kinder, though the grown people snickered it behind their hands where the kids screamed it at me. But I guess I was a stubborn cuss, and I stuck it out. It meant daily fist-fights, but they weren't going to make me run away. So I grew up cocky, bitter, suspicious, and on the defensive, all the time in secret battling that childhood fear I'd developed of being—you might say —"diseased," of carrying the germs of murder in me, inherited from my murderer-father.

Doesn't make much sense, Mr. Queen, does it?

["It makes all kinds of sense, Captain," said Ellery.]

For a time, just before the War, I thought I had its number. That was when Lin and I decided we were in love and had always been. And when on my last furlough before shipping out we decided to get married, and told the folks—my uncle and aunt, Linny's foster-parents—and Uncle Tal was dead-set against it, I was plenty steamed. But Uncle Tal practically predicted what would happen. And Aunt Emily was afraid of the past, too. They knew me better than I knew myself, as it turned out. Or maybe it was a sort of family instinct. I don't know. Anyway, Linny and I had to put the pressure on before they'd say okay.

I found out how right they were, Mr. Queen . . . in China, fighting Japs. And when Lew Binks and I crashed, and I spent that seven weeks in the mountains, hiding from Jap patrols and foraging for food and lugging Binks—his legs were all shot up—on my back, and we wound up with our backs to the wall—a big rock wall, thank God—and they began to run into my tommy-gun fire . . . I guess what I'd been through, the blood bath at the end, seeing the Japs go down like toys under my fire—all that pushed me off the deep end. All through the rest—the hospitals in China and India, Binks's death, the flight back to the States—I could think of only one thing: killing. Killing from a P-38, seeing my wing guns pepper Jap crates—when I could catch 'em—seeing the oily smoke and the death dive— killing from that rocky ledge with a sub-machine gun, killing with ammunition from my .45 and Binks's—killing, killing, killing, the way you sometimes kill in dreams. There's never any end to it. You just kill and kill—nothing can stop you, and everything goes down in front of you. And I was absolutely horrified at myself. Because it proved to me once and for all—I had my father's blood in me, all right. I was a born killer.

When I got home I was still thinking of myself that way—a sort of vague thing—a "born killer"—a killer in *general* terms—not killing individuals, but just . . . just killing, Mr. Queen—I can't explain it any other way. [Ellery nodded.] But after I'd been home a while, I found myself thinking of killing in specific terms. *Of killing . . . Linny.*

[Now Davy was on his feet and Linda was crying inaudibly on the Queen hearth-rug.]

I fought it night after night. But I knew sooner or later I'd lose. I knew I'd do it! I told you, Mr. Queen, it doesn't make sense. God knows I love my Linny; she's everything in the world to me—there isn't anything or anyone else. That's the way it's always been; it hasn't changed a bit. It isn't *Linda,* or anything she's done, or hasn't done. Oh, there was that business about Alvin Cain; he's chased Linny since she was in high school, and somebody sent me some nasty gossip while I was in China, and I've dreamed about him a lot—not very sweet dreams. But I know Lin loves me—I know she's incapable of cheating—and even if she wanted to cheat, I know she'd never pick a specimen like Cain; she has too good taste. No, it's not Linda—I'd let myself be taken alive by Japs before I'd touch a hair of her head . . . I mean, in my right self.

And still, I couldn't stop myself. I knew something inside me—rotten, murderous, strong as the devil in hell —would break out one night and make me kill my wife . . . *the way it made my father kill his.*

And the other night, it actually happened.

Mr. Queen, it wasn't me! It was some other man. I was off on one side, watching him and being sick over what he was trying to do. But I couldn't stop him. You'll have to believe that, Mr. Queen. I just couldn't.

Davy shuffled over to the window and looked down at West Eighty-seventh Street. The hand on the window shook.

"Mr. Queen, you've got to help us," sobbed Linda. "You've got to! It means Davy's sanity. It means the rest of our life together. It means the children we were going to have—"

"It means," said Davy in a dry way, without turning, "Linda's life. Let's face it."

Ellery knocked his pipe against the cold andiron.

"I think," he said amiably, "we can discount your obsession in China, Captain, that you were a 'born killer.' That was the natural climax of eleven years or so of psychological preparation—during your adolescence, incidentally—when you were brooding about being your father's son.

"The important thing is the crystallization of that obsession when you got home. The fear that you're like your father specifically in relation to the 'wife' concept was buried deep in your unconscious, and it was jarred to the surface under stimulus of your war experiences. I'm only guessing, but probably a psychiatrist would say that your father fixation, and your hatred for your mother, caused you to transfer that hatred to Linda . . . that is, that Linda is not the true object of your murder fantasy, but your mother, whom Linda represents."

"My mother!" gasped Davy, blundering about; and over Linda's tear-stained face came a great gladness.

"At any rate," Ellery continued, "such things are far outside my province. Much as I'm inclined to help you, Captain Fox, now that I've heard your story—and to help you, Linda; that goes without saying—I don't see how I can, if the psychiatrists failed, as you told me in your letter."

Linda sprang to her feet. "Mr. Queen, there *is* a way. I'm sure of it, in the light of what you just said. There's a way you can help us!"

Ellery regarded her keenly. "There is, Linda? How?"

"Investigate the case!"

"Case? Which case?"

"The case of Davy's father and mother!"

"I'm afraid I don't quite see—"

"You can prove Davy's father was innocent, Mr. Queen," said Linda eagerly. "Because if Bayard Fox *didn't* murder Jessica Fox, then Bayard Fox isn't a murderer, and Davy isn't the *son* of a murderer. And then all this horrible nonsense about being a 'born killer' and having his father's 'blood' in him and all that—it would go up like smoke, Mr. Queen! Don't you see? Proving Davy's father *didn't* kill Mother Jessica would fix my husband up better than all the doctors in the world!"

Ellery stared at her.

"My dear Linda," he said at last, "only a woman deeply in love would think of such a clever—really a brilliant—solution. But—" he shook his head—"the clippings you sent about the trial, Davy's own story just now, invalidate your whole premise. How could I—or anyone—prove Bayard Fox innocent when the evidence against him conclusively showed that he was guilty? Unless—" and his eyes narrowed—"you have reason to believe he *was* innocent. Have you, Linda?"

Linda's radiance dimmed a little. "Well . . . Tell Mr. Queen, Davy."

Davy came back from the window to pick up his empty glass and finger it. "I have nothing but my father's word."

"I see. Sit down. Sit down, both of you." They seated themselves on the sofa, looking up at him like two people at an interesting play. "Now be explicit. Exactly what was Bayard Fox's attitude at the time of his trial?"

"Daddy Tal and Mother Emily," said Linda, "used to talk about it when they thought I couldn't overhear. They used to say how funny it was that Bayard kept insisting all through the trial that he hadn't done it."

"That's a common phenomenon," said Ellery with a trace of impatience. "Has he persisted in his denials?"

Davy shrugged. "For about two years after he was sent up, Dad bombarded the family and his lawyer with appeals, saying he wasn't guilty, and so on—that they'd let an innocent man be sent to jail. He put up a stiff battle. But everything was done for him legally that could have been; and after a while he just gave up, I guess. Anyway, he stopped appealing to people.

"After Linny and I were married—it was on my way back to camp—I decided to stop off at the State Penitentiary to see him. I guess I had a feeling I ought to, before I shipped over. You know how it is at a time like that.

"It's the only time I've seen Dad since they took him away, when I was ten.

"It was pretty rugged, Mr. Queen. Dad's only fifty-two, but—well, he looked seventy when I saw him." Davy bit his lip, scowling. "He seemed glad I'd come. We didn't have much to say to each other. We just sat there. I hardly recognized him and he—well, I suppose he wouldn't have known me at all if I hadn't announced who wanted to see him. We just sat looking at each other when we thought the other wasn't.

"Just before I had to leave, he took my hand all of a sudden and said to me: 'Davy, you think I killed your mother, don't you?' I wasn't prepared for that, and I guess I mumbled something stupid—I don't remember what. Dad gave me the funniest look. It wasn't sore, or bitter, or resentful. Just . . . I don't know . . . hopeless. He shook his head and said to me: 'I can't understand it, Davy. Because I didn't kill her. I can't have my own son thinking I killed his mother, when I didn't.' And that's all he said. We shook hands and he—he kissed me and I went on back to camp. I was plenty confused. But then I said to myself: 'What else could he say to his son?' But that's what he said, Mr. Queen. It isn't much. I told Linny it didn't mean anything."

Ellery sat down in the hollowed seat of the armchair opposite them, sucking at his empty pipe.

After a while he said: "Davy, supppose I agree to investigate your father's case. Suppose my investigation merely serves to confirm the legally settled fact that he murdered your mother twelve years ago—which, after all, is the greatest likelihood. What would you do then?"

"Leave Linny," cried Davy Fox. "We'll get a divorce.

I'll never see her again. I won't gamble with Lin's life
—I'll take off first!"

"And you, Linda?"

Linda sent him the misshapen gnome of a smile.
"You heard my husband, Mr. Queen. He's a very stubborn guy. It's only on that basis that he'd even consider
coming with me to New York to see you." She paused.
And then she said: "Please?"

"It's a million-to-one shot, you know," said Ellery.

Linda cried: "I want my husband!"

And Davy said miserably: "Lin. Baby—"

But she began to weep again, into her hands, and
Davy stopped, his shoulders sagging.

"Now, now," said Ellery. "Are you two still occupying the same bedroom?"

"Good grief, no!" shouted Davy.

"Good." Ellery rose briskly. "Go back to Wrightsville, both of you. I'll join you there in a few days."

"You're taking the case!" Linda jumped up from the
sofa.

Ellery took her hand. "I like million-to-one shots," he
smiled. "Especially when there's nothing much to go on
but a man's word, and faith in two pretty wonderful
kids."

When Davy and Linda had gone, Ellery shaved, whistling thoughtfully all the while, took his hat, and went
downtown to Police Headquarters.

"Dad," he said, strolling into Inspector Queen's office, "what are my chances of getting custody of a lifer?"

"Aha," said Sergeant Velie, looking as if he smelled
something. "Guinea pigs again."

"Shut up, Velie," said the Inspector. "You, my son
—a civilian? None at all."

"That's what I thought," said Ellery, seating himself
comfortably in the leather chair and putting his feet up
on his father's desk. "So you'll have to do it for me."

"All right, all right," said the old man irritably, "and
watch that varnish, *please*. What lifer, and what's he in
where for?"

"Bayard Fox of Wrightsville. Murder. He's at the State Pen."

"What the blue jinkers would you be wanting with him? Say! *Wrightsville?*"

"The Haight case," said Sergeant Velie with excitement. "Was there a guy named Fox mixed up in that one, Maestro?"

"No, no, Sergeant, no connection. Want with him, Dad? Why, I want him to take a trip back to his home town with me."

The Inspector stared. "Come on," he grunted finally. "Loosen up, Ellery. I can't get on the phone without details."

Ellery gave his father details.

"Sir Galawhoozis on a white horse," said Sergeant Velie, shaking his ponderous head.

"Well, I'll try," said the Inspector without enthusiasm. He picked up one of his telephones. "Charlie. Get me the D.A. of Wright County . . . Probably at the County Courthouse in Wrightsville, you dimwit . . . Yes, I'll wait."

"Too bad Carter Bradford isn't Prosecutor up there any longer," moaned Ellery. "I'd get custody of Bayard Fox in a shot. But Cart had to go and get himself elected to the State Senate."

"What's his name, Charlie?" demanded the Inspector. "Oh. Okay. Put him through. . . . Hello! Mr. Hendrix? Inspector Queen of N.Y.C. police headquarters. Say, can I borrow a lifer who's at State Pen? . . . Bayard Fox of Wrightsville. I want temporary custody. Say for a couple of weeks."

"Fox," said the Wright County Prosecutor. "And what the devil do you want *him* for, Inspector Queen?"

"Reinvestigation of the Jessica Fox murder case, Mr. Hendrix," said the Inspector briskly. "In Wrightsville, where it happened."

"Why, good Lord, Inspector, the woman's been dead and buried for twelve years and Fox hasn't had his nose out since. Reinvestigation?" Prosecutor Hendrix seemed worried. "It's darned irregular. Is New York interested?"

"You might say so," replied the Inspector, winking at his son.

"New evidence, eh?"

"Well . . . yes and no, Mr. Hendrix," said the Inspector, beginning to perspire. "It's not exactly 'new' evidence. It's—a something. That's it. A something, ha-ha."

"Hmm," said Hendrix, sounding not amused. "It's darned irregular, Inspector Queen, without new evidence—"

"Now see here, Mr. Hendrix," said the old man in the voice he usually reserved for the Commissioner. "This isn't a frivolous business, I give you my word. And there's no politics mixed up in it. It's a pure matter of justice—"

"He got justice."

"Maybe he didn't. I mean . . . The point is, technically, you don't ever have to let Fox out of your clutches, Mr. Prosecutor. Why, you can send a detective from your own office up to the Pen and *he* can take Fox into custody on your order, or a court order, or however you choose to work it. See? My deputy will meet your detective up there, and they can all go over to Wrightsville together. Get it?" And the old gentleman beamed at the telephone, won over by his own beautiful picture.

"But without new evidence," began the Prosecutor. Then he stopped. Then he said: "Your deputy? Who is your deputy, Inspector?"

The Inspector laughed falsely. "Funny coincidence. He's got my name. Well, well, let's put all our cards on the table. He's my son, ha-ha! Ellery Queen."

"Oh," said Hendrix, and the receiver was ominously dumb. "I've heard of *him*," he said at last. "Came up here a few years back and played Kelly pool with the Haight case. When Senator Bradford was Prosecutor. So Ellery Queen wants to come up to Wrightsville again, does he?"

"That's it, Mr. Hendrix." Inspector Queen shrugged violently in the direction of his son.

"Well, Inspector, let me sleep on it—"

"Now listen, Hendrix, don't give me any of your fancy upstate brush-offs," snapped the Inspector, assuming his "tough" voice. "You can wangle it, and you know blasted well you can! A thing like this is pretty much discretionary, and if you're going to let personal considerations—"

"Personal! I don't know what makes you say that, Inspector. I've never even met your son—"

"Okay. Then what's to prevent? Ellery's not going to step on anybody's corns. Ask Judge Eli Martin—old Martin'd give you a court order like that, Mr. Hendrix! Dress it up to suit yourself—use my name, if you want —why, with your man having actual physical custody of Bayard Fox, what harm can there be? He can sleep with Fox in the same bed for all we care!"

There was a great deal more of the same, and when Inspector Queen hung up he was mopping his head. "Why, why, why I let you finagle me into doing your dirty work, my son," he snarled, "I'll never know! Okay. It's all set, Your Majesty."

Ellery said absently: "Thanks, Dad. Now all I have to do is prove Fox innocent when he's probably as guilty as Cain."

Sergeant Velie shook his head again, dolefully. "Sir Galawhoozis," he said.

7. The Old Fox Comes Home

THE WARDEN WAS a gentle-shouldered little man who looked more like a pedant than a practicing penologist.

"I'm rather glad you're looking into this, Mr. Queen," he said uneasily. "There's something about Fox . . . He's a quiet one. Been a model prisoner. Pleasant, cooperative, but . . . untouchable, if you know what I mean."

"Untouchable?" Ellery raised his brows. "I'm afraid I don't, Warden, quite."

The Warden shrugged. "I've handled lots of prisoners in my time, Mr. Queen. This man is in a class by himself. At first he wanted help—from anyone—other inmates, guards, me. Very vocal. Sure he was railroaded, and that sort of thing. Like all the rest . . . But then something happened to him. He tightened up. Built a shell around himself. And that's where he's lived ever since. Never lets go. Everything is inside. Deep, Fox is —deep.

"He'll be a few moments yet, Mr. Queen. Meanwhile, there's someone waiting for you in my office."

The Warden held open his office door, and Ellery perceived Chief Dakin of Wrightsville within, smiling at him.

"Dakin!"

"Hullo again, Mr. Queen."

They shook hands with pleasure. Chief Dakin was an elongated countryman with transparent eyes and a large Yankee nose who would have looked perfectly at home behind a plow. But his mouth was almost tender, and there was an air about him—of dependability, gravity, and intelligence—that lifted him out of a type. He was baritone soloist of the First Congregationalist choir in High Village, a tolerant teetotaler, and the best poker player in Wright County. He had been Wrightsville's Chief of Police for over twenty years.

"But why are you here, Chief?" demanded Ellery. "I thought I was to meet one of Prosecutor Hendrix's men."

"You are. Detective Howie—Mr. Ellery Queen."

The man was sitting so still in his corner that he had seemed part of the Warden's office furnishings. Howie was a great fat fellow in a wrinkled blue gabardine suit greasy with age and streaked with old cigaret ash. A once-white handkerchief was stuffed between his wilted collar and his mottled neck; and his puffy brick-colored paws clutched a bundle of blue-backed papers bound with a red rubberband.

He merely nodded at Ellery; he neither rose nor offered his hand.

"I'm happy to make your acquaintance, Howie," said Ellery pleasantly. "We'll be seeing a good deal of each other in the next couple of weeks, so—"

"I got my orders," said Detective Howie in a screeky voice. And his fat lips snapped shut. That was that.

It began to look difficult.

"Howie's a great one for orders," explained Chief Dakin dryly. "I guess that's how Phil Hendrix come to send him on this job, Mr. Queen. It's also one of the reasons I drove up. I didn't want you thinkin' *everybody* in Wrightsville had 'orders.' "

"Thanks," Ellery grinned. Then he said to Detective Howie: "And just what are your orders, Mr. Howie?"

"No funny business." The mouth snapped shut again.

"Right," said Ellery cheerfully. "Now we understand each other. . . . *One* of the reasons you drove up, Dakin?"

Dakin chuckled. "Ain't much bamboozles you, is there? The other reason is I'm sworn to preserve the peace of Wrightsville."

"Oh," said Ellery.

"Expecting trouble, Chief?" asked the Warden anxiously.

"Maybe, Warden."

"But why?" Ellery asked.

"I guess it's because Wrightsville was once pretty riled about Bayard Fox, Mr. Queen. Came close to actin' mighty foolish, the town did. We had quite a time of it."

Ellery nodded soberly.

"I figured," Dakin went on, his light eyes on Ellery, "we'd sort of smuggle him into town by auto through the servants' entrance. They'll be watchin' the trains."

"After twelve years?"

"I'm not sayin' anything's *goin'* to happen, Mr. Queen."

"Dakin, do you think Bayard Fox poisoned his wife?"

The Chief seemed startled. "Why, sure. It was absolutely open and shut. Not a loophole a louse could wriggle through, Mr. Queen. I'm mighty glad to see you, but you're wastin' you time."

Ellery glanced at the fat man in the corner. "And you, Howie? Do you think Fox was guilty?"

Detective Howie spat accurately halfway across the room into the Warden's spittoon. "Are you kiddin'?" he said.

Ellery thought of Linda Fox's tormented face, the shaking hands of Captain Davy Fox.

"All right, Warden," he said with a smile. "We're ready any time your prisoner is."

The man who came into the Warden's office so very correctly was stooped-over and squeezed-looking, as if Time had had him in its vise for more than his span. A brown and freckled scalp glistened through his thin white hair; apparently he did much outdoors work at the prison. He was dressed respectably in a blue serge suit and black shoes, and he wore a white shirt and a neat pin-stripe blue tie.

Ellery noticed a smile of satisfaction on the Warden's

lips, such as mothers smile when they have dressed their young especially well.

"They fixed you up fine for clothes, I see," said the Warden.

"Yes, Warden." Bayard Fox folded his hands before him, looking down at the floor. But Ellery detected a glitter in his eyes, quickly concealed. "Thank you, Warden."

"Hullo, Mr. Fox," boomed Chief Dakin.

Ellery could not decide whether it was the familiar voice or Dakin's use of the word "Mister" that caused the lowered face to come up so swiftly, and the glow to stain the weathered cheeks.

"Chief!" Bayard Fox took a half-step forward. But then he halted and looked down again. "I hardly recognized you, Mr. Dakin."

"How are you?"

"Fine, thank you, Mr. Dakin."

"You're lookin' fit."

"The Warden is kind to me." There was no self-pity in those mumbly accents; merely gratitude. A broken man, thought Ellery, the spirit all but shattered. Or— and he caught himself up—or so Fox seemed.

"And this is Mr. Ellery Queen, Fox," said the Warden. "He's the one responsible for this trip back to Wrightsville."

"How do you do, sir?" Eyes down, but the glitter again.

"You'll technically be in custody of Detective Howie here, of Prosecutor Hendrix's office."

"Yes, Warden."

Detective Howie rose from his mooring.

But Ellery said in the quietest of voices: "Mr. Fox," and waited.

Bayard Fox's glance came up not so much against his will, it seemed to Ellery, as in the absence of it. And when Ellery looked into those encaverned eyes—Davy's eyes, but old, old, embalmed—he felt a pang of pity and knew why the Warden, a sensitive man, had spoken of remoteness. On the surface it appeared that even now, with hope held out to him—such as it was—Bayard Fox had no hope. And yet . . . that glitter. A little shutter-flash. A flash of something that was more life than death.

Ellery frowned: "You know why we're going back to Wrightsville?"

"The Warden told me, sir."

"Please call me anything but 'sir.' And I'll call you Bayard, if I may. We must be friends, or we can't work at this at all. I know your son—"

"Davy?"

That something leaped out of the caverns again—"Quick as a fox," Ellery thought absurdly—and was gone as quickly.

"Am I going to see Davy again, Mr. Queen?"

"Oh, yes."

"My boy's one of the big heroes of the War, Warden," said Bayard Fox with a slightly animated smile. "I've been reading about—"

He stopped. Then he said stolidly: "I don't want to spoil my son's life, Mr. Queen. This can't do any good."

"You mean you don't want your case reopened?"

"Mr. Queen, this can't do any good."

Sincerity or cunning?

Detective Howie spat into the spittoon.

Ellery said abruptly: "Bayard, I don't know whether it will do any good or not. I don't know, from my own knowledge, whether you're guilty or innocent. But I'll tell you this: Your son's happiness—perhaps a great deal more—hangs on this investigation."

The eyes blinked.

"I must have your unquestioning co-operation. Will you trust me—and do exactly as I ask you to?"

That sunken glance went to the Warden, as if—but only as if—for guidance. The Warden, limped soul, nodded with a sore and sympathetic pleasure.

"Whatever you say, Mr. Queen."

The shoulders sagged.

Almost deliberately.

Despite Chief of Police Dakin's precautions, they were spotted driving through Slocum, and by the time they drew up before Talbot Fox's house in Wrightsville a considerable throng had gathered before the big iron gate.

It was neither a menacing crowd nor a compassionate one; simply Wrightsville gaping. But the moment held its terrors.

Detective Howie hustled Bayard Fox up the walk, covering the frail figure with his Himalayan bulk. A faint flush at sight of the rubbernecks on the sidewalk colored Bayard's cheeks; but only for a moment. Then his gaze fixed upon the ivy-disheveled, shuttered house next door, and clung. He actually stumbled on the bottom riser of the Talbot Fox porch steps; Howie had to steady him with a secretly cruel paw.

Ellery had been hopeful of the meeting between Bayard Fox and his family. He sought a hint, the least smear of a clue, from which to direct his researches. But the incident told him less than nothing.

The family was assembled in the parlor in photographic postures. Talbot stood at one of the front windows peering through Emily's faille curtains out at the crowd on the sidewalk. As the four men entered, Talbot turned from the window, a little pale, and hurried forward with a forced smile.

"Hello, Bay."

Bayard Fox regarded his elder brother for an instant without recognition. Then he mumbled: "Tal," and looked away—searching. The vague glance rested on his sister-in-law, and awareness flickered again. Emily crept forward to cling to her husband's arm. "Bayard, I'm so glad—" She stopped in a sort of terror, and his glance wavered on—and then that glitter Ellery had noticed in the Warden's office sprang into the sunken eyes as they found Davy in a corner, his arm tightly about Linda.

"Son!"

Davy managed a grin. "Hello, Dad. Meet your daughter-in-law. Remember little Linny?"

Linda ran to the white-haired prisoner and threw her

arms about him. From the way he stiffened, she realized
she had made a serious mistake. Linda recoiled, smiling
to conceal her confusion.

"So you're Linny," said Bayard. "So grown-up." And
his eyes dismissed her. "Davy."

"Dad."

They glanced at each other, and then away.

That was all.

A very bad scene, Ellery thought with irritation. It
lacks color, drama, and above all significance. A man
comes back from the dead and everyone is embarrassed,
including the corpse, although he less than anyone.

As Chief Dakin pushed a chair forward, Bayard
smiled his vacant smile and sat down in it to fold his
hands and rest them in his lap and look around with a
certain pleasure of recognition—yes, there's the grand
piano with the same Spanish shawl all fringed with silk
Emily used to have—I remember that—there's the daguerreotype of Great-grandmother Finggren who went
out to Illinois as a "Latter-day pioneer," as Grandmoth-
er Harrison used to say—Talbot's Harvard Classics on
the mantelpiece, and the Danish meerschaum that came
over from the old country with somebody's great-uncle
—they've changed things around a bit, but it's pretty
much the same. . . . Ellery thought how perfectly calculated this bit of nostalgic by-play was to arouse the
sympathy of an audience—the brittle, frail figure in the
too big tapestried chair, smiling sadly at familiar things
all but forgotten.

If it *was* calculated.

They were all talking now, all but Bayard, talking
with great liveliness, about the dry spell since the bad
storm, about Chief Dakin's daughter Elvy who had just
married a Slocum boy, about the triplets old Doc Willoughby had delivered over at Farmer Hunker's—about
everything but what was on their minds.

"May I suggest," said Ellery, "that we call the meeting to order?" He smiled at Bayard, who started nervously. "Bayard, your sister-in-law has offered her home

here as our headquarters. Very generously. However, if you have any objection—you see, Mrs. Fox, I'm being brutally frank—we'll take rooms at the Hollis or Upham House and operate from there. Which would you rather do, Bayard?"

"Which would . . . *I* rather do?" The question seemed to confuse him. He paused helplessly, then he said: "This is very kind of you, Emily." He repeated, "Very kind of you."

"Oh, Bayard!" Emily burst into tears.

"Now Emily—" thundered Talbot.

"I'm sorry, I'm sorry." Emily swabbed her eyes with a handkerchief that was already sodden.

Detective Howie looked about, as if for a spittoon.

"Before we begin, Bayard," said Ellery. "Have you anything to tell us?"

"Tell you?" Bayard blinked.

"Well," said Ellery, "you might tell us whether you poisoned your wife twelve years ago."

Linda sucked in her breath; it was the only sound in the room.

"I guess you all think I want to be freed," Bayard began slowly. "But I don't know. Once I did, but maybe now I'd rather stay where I am. It's gotten to be sort of like home." He sighed. "Davy, Mr. Queen told me on the drive over from the prison all about what's happened to you . . . what you almost did to your . . . wife, and why. Mr. Queen says this investigation means —well, Davy, I guess if it means all that to you and Linda, I'll do anything." And now that tantalizing glitter was in his eyes again. "All I ask is that everybody tell the truth. That's all I ask. The truth."

"But Dad." Davy was shaking. "You haven't answered Mr. Queen's question."

Bayard regarded his son with the unconcealed tenderness of a woman. "I did not kill your mother, son."

It sounded like a man stating a truth. There was no slightest timbre of falsity. A simple and direct and—yes —hopeless statement of fact.

Or was it the quintessence of cleverness? The man, thought Ellery, is either the victim of the foulest circumstances, or an astounding actor.

"All right," said Ellery; his voice told nothing of his thoughts. "Then here's my program. I'm going to spend a few days examining the court records of the trial. Then we'll all get together in the house next door and retrace every step of the events of a dozen years ago. Every action, every statement, every remembered thought as far as possible. I propose to pull time back. Maybe in making history repeat itself we can get it to shout something now that it only whispered then, or was silent about altogether.

"There are certain dangerous implications in what I'm trying to do here. The people involved are very few in number. And tied to one another by blood or marriage. If Bayard Fox is innocent, as he claims to be, then we may be faced with a most unpleasant situation."

It was unnecessary to belabor the point. Their eyes mirrored the possibilities.

"One thing more." Ellery smiled at Davy and Linda. "These two young people have a tremendous stake in this investigation. They were virtually babies when Jessica Fox died. It isn't fair or right that they should be made to suffer as adults for someone's duplicity when they were children. I'm not saying there was duplicity; I just don't know. But if there was, I warn you now—I'll follow this through till I corner the truth. No matter where it leads. No matter whom it hurts.

"Is that clear? To everyone?"

No one replied; no one had to.

"Thank you," said Ellery, with a smile. "And now I've got to get busy with those trial records."

PART TWO

8. Fox-Love

THE NEXT MORNING, having a half hour before his appointment with Prosecutor Hendrix, Ellery renewed his acquaintance with Wrightsville.

It hasn't changed much, he thought as he roamed about High Village. Some new stores; a busy new City Parking Lot abutting Jezreel Lane, behind the Post Office and the Five-and-Dime; Andy Birobatyan's Florist Shop in the Professional Building adjoining the Kelton on Washington Street wore a different-colored paint; Dr. Emil Poffenberger's dental offices had disappeared; the Hollis Hotel displayed a new marquee, very elegant; in store windows on Lower Main and along Upper Whistling Avenue hung banners boasting one or two or three blue stars. But behind the plate-glass front of the *Wrightsville Record*, where Lower Main fed into the Square, Ellery could spy old Phinny Baker shining up the presses, as of yore; Al Brown was serving New York College Ices in the ice-cream parlor next to Louie Cahan's Bijou to boys and girls of Wrightsville High, as if he had never stopped; and in the Square, which was round, Founder Jezreel Wright still brooded over the stone horse trough, his nose and arms decorated with bird-droppings and his verdigrised back set against John F. Wright's Wrightsville National Bank on the northern arc of the Square—adjoining the grounds of the red-brick Town Hall, where State Street began.

It was very like the Wrightsville Ellery had known; it must be, he perceived, very like the Wrightsville Jessica Fox had known.

Ellery strolled up State Street under the venerable trees. He passed Town Hall and glanced across the street to the Carnegie Library: Was Miss Aikin still enthroned there, he wondered, behind the stuffed eagle and the moth-eaten owl? And then he reached the "new" County Courthouse. It did not look so new now: the granite was dingy and the bronze letters over the Doric columns were in need of polishing, the broad flat steps were a little down at the heel. But the bars on the top-floor windows, where the County Jail was, looked the same; and for an imaginative moment Ellery almost saw Jim Haight's tortured face glaring down at him from one of them.

Prosecutor Hendrix was definitely cool.

"Sure, we're provincial," said the Wright County Prosecutor severely. "We don't like outsiders muscling into our town and shaking us up, Mr. Queen. I'm an outspoken man. Bayard Fox got a fair trial twelve years ago; the case is practically ancient history. Where's the point?"

"There's a bit more at stake, Mr. Hendrix, than the provincialism of Wrightsville—or even Bayard Fox."

"What?"

In confidence, Ellery told him.

"Well." Hendrix pursed his Yankee lips. "I must say it's a darned funny kind of therapy." He did not bother to disguise his hostility.

"Captain Davy Fox," Ellery pointed out slyly, "is currently Wrightsville's proudest possession."

"Yes. Of course." Hendrix looked uncomfortable. "I'm sorry to hear about his condition. But this is the wildest jump in the dark, Mr. Queen. Your investigation won't do the boy anything but harm, because it'll only raise his hopes and you can't help but disappoint him.

"Bayard Fox murdered his wife twelve years ago, and that's all there is to it. You're wasting your time." He did not add "and mine," but that was what his tone implied.

It had begun to be an annoying refrain, and Ellery

scowled. "By the way, Mr. Hendrix, who was Prosecutor of Wright County during the Fox trial?"

"Tom Garback."

"Garback?"

"He was one of Judge Eli Martin's bright boys—the old fellow used to handpick 'em and train them himself. Made a good Prosecutor, too, Tom did, even though it wasn't my party."

"Garback," mused Ellery. "Wasn't there a Garback —Myron! Myron Garback was a witness in the Haight case—owns the High Village Pharmacy. Any kin of the Garback who prosecuted Fox?"

"Tom's older brother. Incidentally, Myron doesn't own the High Village Pharmacy any more. He dropped dead of heart disease late in '42 or '43, was it?—and his widow sold out to Alvin Cain and moved to California."

"Alvin Cain." The name struck a soft pedal. Cain? Then Ellery remembered the look on Davy Fox's face in the Queen living room in New York. "Oh, yes. Well, Mr. Hendrix, it may be necessary for me to talk to Tom Garback. Where can I find him?"

"Ask the White House," grinned Prosecutor Hendrix. "Tom was called to Washington years ago—confidential work on Pennsylvania Avenue. Last I heard, he was off somewhere on a mission for the President. He might be in Paris, or Moscow, or where-have-you. Local boy makes good!"

"You sound bitter," grinned Ellery. "In that case, Mr. Hendrix, I'm confident *you* won't mind making all the official records of the Fox trial available to me . . . eh?"

The Prosecutor threw up his hands.

Four days later, Ellery dropped into Chief of Police Dakin's office.

"I was wonderin' what happened to you," said the Chief. "Boned up, have you?"

"I've been studying the old court records."

"Nose out anything?"

"If you mean errors—no."

Chief Dakin sighed. "I told you, Mr. Queen. It was an open-and-shut case."

"Oh, certainly." Ellery stared out the Chief's window at the Wrightsville Light & Power Company and the Northern State Telephone Company buildings across State Street. The serene old elms he remembered intervened, but they were agitated this morning; it was a sunless, blustery day. "But then I didn't expect to find anything startling. I've assumed all along that if there's anything to be found, it will take more than library work."

"How's Bayard behavin'?"

"Very well, I must say, considering that Detective Howie's taken his orders literally and insists on occupying the same bed. Emily Fox has given them the south room on the first floor."

"Tough on Bayard," said Dakin.

"He's up to it. Not so shy—he's loosened up considerably, though there's a good deal of strain between him and his brother Talbot. I wonder if there's anything behind that. Was there, ever?"

"Not that I know of. They always got along in business fine."

"So I understand. Anyway, Bayard sits around all day talking over old times with Davy—when Davy's around, which isn't often; it's not easy for Davy—or getting acquainted with Linda, to whom he's taken a shine, and filling out on Emily's fruit pies."

"That woman bakes a fillin' pie." The Chief grunted. "So now what, Mr. Queen?"

"This."

Ellery handed him a typewritten list of names. Dakin scanned the list slowly.

"You want these people?"

"Yes."

"When?"

"On call from now on. They're still in town?"

"Yep. Even young Jackson, the Negro boy."

"That's more than I could have hoped for. Why do you say 'even' young Jackson?"

"Abe L.'s in the Army—he's Henry Clay Jackson's

son, the buttlin' Jackson." Ellery nodded, grinning. He recalled old Henry Clay in his buttling suit announcing dinner at the John F. Wrights' when Hermione Wright had introduced Ellery to her *"intime"* Wrightsville friends during his first visit to the town. "But I saw Abe on State Street only this mornin'. You're holdin' your get-together at the Bayard Fox house, Mr. Queen?"

"Oh, yes. I believe in atmospheres, Dakin." Ellery drummed softly on the Chief's desk, staring out the window again. "Authentic atmospheres . . . It's going to be on the gruesome side," he muttered.

Dakin winced. "Must you?"

"It's where the murder took place."

"But that house is a tomb, Mr. Queen. It's been sealed up for a dozen years. I'd feel like a grave-robber."

"Let's both feel like grave-robbers."

The Chief stared.

"Because I need a friendly presence," complained Ellery. "I'm out to save two young people from a fate at least as bad as death, Howie is a depressing leech, and I need a friendly presence, Dakin."

Dakin reached for his visored hat. "May's well be hanged for a fool as a jackass," he grunted, shrugging. "Okay, Mr. Queen, let's go rob that grave."

Later that morning, Ellery led a nervous procession across two lawns to the stained and weather-cracked door of Bayard Fox's house.

An impression, almost an impact, of frozen life struck Ellery the instant he unlocked the door with the tarnished key Emily Fox had preserved in her "trinket box" next door for twelve years. As he pushed the door open, it screamed. It was as if the house itself were screaming at being awakened from its long sleep. And when they walked into the musty foyer the feeling was intensified. For the drawer of a mahogany reception table gaped, as if it had just been jerked open. Inside they could see a puppy's leather collar, a frosted electric bulb, a mess of papers—greeting cards, laundry bills, scribbled housekeeping memoranda, old letters—a torn hairnet, some marbles, a *Wrightsville Record* dated June

2, 1932, some cracked snapshots . . . the litter and clutter of a "rumpus" drawer such as all living households, no matter how efficiently managed, cannot escape maintaining. And on the plum-striped satin seat of a mahogany chair beside the table lay a boy's pullover red sweater, where it had been cheerfully tossed as if only yesterday—a sweater which at Linda's touch expelled a fine dust and a swarm of moths, and collapsed.

One corner of the domestic Oriental rug lapped over where a hurrying foot had tripped over it twelve years before. A Maxfield Parrish reproduction ogled them from the streaked wallpaper above the table, in need of a decent leveling touch. Through the blanket of gray dust and the webs of spider generations which choked the corners of the hall ceiling they perceived a house, not in death, but in suspended animation.

"The dirt," said Emily Fox. "Talbot, I *told* you we should have kept the house up—"

Talbot shook his head, peering about. Davy and Linda kept close together, almost furtively.

But Bayard Fox had come alive. His cheeks shone, his sunken eyes sparkled. He stood there looking around and sniffing, almost tasting, his house.

"It's just the same," he said in a pleased voice. "It's exactly the same."

Bayard broke into a curious little run, making for an archway to the left of the foyer. Detective Howie, startled, took a heavy step in pursuit. But he stopped short, for Bayard Fox had stopped short . . . stopped to gaze into a room, an ordinary enough room, a typical Wrightsville Hill living room, but Bayard was looking at it as if therein lay the secret of all his lifetime and he was viewing it from some afterlife, with humility and wonder.

He went in; and, infected by his mood, they followed him almost on tiptoe.

Muttering, Chief Dakin hurled the windows and shutters open. A breeze blew in, and the sour air stirred sluggishly. And after a while it became almost breathable.

"I want the picture," said Ellery. "I want the picture of Jessica Fox as she was just before the tragedy."

He glanced at Bayard; but Bayard's eyes were on the sofa, a French-provincial reproduction. Ellery wondered what there was in that undistinguished piece of furniture to attract the man. But then he realized that Bayard was not looking at the sofa, but at the afghan that lay upon it. It was imaginatively made, the work of a woman clever with her fingers. It lay on the sofa, its colors unfaded, and one had merely to squint in order to see a pallid woman with clever fingers lying under it there, in the dust.

"Jessica had been sick for months," began Davy's father in a warm voice, studying the afghan. "She'd had pneumonia—lobar, I think Dr. Willoughby called it—and it was a wonder she didn't die of it, because she never was what you'd call a well woman, Mr. Queen—always delicate. Remember, Davy?"

And Davy mumbled: "I remember, Dad."

"For the first two months I'd had both a day and a night nurse for her. The day nurse was Miss Hinchley, I remember, of the Junction Hinchleys, a very nice woman—Jessie liked her. The night nurse I can't recall."

"Mrs. Grueniger. That bossy old fat nurse," said Emily unexpectedly. Then she blushed and shrank into a shadow.

"That's right, Emily," said her brother-in-law, nodding. "Mrs. Grueniger. Jessie thought she was an old witch. But we couldn't get anyone else, and besides the woman knew her business. Dr. Willoughby recommended her highly."

"Excuse me," said Ellery. He asked Chief Dakin: "Have you got in touch with Dr. Willoughby?"

"He's at the hospital, operatin'," replied Dakin. "Doc'll be here soon as he's through, Mr. Queen."

"Go on, Bayard."

"But after two months, while Jessie was still pretty sick, I sent the nurses away." Bayard was addressing the afghan. "Jessica was a sick girl, but I sent them away."

For a moment the silence was disturbing.

"I recall that from the trial transcript," murmured El-lery, "although I don't recall any explanation. There was a special reason, Bayard?"

Bayard said: "Yes, Mr. Queen, there certainly was."

Someone in the room choked, but when Ellery looked around they were all as before, tense and uniformly pale. He glanced at Dakin. The Chief nodded ever so slightly in the direction of Talbot Fox.

"I fired the nurses," continued Bayard softly, "and I decided to take care of my wife myself. My brother and I were in business together and there wasn't any great problem about my staying home during a crisis. We agreed Talbot was to keep the shop going by himself till I got Jessie on her feet again."

Talbot had to hawk several times before he could say: "That's right. And I did, too. Pulled for both of us." There was the most curious note of defensiveness in his voice.

"Yes, Tal, I must say you did," replied his brother.

By the prickling of his wrists Ellery knew that at the very outset he had struck something—something that had not come out at the trial. Why it should emerge now he could not fathom, except that twelve years in a prison cell may well change a man's sense of values, and what was cause for silence then might be cause for speaking now.

Talbot kept clearing his throat.

"I remember the day just as plain—" continued Bay-ard.

"Which day, please?" demanded Ellery.

"The day Jessica was strong enough to come down-stairs for the first time, Mr. Queen. It was a fine warm sunshiny morning early in June . . . well, not early, maybe. The fourteenth of June, it was. I don't suppose I'll ever forget that date. June 14th, 1932."

Looking about him, Ellery thought: No, nor will these others.

"The room looked . . . just the way it looks now. The windows were open, the curtains were blowing in, and I fixed my wife up snug on the sofa there. I tucked the afghan around her. Jessie was awfully proud of the afghan. She'd made it herself."

"I remember," murmured Linda; she was hanging onto Davy's arm, the motheaten sweater clutched to her breast. "I used to ask her if I couldn't take it to play house with, and Aunt Jessie'd always say: 'Now baby, you'd only get it dirty,' and give me a cookie to make up for things."

Bayard smiled faintly. "Yes, Jessica was a great one for not letting things get spoiled, Linda. Anyway, she was feeling pretty well that morning. Had fine color in her cheeks. I guess she was excited, coming downstairs after that long bout in bed, because she didn't want any breakfast—said she wasn't hungry. I was worried about that, because Jessie hadn't eaten since supper the night before, and she needed to build up her strength. When I started to insist she eat some eggs, or at least a piece of buttered toast, she got a little peeved with me. Doc Willoughby had told me not to get her excited, so when she compromised by letting me talk her into having at least some grape juice, I let it go at that."

"I believe you had no help in the house at that time?" Ellery said.

"Not steady help, Mr. Queen. We'd lost Maizie Le Roche, our servant girl, and Jessie'd had a time getting another good one, and then she came down with the pneumonia, so through Emily I hired one of the Polish women of Low Village who work out part-time to come in twice a week to clean up—just a few hours a week. Davy and I used to make the meals and wash the dishes —remember, Davy?"

And again Davy said: "I remember, Dad."

"This particular morning the part-time cleaning woman was not in the house?"

"No. She wasn't due for a couple of days."

"As I recall the testimony, Davy was at public school."

"Yes. Up here school doesn't let out for the summer till the end of June. My wife and I were alone in the house."

Chief Dakin coughed. "Excuse me . . . That's not exactly so, Mr. Fox. Wasn't your brother here, too?"

"Oh, yes. I thought he meant when I first brought Jessie downstairs. Yes, Talbot was here, too, a little later."

"That came out in the trial," Emily Fox said in a smothered voice. "And for that matter, I was here, too. I'd dropped in with some flowers for Jessie—"

"First things first, Mrs. Fox," smiled Ellery. "Yes, I remember the testimony on that point. Your husband had dropped to discuss some matter concerning the machine-shop with your brother-in-law. Isn't that so, gentlemen?"

"No."

Bayard almost snarled it.

"No?" said Ellery.

"No! I said I'd tell the truth, and I will. And Tal, you'd better, too! I don't know what it means, if it means anything, but Mr. Queen wanted the truth and, by God, that's the truth! I've had twelve years in prison, Tal, and Jessie's been sleeping under a tree on Twin Hill for twelve years. Nothing can hurt *us* any more! And if this hurts you and Emily . . . I'm sorry, Tal, but my son means more to me than anybody!"

Talbot, who had opened his mouth, now closed it without having employed its mechanism for his intended purpose. His features were darkly crimson; he was perspiring.

"You mean, Bayard, that your brother *didn't* drop in that morning to discuss a business matter?"

"He didn't 'drop in' at all. I phoned him and told him to come over for a talk without fail. And no—it wasn't about business."

Davy was glancing from his father to his uncle in absolute bewilderment.

"But Talbot testified on the stand," said Ellery mildly, "that it *was* a mere business conversation. I recall no contradiction, Bayard, of your brother's testimony."

Bayard grinned—how like a fox, Ellery thought; it's true; in a queer way he looks like one. "At the time, I thought it was better to let it go at that. Jessie wasn't dead very long, and I couldn't bring myself to drag something out in court that gossips like Emmeline DuPré would use to throw at my wife's grave."

"The other man!" burst out Emily.

Talbot's wife had been standing there quietly, but holding herself in, growing paler and paler. Now, when she gave voice to that agony, it was as if a dam had burst somewhere deep within her.

And so it came out—at the beginning of Ellery's probe it came out—and he stood back and let it come, effacing himself.

At the trial there had been testimony about "another man," but despite the most strenuous efforts of the prosecution—and indeed of the defense attorney, although for a different purpose—the mystery of the "other man's" identity had not been penetrated. And in the end it had been dropped, unsolved. But not before the jury had been persuaded that Jessica Fox and Bayard Fox and the unknown male had formed the familiar triangle, thus supplying a motive for the husband to have sought the wife's life which even the dullest-witted talesman could grasp. The major fact had been the outstanding fact: Only Bayard Fox could have poisoned his wife. And for this fact there had been ample and unbudging evidence.

Nevertheless, to discover now, of a sudden, after twelve years, that the "other man" had been, not some stranger with a blank face, but Bayard Fox's own brother . . . somehow the motive loomed larger.

Ellery put the pieces together from the sidelines of that damp, dusty room. Bayard had been forty, Talbot forty-one, Jessica and Emily each thirty-five, Davy and Linda ten and nine. Two families, living next door to each other—a vigorous, handsome Talbot Fox and a timid, rather faded Emily, with Linda romping about their house; and next door slim, shut-in, a little sad, Bayard Fox, and the tall, passionate woman who was his wife, with little Davy.

It should have been, Ellery thought, fairly obvious.

And yet, from the trial records and the contemporary newspaper accounts, no one had suspected. Truth will out, he thought, but it takes its sweet time about it sometimes.

"I first got wind of it," Bayard declared calmly, "in the early stages of Jessie's pneumonia. She was delirious at night sometimes, and once, while that fat nurse—Mrs. Grueniger—was resting in the next room and I was alone with my wife, she called out in her delirium for my brother. I couldn't be mistaken about why she'd called out. I watched like a detective after that, and as soon as I could I got rid of both nurses, as I said a few minutes ago. I didn't want talk.

"Then it happened again. My eyes had to stay open, whether I wanted them to or not. And so I began to notice things—a lot of things—little things—things I'd been blind to before. My brother's concern about my wife. The way my wife looked at him when she thought nobody was watching. The way Tal would phone. Things like that.

"By the time Jessie was well enough to get out of bed, I knew practically the whole story without ever having said a word either to her . . . or to him."

"It's past. It's past and done with," choked his brother. "Bay, for the love of heaven, what's the sense of raking all that up now?"

"He wanted the truth," said Bayard with that same odd vulpine grin. "It's the truth, isn't it, Talbot?"

"Yes!" his brother shouted. "Yes, it's the truth, damn it! All right, it's the truth!"

"And I've lived in your house all these years," said Davy Fox to his uncle with his sweet smile.

"Davy! Mother, please—" began Linda wildly. But Emily had dropped onto the dusty seat of one of the chairs and was staring out the window.

"Now Emily," groaned Talbot. He stopped, very pale now.

"I didn't say or do anything about it," continued Bayard almost gently, "till that morning when I brought Jessica downstairs. Just before I brought her down, I phoned Tal next door and asked him to drop by on his way to the shop—told him to be sure to come in by the kitchen door so Jessie wouldn't hear us. I tucked her in on the sofa and went into the kitchen to get her grape juice, and while I was there Tal came up the back porch and we had it out. In the kitchen."

Tal said hoarsely: "Now wait a minute, Bay." Bayard waited. The bigger brother wiped his forehead and neck with a handkerchief that shook. "All right, so it's come out . . . Emily. I'm talking to you, too."

"I'm listening, Talbot," said his wife without taking her eyes from the lawn.

"You mustn't get the wrong idea about this, any of you. Any of you. Davy, don't glare at me so. Your mother and I—we couldn't help it. Those things happen, Davy. Emily, they happen. It doesn't make a man a skunk or a woman a—a floozey when they do. I swear to God Almighty there was nothing between Jessie and me that either of us could have been ashamed of—at any time. Do you hear me? The lot of you! You've got to believe it. Emily, you've got to! You've lived with me enough years to know what I am. I have no backbone sometimes but—you know what I am. And you know what Jessie was—how fine, what a lady. We fell in love, and we fought it like fury. But we fought a losing battle. We lost out. All without so much as touching each other's hand, I tell you!"

Talbot stopped. He was about to say more. But then his mouth tightened.

Emily sat in her bitter corner, hands in her lap, staring out Jessica Fox's window.

"We had it out," said Bayard, as if his brother had not spoken at all, "right there in the kitchen. I told Tal what I'd found out, and he admitted it right off. I'll give him that. He told me almost exactly what you just heard. And I believed him. I wasn't mad. I was hurt, I guess, but—not mad. Tal was my elder brother and a darned fine man, and he'd never done a thing to me that I could call mean or underhanded. So I couldn't be mad."

Then why is there that excited triumph in your voice, Bayard? Ellery thought.

He could see them, the big handsome brother and the frail plain one, facing each other in Jessica Fox's kitchen while she lay on the sofa under the afghan in this very room, tasting the joy of life regained. Ellery almost heard their inflections. Two intelligent men, brothers, discussing a cruel and surprising problem, and both too uncomfortable about it to take bold slashes at the tangle in which they stood trapped.

At least that was the picture as Bayard painted it; and Talbot nodded almost with eagerness.

"I told Bayard I loved Jessie," Talbot put in at one point, "and that I didn't know what to do about it. And I told him Jessie was mixed up and undecided, too. We both had our families to think of—"

"Thank you," said Emily, "Talbot."

Talbot reddened. "It was the contact that made it so bad," he went on doggedly. "Living next door—Bay and I tied by a successful business partnership—and Jessie and I feeling we couldn't go on living like liars, either—without each other, and still practically touching each other. It was plain hell, and I was glad to get it off my chest and tell Bayard about it."

"We worked it out," said Davy's father dreamily. "We agreed the decision had to be Jessie's—that whatever Jessie decided, Tal and I would stick by."

But one of you did not, thought Ellery. Or did you both?

"We decided," Bayard went on, "that we'd do nothing at all till Jessica got completely well, unless she did something about it herself beforehand." He pressed his thumbs to his eyelids in a gesture of weariness. "Tal, what was it we agreed on exactly?"

"That if Jessie decided to stick by you, Bay," muttered his brother, "I was to sell out my share of the business to you and move my family from Wrightsville. Out of the state. Make a clean break. For good."

"That's it," nodded Bayard. Had he really forgotten?

"And if she picked Tal, I'd step out—sell out to Tal, arrange for a divorce, and go away with Davy."

"And me?" asked Emily. "What was to happen to me and Linda? Did you two agree on that, too?"

"Well, now," replied her husband in a mumble, "if Jessie decided to leave Bay and marry me—why, Emily, naturally I'd have provided for you and Linny—"

"Thank you," said Emily. "That was considerate of you, Talbot." She kept looking out at the sunless world.

"Emily! I couldn't help it!"

"Mother," said Linda. "Please, Mother."

"I couldn't help it, Emily!"

His wife turned from the window then. "No, Talbot, I expect you couldn't. I just wish you hadn't kept it from me—I wish you hadn't kept quiet about it all these years. I wish you'd been as honest with me then as you were with Bayard—and Jessie."

"But then she died, Emily! And what good would it have done to hurt you?"

"I wish you had told me," said Emily.

"And when she died, I saw how wrong it had all been—"

"Oh, did you?"

"Wrong, and still *right*. How can a man get out of a mess like that? Wrong, and right, too! And afterwards, when Bay was sent up to . . ." But Talbot did not pursue that spoor. "I felt I had to make up—for the part that was wrong. Some way. To Bayard—by taking his son into our home and bringing him up as if he were my own. To you, Emily—by being the husband you'd a right to expect me to be. And I *have* been, Emily, you know that—"

"Did you love Jessie very much, Talbot?" Her tone was curious.

He paled. "Don't ask me that, Emily—"

"Do you still love her?"

"How can you ask me that?" he cried. "Twelve years, Emily!"

"You always were a weakling in some things, Talbot," said his wife with a sort of contempt.

His glance fell. And in the uncomfortable silence they became conscious of an incongruity. They looked about, blankly. But it was only Detective Howie. He was whistling a merry, jeering little tuneless tune through his fat lips.

"We decided not to tell you anything, Emily," said Bayard, "till the time came. Because maybe the time would never come—maybe Jessie would choose to stay with me. And then you wouldn't have had to know at all. I'm sort of sorry you had to find out now, Emily. After all these years. But Mr. Queen wanted the truth."

Emily Fox gripped the arms of her dead sister-in-law's chair. "You men," she cried in a passionate voice. "You think you know it all. You think you can make a woman or break her. You think the whole world revolves around you. Find out *now*, Bayard? I've known all about Talbot and Jessica for twelve years!"

"You . . . *what?*" Talbot Fox feebly asked his wife.

"Do you think I was deaf, Talbot, or blind?"

"But you never said a word. You never let on, Emily —not once—"

She sat up stiffly in the chair, as if her back hurt. Her hands lay limply in her lap.

"I suppose I loved you."

Talbot groped toward the window nearest him and stood there, his back to the room.

"Anyway," said Bayard with a deep sigh, "that's what Talbot and I talked about in the kitchen that morning while I was preparing a pitcher of grape juice for Jessica."

"Ah, yes," said a cool voice; and they all started.

But it was only Ellery, emerging from the corner shadow in which he had been standing.

"Yes," he said. "That brings us to the grape juice."

9. Foxglove

CHIEF DAKIN SAID: "Hold it, Mr. Queen," and lumbered from the room. When he returned, he had big old thick-chested Dr. Milo Willoughby in tow.

"Thought I heard that jalopy of yours laborin' up the Hill, Doc," the Chief was saying.

"I got here soon as I could, Dakin," growled Dr. Willoughby. "Three appendectomies this morning—they always come in bunches, like grapes. Well, Mr. Queen!"

"Hello, Doctor." They shook hands warmly. Ellery had been fond of the blunt old physician, and it was pleasant to see him again. But Dr. Willoughby's heavy shoulders were drooping this morning. He glanced around the room, it seemed to Ellery, with an unaccustomed lack of ease. It brings back memories to Doc Willoughby, too, Ellery thought.

"Hello, Bayard," said the doctor quietly.

"Hello, Dr. Willoughby."

Neither man offered his hand.

After the doctor had nodded to the others, he said to Ellery: "I didn't mean to interrupt anything."

"You know what we're trying to do, Doctor?"

"Dakin told me when he phoned."

"Could you hang around for a while?"

"I'm afraid not. I have a few calls to make, and then I must be getting over to my office for my regular office-hours."

"You'll be there the rest of the afternoon?"

"Unless Mrs. Malakowski in Low Village decides to have her twins today instead of tomorrow."

85

"All right, Doctor, I'll probably call you later."

Dr. Willoughby left Bayard Fox's house in what Ellery thought was considerable relief. And after a very few moments they heard his car scuttling down the Hill. Did Dr. Milo Willoughby, who knew more secrets about more people in Wrightsville than even Emmy DuPré, know something about the death of Jessica Fox which he had never disclosed? It seemed improbable. Still, Ellery made a mental note.

"I think we can proceed," he said briskly. "Bayard, tell me precisely what happened when you went into the kitchen that morning twelve years ago to prepare your wife's grape juice."

"But if you've read the testimony, Mr. Queen—"

"I want it all over again, from you, Bayard. In the most finicking detail."

Bayard frowned. "When I first went into the kitchen —before Talbot dropped in—and looked in the kitchen-supply closet for a bottle of grape juice, I found we'd run out. Jessie'd always loved grape juice, and we used to go through a lot of it, especially in the summer time. Anyway, I phoned the grocery to send up half a dozen quart-size bottles right away."

"Logan's Market, the one on the corner of Slocum Avenue and Washington Street?"

"That's right. We bought all our groceries and meats there. After I phoned the order—our phone was in the hall just outside the kitchen, Mr. Queen—I went back into the kitchen and got a pitcher and tumbler down. It's while I was doing that that my brother came in and we had our talk."

"So we have you and Talbot in the kitchen, over the pitcher and tumbler, discussing the quadrangular problem of your households, while you waited for Logan's to deliver a fresh supply of grape juice. Now, Emily Fox. It was brought out at the trial that during this period—before the delivery of the grape juice—you also stopped in."

Emily turned from the window. "I beg your pardon?"

"You dropped in, Mrs. Fox. You began to tell us about that before."

"Oh. Yes," said Emily. "I'd picked some branches of white and purple lilac in my back garden. I knew Jessie was to come downstairs that morning and I thought she'd enjoy having some fresh flowers. So I walked over with them."

"You entered this house—let me see . . . was it by the front door, Mrs. Fox, or the rear door?"

"The rear, Mr. Queen. Through the kitchen."

"Then you must have run into your husband there, talking to your brother-in-law?"

"Yes." Emily's back became straighter. "I was surprised, because I thought Talbot had gone directly to the shop. But Tal said he'd stopped by to discuss some business with Bayard, and Bayard didn't contradict him, so I went on into the living room, where Bayard said Jessica was lying down. She was resting on the sofa, the afghan over her legs. She made a nice fuss about the lilacs, I remember. I went upstairs to the bathroom, filled a vase with water, brought it back down, and put the lilacs in. We talked a while."

"About what, Mrs. Fox?"

Emily started. "I don't really recall, Mr. Queen. Nothing important, I'm sure."

Ellery smiled. "Your testimony on the witness stand twelve years ago was that you talked about how Jessica felt after her long illness, about spring cleaning—which was long overdue in Jessica's establishment and about which she felt badly—about how nicely Linda and Davy got along, considering that they were at the boy-hates-girl age—" Davy and Linda gripped hands furtively—"and about how bad your husbands kept saying business was."

"It's so long ago," sighed Talbot's wife.

"Nothing important, as you say, Mrs. Fox. And then you left?"

"Yes. I was there only a few minutes."

"By which door did you leave, Mrs. Fox—can you recall?"

"The front, I think . . . yes, the front." Ellery nodded; that had been her testimony. "I remember I didn't go out through the kitchen way because I didn't want to disturb the men's . . . business talk."

"Oh, that was the reason? By the way, Mrs. Fox, do you happen to recall this? On your way *into* the house —when you first came through the back yard approaching the kitchen door with the lilacs for Jessica—were the kitchen windows open or closed?"

"The kitchen windows?" Emily shook her head. "I really can't say, Mr. Queen."

"I don't blame you," said Ellery with a smile. "Such a trivial detail. But try to think, Mrs. Fox. For instance, as you approached the kitchen door, could you hear your husband and Bayard talking inside? From the back yard? From the back porch?"

"Well, now . . . wait. Yes. I think I did hear their voices. Mumbly, sort of. You know how you hear voices sometimes without being able to make out the words."

"As a matter of fact," Bayard said suddenly, "the windows *were* open, Emily. I remember because it had rained during the night and I'd had to get up about 3 A.M. and go around the house closing all the windows. So when I got up that morning the first thing I did was open them all again, throughout the house."

"Then the kitchen windows were open," said Ellery. "I'd been wondering about that." He did not explain why he had been wondering about it, but continued pleasantly: "Suppose we all go into the kitchen. We'll continue our investigation there."

Wrightsville's ladies are proud of their kitchens, even the ladies who live on the Hill. No skimpy ten-by-ten city "boxes" for them, thank you! In Wrightsville the kitchen is the hearth and the refuge—the tavern, as it were—of the family group, and it is built to generous dimensions, to take a big range and a big refrigerator and a big table and many kitchen chairs. There are cupboards and closets for every culinary and housekeeping purpose—and then room to spare.

The dead woman's kitchen would have been approved by the most exacting matron in town. Even through the dust and rust and tarnish of a dozen untended years its sturdy housewifely character shone. One long wall was all cupboard-unit, built around a double porcelain sink: cabinets above, and cupboards below, the cupboards divided into numerous drawers, the cabinets an army of glass-fronted housewife's delights, their shelves daintily edged with scalloped blue-and-white oil cloth and crowded with dishes, ordinary and "company," glassware likewise of the "common" or everyday and the "good" or Sunday and special-occasion varieties, cooking utensils, gadgets, spices, condiments, "pickles," herbs, cereals, and all that endless array of accessories to good housekeeping without any one of which the Wrightsville matron would have felt positively impoverished.

On the opposite wall stood a large white range with two ovens and a warming oven and six burners. A double-doored, six-foot electric refrigerator stood against the same wall. A vast porcelain-topped table occupied the axis of the kitchen, and strong white wooden chairs were neatly tucked beneath it.

Above the double sink was a double window, looking out upon the other side from the Talbot Foxes'. A door, fitted out with an accessory screen door for summer use, was set into the rear wall. Chief Dakin had opened the solid door as well as the windows, and they could see through the rusted screening the back porch and the garden, now a lofty forest of weeds, and the walk curving off through it toward the corresponding garden at the rear of the Talbot Fox house.

"Well, I'll be—Linny, look. Dad." Davy Fox grinned feebly. "There's my old checker game."

It was on the kitchen table, its black and red discs still in position on the board—a game which had been begun twelve years before and had never been finished.

"It's weird," said Linda with a little shiver.

"We played that previous night, Davy," said Bayard with a smile. "But we stopped in the middle because you had to go to bed."

"It's kind of dim, Dad."

"You accused me of stopping the game because you were licking the pants off me. And you were, too." Bayard looked about, still smiling faintly. There were two copper-bottomed pots on the range, green-black with age. The handles on the refrigerator were tarnished to the color of gunmetal. The dampness of twelve unheated winters had warped and cracked the blue-and-white squares of the floor linoleum, and dust covered everything. But Bayard did not seem to notice. He just kept looking around, with that faint pleased smile.

"These windows. The screens," said Ellery.

They were the full-window type of screen, which fits on like a storm window, fastens to the inside by a hook, and does not interfere with the opening or closing of the window.

"Are these the identical screens which were on the windows that morning twelve years ago?"

"Yep," said Chief Dakin. "If you're thinkin' maybe the kitchen screens—or any of the other screens in the house—were tampered with from the garden or the drive out there . . . from outside . . . I can promise you they weren't, Mr. Queen. I checked 'em all myself first thing, in the original investigation."

Ellery dismissed the mysterious subject of the kitchen windows abruptly. "All right, Bayard. Let's go through the business. I assume the original pitcher and tumbler you used that morning in preparing the grape juice aren't here—"

"They were evidence in his trial," said Detective Howie. The sound of his own voice seemed to startle him. Abashed, he sneered defensively.

Ellery ignored him. "Bayard, is there another pitcher and tumbler here like the ones you used?"

"There can't be another pitcher," replied Bayard. "It was part of an iced-drink set—one pitcher and eight tumblers. There ought to be some of the tumblers on the shelf here, though." He scanned the glass-paned wall cabinet immediately to the left of the sink. "Yes. There they are, Mr. Queen."

Ellery went to the cabinet and tried to open it. But it was stuck fast; dampness had swollen the wood frame. Chief Dakin produced an all-purpose pocket knife, and between them they managed to pry the cabinet door open.

Ellery took down one of the tumblers which Bayard had indicated and blew the dust from its surface. It was a heavy glass, dark purple in color and virtually opaque; its massive exterior had been cut in an ornate bunch-of-grapes pattern which spread all over the glass.

He hefted it thoughtfully. "This is exactly like the one you used that morning, Bayard?"

"Oh, yes. Part of the same set."

"Was the pitcher of the identical color and design?"

"Yes."

"Too bad we haven't the original pitcher. Well, we'll make shift with a substitute. This one up here should do."

Ellery took down a very ordinary two-quart pitcher of clear glass, blew on it, and handed it to Bayard with the purple tumbler.

"Now show me just what you did when you took the original pitcher and glass from the purple iced-drink set out of this cabinet."

Bayard set them down on the porcelain drainboard of the sink.

"Oh, no," said Ellery with a smile. "The testimony was that you rinsed both the pitcher and tumbler at the sink just after taking them from the cabinet."

Bayard reddened. "Is that so? I've forgotten."

"Naturally. That's all you took down—just the pitcher and glass?"

"That's all."

"Was anything else standing on the drainboard or in the sink, Bayard?"

"No. I'd washed and wiped Davy's and my breakfast dishes that morning after Davy left for school, but before Jessie came downstairs. The drainboard was bare. There wasn't anything on it but the pitcher and glass."

Ellery stood ruminating over what he knew of the story from having studied the trial records.

Jessica Fox had had no breakfast that morning. Her last meal had been eaten the night before, a meal shared by both her husband and her son, and from which none of them experienced ill effects. She had awakened the next morning fresh, strong, and elated over the adventure of going downstairs for the first time in months. The first and the only substance Jessica had put into her stomach that morning was the grape juice Bayard prepared for her.

Two hours later she became violently ill.

The fact that nothing had passed her lips that morning except the grape juice had been established by Jessica herself, according to the testimony of her physician, Dr. Willoughby, to whom she had confided that all-important piece of information when the doctor arrived at Bayard Fox's house in response to Bayard's frantic summons.

Apparently Dr. Willoughby had not suspected foul play at the very beginning. But a later piecing together of the evidence indicated beyond question—or at least to the satisfaction of an impressive parade of medical luminaries—that Jessica had died of digitalis poisoning.

The source of the drug was no mystery. A bottle of it, nearly full, had stood in the medicine chest in the upstairs bathroom. Jessica's heart, never too strong, had weakened further under the strain of resisting the pneumonia, and Dr. Willoughby had prescribed for a very short time a daily dose of tincture of digitalis—a powerful cardiac stimulant, dark green in color, derived from the purple foxglove, which is commonly used in diseases of the heart to correct lost compensation. Jessica herself informed Dr. Willoughby that she had followed his orders and discontinued the prescribed dosage of digitalis exactly two weeks before, on Memorial Day.

Yet both official and unofficial medical opinion, based upon the symptoms as later reviewed, and one salient fact, had been that Jessica Fox's death was caused by a huge, killing overdose of digitalis, which must have been taken that morning.

It was obvious, then, that she had not been the victim of an accidental overdose at her hand in the normal course of "taking her medicine"; it was equally obvious that the overdose had been deliberately given to her in something she had eaten or drunk that morning. And since by her own testimony the only thing she had eaten or drunk that morning had been the grape juice, it was elementary that the overdose of digitalis—the poisonous potion—had been administered to Jessica Fox *in the grape juice.*

QUESTION: Exactly how did the poisonous overdose get into Jessica's grape juice? It all simmered down to that.

10.   The Fox and the Grapes

ELLERY ASKED CHIEF Dakin: "Are Mr. Logan and Abraham L. Jackson here?"

"I've got them waitin' on the porch."

"I'm ready for them."

Dakin went out. He returned shortly with a hatless, middle-aged white man with empurpled hands and face, who wore a bloody butcher's apron over which he had hastily thrown a Norfolk jacket, and a nervous young Negro in Army uniform.

"You're Mr. Logan," said Ellery, addressing the aproned man, "proprietor of Logan's Market in High Village?"

"I am," said Mr. Logan, wetting his lips. "I am."

"Do you recall testifying in the trial of Bayard Fox twelve years ago, Mr. Logan?"

"I guess I do. Yes, sir, I do."

"You were questioned specifically at that time about taking a telephone order from Mr. Fox for six quart-sized bottles of grape juice, on the morning of the day Mrs. Fox was allegedly poisoned. Do you remember that, Mr. Logan?"

"I sure do."

"I'd like to hear that testimony again, as accurately as you can recall it."

"Well." Mr. Logan's shrewd little eyes became reflective; his first nervousness gone, he meant to make the most of his moment. "Near as I can recollect, I answered the phone in the store and Mr. Bayard Fox said to me: 'Mr. Logan, we've run out of grape juice and Mrs. Fox is downstairs this mornin' for the first time since she's been so sick and she wants grape juice. Could you do me a special favor and send six quart bottles up the Hill right away?' It wasn't our regular delivery time, y'see, and Mr. Fox knew that, because he'd been doin' the orderin' for months. 'Why, certainly, Mr. Fox,' I said. 'Glad to oblige. Will there be anything else?' But he says no, he'll phone me their regular midweek order next day. I didn't mind, because my customers are nearly all on the Hill, and I've always found it's good business to—"

"Yes, yes, Mr. Logan. Tell me—how did Bayard Fox sound over the telephone?"

"Sound?" The tradesman blinked. "Why, all right, I guess."

"Did he seem happy?"

"Well . . . Mr. Fox never did sound exactly *happy*."

"You don't remember."

Mr. Logan grinned weakly. "I guess you got me."

"What happened when you hung up?"

"I filled the order."

"Yourself."

"Yes. My clerks were all busy at the time, so I went over to the grocery department—usually I stay behind

the meat counter—and took six quart bottles of grape
juice off the fruit-juice shelf—"

"A national brand."

"Oh, yes."

"They were in metal-capped bottles?"

"That's right."

"The bottles were in perfect condition when you took
them off the shelf, Mr. Logan? You didn't notice anything wrong with one of the caps, for instance?"

"No, sir. I've sold I'd say thousands of bottles of that
brand of grape juice in my time, and I've never had a
complaint yet."

"Then what did you do?"

"Why, I said to Abe L. here—" The soldier started
and tugged at his tunic—"Abe was a delivery boy for
me at that time—'bout fourteen, Abe, weren't you?"—
The soldier nodded vigorously—"I said to Abe: 'Abe
L., you take the Ford truck and run these bottles of
grape juice up the Hill to the Bayard Foxes'. They want
'em right off.' So Abe says 'Okay, Mr. Logan' and the
last I see of 'em Abe's stowing 'em in an empty carton."

"Thanks very much, Mr. Logan. That's all."

Mr. Logan lingered. "You won't need me any more?"

"I'm sure we won't. Thank you."

"Well." The tradesman looked disappointed. He
glanced jauntily in the direction of Chief Dakin, but the
Chief did not smile, so Logan slapped the soldier on the
arm. "Don't let 'em court-martial you, Abe. Good
luck!" he said and he went out, chuckling over his sally,
which Ellery felt certain he would repeat to his clerks
and customers for weeks to come.

The soldier, thus deserted, gulped several times and
then stood at attention.

"Well, Corporal," said Ellery with a grin, "I see
you've changed employers in the last twelve years."

Corporal Jackson looked astonished. Then he grinned
back. "Yes, sir. I used to drive a delivery truck for Mr.
Logan, now I'm driving ditto for Uncle Sam."

"Home on leave, are you?"

"Yes, sir."

"Hi, Abe L.," said Davy. "Remember me?"

Corporal Jackson showed his teeth. "Yes, *sir*, Captain. You sure showed those Japs, didn't you, Captain?"

"I sure did," said Davy. "How's Rose-Ann?"

"She married me."

"She always said she would!"

"Got a couple of kids," said Corporal Jackson proudly.

"Good for Rose-Ann."

"Good for me!"

And suddenly everyone, even Bayard, was smiling, in a sort of happiness, and Corporal Jackson was no longer nervous.

"We won't keep you from your family long, Corporal," said Ellery. "Do you remember delivering the grape juice to this house that morning twelve years ago?"

"Yes, sir. I remember the whole thing plain."

Ellery silently blessed the circumstance that had set the crime in Wrightsville rather than a large city. Any murder case in a town of ten thousand souls, half-industrial, half-rural, would be bound to become a *cause célèbre,* details of which would be repeated for years by those lucky enough to have been involved, and so perpetuated. If there was the inevitable danger of details becoming distorted and the various stories enlarged through repetition, there was also the contemporaneous testimony in the trial records as a frame of reference. It was not wonderful that the colored delivery boy of fourteen should, as a responsible citizen of twenty-six, recall the details of that grape-juice delivery twelve years before; it would have been wonderful had he not done so.

Corporal Jackson told his story with dignity, relish, and some transparent embellishment; but the essence of it was an exact distillation of his testimony as a boy.

He had placed the six bottles of grape juice into an empty carton at Logan's Market. He had carried the carton out to the Ford truck parked in the narrow alley behind the store—the alley which the market shared with the side entrance of Upham House and the fire-exits at the rear of the Bijou Movie Theater. He had climbed behind the wheel and set the carton beside him on the empty companion-seat. He had *not* left the carton there and returned to the store, or gone around the corner to Al Brown's for a soda—Corporal Abraham L. Jackson was most vehement on that point (as he had been on the witness stand under fire). After depositing the carton with the grape juice (visible to him at all times, he insisted) on the seat beside him, he had driven directly out of the alley into Washington Street, into the Square, into Lower Main, into Upper Whistling, and straight out Upper Whistling towards Hill Drive in the northeastern section of town.

He had made no stopovers of any kind, for any purpose. ("Once I got on Upper Whistling I didn't even shift gears till I got to the bottom of the Hill, and then only to go into second because the old truck wouldn't make it on high," asserted Corporal Jackson.) No one had hopped onto his running-board en route. No one had "hitched a ride" in the seat beside him.

"Those bottles of grape juice were right alongside me till I drove into Mr. Fox's driveway and stopped the truck and jumped out and lugged the carton into the kitchen through the back porch."

He had found the Fox brothers, both of whom he knew well, talking in the kitchen; yes, he had noticed a purple pitcher and a purple glass on the drainboard, because as he set the carton down on the table he remembered Mr. Bayard Fox saying: "You got here almighty fast, Abe L.—thanks a lot. I've got the pitcher waiting!" And then Abe L. had handed Mr. Bayard the carbon copy of the bill Mr. Logan had made out and Mr. Bayard had said to tack the grape-juice charge onto the next regular-delivery bill, and Abe L. left by the back door just as Mr. Bayard was hoisting one of the quart bottles of grape juice from the carton.

When Corporal Jackson had left, Ellery said to Bayard: "You took one of the six quarts of grape juice out of the carton. Did anything happen, Bayard—please try to remember—that *dictated* your choice of the bottle you selected?"

Bayard shook his head. "There were six, and they were all alike, and I simply took the first one my hand lit on."

"The other five bottles, Mr. Queen," Chief Dakin interposed, "were all analyzed by the Sieglitz Labs over at Connhaven. And so was the grape juice that was left in the quart bottle after Mr. Fox poured some off for Mrs. Fox's drink. The Sieglitz Labs gave *all* the grape juice left in the bottles a clean bill. Absolutely pure, their report said."

"I know, Dakin," said Ellery gently, "but you'll forgive me if I go over the ground myself, in my own way." Dakin colored and coughed. "So, Bayard, you took one of the bottles out of the carton *at random.* Then what?"

"Then I went to one of those drawers—" Bayard at the many drawers in the cupboard-unit, then shook his head—"I've forgotten now which drawer it was kept in —and took out a bottle opener and with it I removed the metal cap of the bottle. And then I poured enough grape juice out of the bottle into the glass to fill it to the brim —the first of the two glassfuls of grape juice I poured from the bottle."

"Do you recall Bayard's doing that, Talbot?" asked Ellery suddenly.

Talbot started. "Yes. Yes, Mr. Queen. That's just what he did. I was standing right here when Bay filled the tumbler."

"It was at about this time, wasn't it, Bayard, that there was another interruption?"

"Interruption? Oh. Yes. The drugstore delivered a bottle of aspirins."

Ellery glanced at the Chief of Police. "I'd like to talk to Alvin Cain, please," he said.

Ellery beheld a man in a sculptured linen suit, panama in hand, hair combed carefully over a thin spot, who came in with a bounce, stopped short, and then looked around with quick little glances. There were brown wrinkles at the corners of his eyes and purple pads beneath them. The pallor under his swarthiness gave his skin a lavender look.

"Hello there, Linny." Pharmacist Cain was nervous.

"Hello, Alvin."

"Davy. How's the boy?"

Davy did not reply.

Cain's glance darted at Bayard. He did not greet Davy's father. He nodded respectfully, however, to the Talbot Foxes and then stood there, clutching the brim of his panama.

Pharmacist Cain must have been just under thirty during the trial, thought Ellery. The super-fastidious type . . . on the surface; one could not be sure of what lay beneath. Shoetips glistening. Clothes without wrinkles and immaculate. Deeply burned by the sun; he would play a desperate, swashbuckling, ineffectual game of golf. The small-town Beau Brummell, ever ready with a wisecrack, ever yearning for big cities, always avoiding them; the joy of the local haberdashers.

"Mr. Queen." Chief Dakin beckoned.

Ellery excused himself and joined Dakin in a corner.

"I thought you ought to know," whispered Dakin. "Cain was mighty sweet on Linda Fox all the time she was growin' up. I guess he still is."

"Davey mentioned something about it. But I didn't take it seriously. Linda—and that oaf?"

"Oh, it's never meant anything to little Lin. But Cain —he's the type thinks girls can't resist him."

"But he's old enough to be her father."

"Alvin spends a lot of money preservin' himself," said the Chief dryly. "Anyway, his ideas ain't paternal."

"He's serious about Linda?"

"As serious as he could be about any woman."

"Thanks, Dakin."

They returned to the group.

"I shan't keep you long, Mr. Cain," said Ellery smoothly. The man's nervousness had increased during the whispered interchange between Ellery and the Chief. "Do you know what it is we're trying to do here?"

"The Chief told me when he phoned me."

Ellery could detect nothing in the man's tone; it was perfectly proper.

"I take it you know what this means to Davy Fox—and Linda."

"It sounds squiffy to me," said Alvin Cain. "But if you say so, pal—okay." He smiled at Linda, showing his dimple. "I'll do what I can, baby."

"Thanks, Alvin."

Davy swallowed—hard.

"The only thing is," said the pharmacist jauntily—"what?"

He flings a wisecrack, Ellery thought, into the very teeth of a serious moment; this makes him feel superior to the situation; in reality, he is frightened and uncertain.

"What you can do, Mr. Cain, is only what I'm asking everyone to do: Tell the truth."

"Sure. Say!" Alvin Cain flushed. "Why shouldn't I tell the truth? I've got no reason not to!"

And Mr. Cain carries a chip. It might mean something.

"I'm sure you haven't," smiled Ellery. "Well, let's get on. You own the High Village Pharmacy now, I understand, but at the time of the Fox trial twelve years ago you were merely a clerk there?"

Alvin had recovered. "Slaved for old Myron Garbage for twenty-eight seeds per," he said smartly. "I bought the store out—lock, stock, and good will—a couple of years ago when Garback dropped dead. Always said I would."

"You were a witness at Mr. Fox's trial."

"Yeh man. About the aspirin."

"But your testimony," interposed Chief Dakin slyly. "It was kicked right out the court window, Alvin."

Cain's smile was half a snarl. "I can't help that, Chief. They subpoenaed me. I told 'em what I knew. Who cares what they did with it?"

"The aspirin," said Ellery gently. "Oh, just a minute. Bayard, how did Alvin Cain come to deliver a bottle of aspirins that morning?"

"I'd phoned the High Village Pharmacy the night before," Bayard explained. "Jessie'd had a slight headache and wanted an aspirin, but when I went to look for some in the medicine chest, I couldn't find any. So I phoned the Pharmacy. Alvin here answered—the clerk. I asked him if he'd send over a bottle of 100 tablets right away. Alvin said he couldn't leave the store alone— Garback'd gone home early—but he'd deliver a bottle in the morning. I hung up and ran over to Talbot's next door and got a few aspirins from Emily—remember, Emily?"—Emily Fox barely nodded—"and gave Jessie two, and it cleared up her headache in a half-hour. Then the next morning, while I was pouring the grape juice into the glass in the kitchen, and talking to Tal, Alvin delivered the bottle of 100 tablets."

"Wasn't there something more, Bayard?" Ellery asked. "Something about an argument between you and Cain over the phone the preceding night, when you called the Pharmacy?"

"Oh, that." Bayard smiled a little.

"You sure bawled me out, Foxy," said Alvin Cain. There was contempt in his patronizing tones—quite unconscious, Ellery felt sure. Davy stiffened; but Linda put her hand on his arm, and he relaxed.

"What was the argument about, Mr. Cain?"

"When Fox asked me on the phone that previous night to deliver a bottle of 100 aspirins, I said: 'Say, Mr. Fox, what do you do with that stuff—eat it?' You know, cracking wise. But he gets sore and wants to know what 'right' I have talking to him 'that way,' and a lot more gilhooley like that. So I said, look, I delivered some rubbing alcohol and mouth wash and iodine and stuff to your house only yesterday, and in the order was a bottle of 100 aspirins. Don't tell me you've used 100 tablets in less than two days! He got nasty and said nobody had to give me an accounting and what did I mean by keeping 'tabs' on him that way, and I'd better send a bottle over right away or he'd report me to Mr. Garback. That got *my* monkey up. Look, Foxy old boy, I said, I don't need Myron Garbage and I don't need *you*, and as far as this job is concerned, Garback knows what he can do with it. And a lot more like that—about crabby customers, and so forth. Well, we had it out for a while, then we both cooled off and apologized, and finally I said I'd run the aspirins over first thing in the morning, which I did. That's all there is, there isn't any more," concluded Alvin Cain with a wink.

"When you delivered the aspirins the next morning, you came through the rear—directly into the kitchen?"

"That's the ticket, friend. The Fox brothers were in here, jawing about something, and Bayard was just pouring grape juice from a full bottle into a purple glass —filled it right up to the top. I tossed the aspirins on the table—right here—and I said: 'No hard feelings, Mr. Fox. About last night, I mean,' because the truth is I'd had a few beers over at the Square Grill for supper the night before and they'd gone to my head, ha-ha!—and Foxy said: 'No, of course not. Just charge this to my account, Alvin,' and then I left."

"Bayard Fox didn't leave the purple tumbler full of grape juice even for a moment? Didn't turn his back on it, for instance?"

"He couldn't have. He was pouring it in while he was talking to me. When I left he was filling the glass from the bottle a second time."

"Thanks, Mr. Cain. That's all."

"Keep the change, old-timer. Well, Linda, I'll be seein' you! Drop around sometime—with or without friend husband!" And Alvin Cain left, adjusting his panama to a carefully dashing angle.

"Someday—soon," Davy remarked in a quiet way— "I'm going to knock that hat off his head and ram it down his throat."

Ellery stood frowning for a moment.

Then he said: "About those aspirins, Bayard." The aspirins seemed to bother him. "What did happen to the bottle of 100 tablets Cain had delivered the day before?"

"I don't know. I'd unwrapped the package myself, and the various things in it—the iodine, mouth wash, aspirin, and so forth—I stowed away in the medicine chest in the bathroom upstairs. But that evening, when I went for the aspirins, as I've told you, for Jessie's headache, Mr. Queen—the bottle wasn't there."

Ellery glanced at Chief Dakin. "I don't recall anything in the trial transcript about a missing bottle of aspirins, Dakin. Why the omission?"

"Because it couldn't have had anything to do with the death of Mrs. Fox," retorted the policeman. "That's why Cain's testimony wasn't admitted, either . . . about the aspirins, I mean. The phone call and the argument, of course, was."

"The autopsy revealed no unusual quantity of aspirin?"

"That's right."

"And of course," said Ellery fretfully, "there's no medical connection that I know of between aspirin and digitalis." He shook his head. "It's a peculiarity," he complained. "A loose end. Why should a fresh—in fact, unopened—bottle of 100 aspirins be missing?"

He had not been addressing Bayard, but it was Bayard who answered. "We just didn't bother our heads about it, Mr. Queen. We took it for granted that the bottle was mislaid somewhere in the house."

Ellery sighed. "Well, let's get back to the preparation of the drink that poisoned Jessica Fox.

"Our investigation so far," Ellery said reflectively, "has demonstrated that the digitalis couldn't have been in the bottle of grape-juice concentrate from which Bayard filled the purple tumbler. The quart bottle was one of six freshly delivered from Logan's, Bayard selected it from among the six wholly at random, he uncapped it, he poured out the first tumblerful. To that point, then, the grape juice was unadulterated. But how about the tumbler itself?"

"The trial went into all that, Mr. Queen," said Chief Dakin patiently.

"But let's follow through. Could the *tumbler* into which you poured the grape juice from the bottle, Bayard, have contained the poison?"

"Impossible," said Bayard. "I'd thoroughly rinsed the tumbler at the hot-water tap before I filled it with juice."

"Talbot, you saw your brother do that?"

Talbot Fox nodded.

"Clearing the tumbler. Now. *Could the water from the sink tap have been poisoned? The water with which the glass was rinsed?*"

The Chief of Police shook his head. "If you'll recall the testimony, Mr. Queen, we'd had the Sieglitz Laboratories analyze the water from both kitchen taps. It was also checked by the Chief Chemist of the State Water Department. Both reports gave the water—hot *and* cold —a clean bill."

"All right," nodded Ellery. "So we now have unpoisoned grape juice in an unpoisoned tumbler which was rinsed with unpoisoned city water. Bayard, what did you do next?"

"I poured the grape juice from the tumbler into the pitcher, the pitcher from the purple set. And then—"

"Stop. Logical question: Could the *pitcher* have contained the poison?"

Bayard shrugged. "I'd rinsed the pitcher in hot water at the same time I rinsed the glass."

"I'll testify to that," added his brother. He grinned a little. "In fact, I did testify to it."

"So the pitcher is eliminated. Keep going, Bayard. What did you do then?"

Bayard explained with the first note of impatience he had displayed since the investigation began. Apparently Detective Howie, who had been a sphinxian auditor of the proceedings, mistook impatience for desperation; the fat man roused himself and jabbed Bayard's thin shoulder with his forefinger, as if to remind him that he was a prisoner of the law and that any suspicious move would evoke instant and merciless consequences. But Bayard merely shrugged the finger off.

Jessica, he said, had always preferred her grape juice diluted with water in a 50-50 ratio: half grape juice, half water. After pouring two full tumblers of grape juice into the pitcher, he had refilled the tumbler twice with cold water from the tap and poured this water into the pitcher after the grape juice.

"And since the water from the cold tap was also pronounced pure by the chemists," mused Ellery, "then at this point the contents of the purple pitcher—half grapejuice concentrate and half cold water—were still unpoisoned." But then Ellery narrowed his eyes. "No. Not necessarily. Logically the poison could still have been in that cold water."

"But I tell you the cold as well as the hot was okayed, Mr. Queen," objected Dakin.

"Nevertheless."

"How come?"

"The tap, Dakin. It's an old trick—putting poison under the filter, say, of the tap, so that when the tap is turned on the poison is washed into the container along with the water."

But the Chief only smiled. "We didn't miss up on that one, Mr. Queen, though it's a fact it didn't come out in the trial—the defense never brought it up. I had both taps taken apart and thoroughly examined. Given a chemical analysis, as well. My reports said there had been no poison in either the hot or the cold tap, digitalis, or any other foreign substance."

Ellery made a face. "Too bad. By the way, the purple tumbler holds about a half-pint, doesn't it?"

"Exactly a half-pint, Mr. Queen."

"So we now have a full quart of liquid in the pitcher —two tumblers, or one pint, of grape-juice concentrate and two tumblers, or one pint, of cold water—and all the contents have been proved free from digitalis, as well as the tumbler and pitcher themselves. What happened next, Bayard?"

"I added the ice—"

"Ice!" Ellery glanced swiftly at the tall refrigerator. "Ice from an automatic refrigerator! Another old trick. *The digitalis had been mixed with the water in one of the ice trays.* The water froze into cubes, and when you used those cubes, Bayard, they contained the poison. Poison in the ice!"

Before the excitement could begin to rise, Chief Dakin crushed it. "I went into that, Mr. Queen," he said simply. "But Bayard Fox didn't use ice cubes from the electric refrigerator that mornin'. He'd defrosted the box the night before."

"Then where did he get the ice to put into the pitcher of grape juice, Dakin?" demanded Ellery with a scowl.

"In the summer time the Foxes used to keep an old-fashioned ice chest on the back porch there, as a sort of extra storage box for beer, watermelon, and other bulky summer items—most folks up here do.

"The Wrightsville Ice Company—it's a big outfit, Mr. Queen, absolutely reliable, got a great big modern purifying plant—they'd delivered two fifty-pound cakes only the day before. You could hardly say someone'd frozen digitalis into a fifty-pound cake of ice!

"Mr. Fox chipped a piece off one of the cakes with the icepick the Company provides, ran cold water from the same tap there over it to clean the ice, and dropped it—one big chunk—into the pitcher.

"It all came out in the trial, but for some reason or other was ordered struck out by Judge Newbold, so it doesn't appear in the transcript you read."

"Eliminating the ice," growled Ellery. "All right, Bayard, you now had the purple pitcher containing a quart of dilute grape juice and some ice—or rather, one chunk of ice—and at this point the contents of the pitcher were still pure. What was your next step?"

Bayard had taken a fresh glass, another of the purple iced-drink set, down from the kitchen cabinet.

"Could the digitalis have been in that second glass?"

No, this tumbler too had been thoroughly rinsed by Bayard—"Neither Davy nor I," Bayard smiled, "were what you'd call expert dishwashers, and I usually rinsed everything before using it—during that time when Jessie was sick—just to make sure it was really clean. Tal saw me rinse that second glass."

Ellery nodded. "It was at this point, I believe, that your brother left the house?"

"Yes. I'd just rinsed the second glass. We'd got to the

end of our talk. Tal said something about being pretty late—he'd have to be getting down to the shop—and I said all right, so Tal walked out of the kitchen, down the back porch, back across the two gardens to his garage, and a couple of minutes later I heard him drive out to the road and down the Hill. . . . You asked for every detail," Bayard added, rather suddenly.

It seemed a queer thing to say. And all at once an impression which had been gathering texture in Ellery's mind was complete, to the selvage. Bayard Fox's talk was striking, and had been striking from the first, at his brother Talbot . . . as if in Bayard's thoughts Talbot Fox was not in the least what he seemed.

The question was: Was this really what Bayard was thinking, or was it a cunning attempt to project suspicion against his brother into Ellery's brain?

And now their interest surged back, after its natural flagging during the long interrogation, for this was the crucial episode: The husband alone in the kitchen for the first time with the pitcher of grape juice, the wife in the living room resting on the sofa, and not another soul in the house.

"I carried the pitcher and glass into the living room," said Bayard somberly, "and I set them down on the coffee table in front of the sofa. I asked Jessie how she felt. She said fine, it was good to be downstairs. She was very nice about my having made her the grape juice. She did remark that maybe it wouldn't be too good for her to drink it iced—Dr. Willoughby was dead set against iced drinks for anybody, let alone sick patients—I'd forgotten that—so I fished the chunk of ice out of the pitcher with the rim of the glass. The ice hadn't been in the pitcher more than a few minutes, so the grape juice wasn't cold—"

"Also it hadn't been in long enough to have melted appreciably," Ellery pointed out. "Meaning that there was still almost exactly one quart of liquid in the pitcher. You filled the glass after fishing the ice out of the pitcher, Bayard?"

"Not right off, no. The empty glass just stood on the coffee table, next to the pitcher, till later."

"I see. The pitcher, too, remained on the coffee table? All the time you were in the living room with your wife?"

"Yes."

Ellery scowled, jamming his hands into his pockets. "All the materials have been proved pure. All the containers used in the preparation of the grape juice have been proved pure as well. Yet the facts say beyond argument that the overdose of digitalis *must* have been taken in the grape juice, since that was the sole substance that passed Jessica Fox's lips before she became so violently ill. Only possible conclusion: The poison must have been *dropped* into either the pitcher or the glass from which she drank—dropped in *after* the pitcherful was prepared."

Dakin nodded grimly. "That's it, Mr. Queen. Now you've got it. It was dropped in by Bayard after Talbot left the house and—"

"Please, Dakin." Dakin stopped. "Let's see if we can't narrow the possibilities down to either the glass or the pitcher. The testimony said something about the tumbler's breaking, I believe?"

"Yes," said Bayard. "After we'd been sitting in the living room a few minutes, talking, Jessie leaned over to pick up the glass so I could fill it for her. But she was still pretty weak, and the glass was heavy. It slipped out of her hand, hitting aginst the edge of the coffee table, and broke."

Bayard had picked up the fragments of the broken tumbler and taken them back to the kitchen. Jessica went with him.

"I'm going with you," Jessica had said. "I'd like to see what my kitchen looks like. I can imagine the mess you and Davy have made of it, Bay!"

So husband and wife had gone from the living room to the kitchen together. And while Bayard threw the pieces of the smashed glass into the kitchen garbage pail, Jessica with her own hands took a third glass from the same iced-drink set down from the cabinet. They had walked back to the living room slowly, Jessica herself carrying the tumbler; and then Bayard had picked the pitcher up from the coffee table and poured grape juice into the tumbler as Jessica held it out to be filled.

And Jessica drank.

"You were with your wife every moment from the time you first brought the grape juice into the living room?" Ellery asked Bayard sharply.

Bayard nodded.

"Your wife was never alone with either the pitcher or the glass from which she drank?"

"Not for a second, Mr. Queen."

"On your walk back from the kitchen, did anything happen—anything at all—that might have caused you to turn your head for a few seconds, sidetracked you?"

"No, Mr. Queen. Jessie had to take it easy, and as a matter of fact I had my arm around her waist all the way, supporting her. I didn't lose sight of that glass she was carrying for a second."

"In other words, Bayard—and this is tremendously important, so think carefully before answering—in other words, it's your opinion that your wife could not *herself* have dropped the overdose of digitalis into the pitcher, or into the glass from which she subsequently drank?"

Bayard shook his head emphatically. "It's not a matter of 'opinion,' Mr. Queen. She just didn't. If she had, I'd have seen her do it. She couldn't even have done it while I was picking up the broken glass in the living room, or throwing the pieces into the garbage pail in the kitchen. I'd swear to that. I did swear to it. I went through this whole business at the trial, and before the trial with my lawyer. Jessie just didn't do it herself."

"I can see why your attorney," said Ellery through his teeth, "was exasperated with you at the trial."

"I told the truth. I'm still telling the truth."

"So the overdose wasn't self-administered—Jessica did not commit suicide." Ellery was silent. Then he tried again. "Let's see where we stand now. We established that the digitalis must have been dropped into either the pitcher or the glass. The broken tumbler is out—it was never used.

"Was the poison slipped into the tumbler that *was* used? The only person who touched or handled that tumbler was Jessica herself, and here you are, Bayard, protesting that she couldn't possibly have put the poison into that glass without your knowledge. So—the poison wasn't dropped into the *glass*.

"Then it follows that it was the *pitcher* into which the digitalis had been dropped—the pitcherful of grape juice. So when you and your wife returned from the kitchen to the living room and you filled the glass she was holding out, *the grape juice in the pitcher was already poisoned*.

"The question is: *When* had the digitalis been dropped into that pitcher? One of the first things that occurred to me, Dakin, in searching for a loophole in the case against Bayard Fox, was that *there was one interval during which the pitcher of grape juice was out of sight of Bayard . . . and of Jessica, too*. During that interval, the pitcher was alone and unguarded."

"When was that?" asked the Chief of Police quickly.

"The short period, after Jessica accidentally broke the glass, during which she and Bayard went to the kitchen for another one. The pitcher of grape juice was left on the coffee table in the living room, *alone*. It was conceivable that while the Foxes were in the kitchen, someone had entered the house either through the front door or one of the downstairs windows, perhaps a living-room window—that's one reason I was so interested in the question of the screens, Dakin—and poisoned the contents of the pitcher, escaping the same way."

"Oh, that." Dakin shook his head.

"Yes, I know. I found out in reading further in the trial records. There were three witnesses to cross-testify that no one did gain entry to the house during that period: Emily Fox, who after visiting Jessica was trimming the rose bushes in her front yard, which is adjacent to the Bayard Fox front yard and one side of the house; Hallam Luck, president of the Public Trust Company in the Square; and Mrs. Luck. The Lucks had been driving down the Hill towards town and had stopped to chat with Emily Fox in her front garden."

Emily nodded. "The three of us could actually see into the living room through Jessie's open windows as we talked. Nobody could possibly have entered her house while we were out there, either from the side visible to us, or the front. Anyway, nobody did. We saw Bayard come into the living room with the pitcher and glass, we saw Jessie drop the glass, we saw them both leave the room, and we saw them come back and Bayard pour grape juice from the pitcher on the coffee table into the glass Jessie'd brought back with her. We even saw Jessie drink." Emily shivered. After a moment, she continued: "Anyway, a minute or so later Mr. and Mrs. Luck drove on down the Hill, and I left a few minutes after that to go down to the Village to attend an Eastern Star luncheon."

Ellery looked lugubrious. "So that logical possibility was removed. I've already spoken to Mr. and Mrs. Luck and they confirm their original testimony to the letter. There's no doubt on that point whatever. You and Mr. and Mrs. Luck had the front and one side of the Bayard Fox house in full view, and the Bayard Foxes, from the kitchen, the rear and other side. Besides, you three—Emily Fox, and Mr. and Mrs. Luck—all swore no one did enter that living room while Bayard and Jessica were out of it.

"So the grape juice in the pitcher must have been poisoned *before* Bayard brought it into the living room to Jessica."

The atmosphere in the damp and dusty kitchen was thickening. Davy stood gnawing at his underlip. His father was detached and lax, that faint smile twisting his mouth. These two were looked at; they did not look at each other.

"Which brings us to the all-important question of opportunity. Who had opportunity to drop a large quantity of digitalis into that pitcher of grape juice?

"Jessica? Bayard himself says she had no opportunity.

"Emily?" Emily gasped, stiffening in her chair. Her nearsighted brown eyes flashed indignation. "Emily had left the house," Ellery went on calmly, "even before Bayard prepared the grape juice. In fact, before young Jackson drove up with the six bottles from Logan's Market."

"Well, I should think so!" snapped Emily. "Of all—"

"Talbot Fox?" Talbot had had time to brace himself; he did not react visibly. "True, Talbot was present in the kitchen throughout the preparation of the grape juice, but his testimony at the trial was that he had not once been in physical contact with either the ingredients or the containers—had not once touched anything, or been near enough to touch anything, connected with the drink Bayard was preparing." Ellery glanced sidewise at Bayard. "I seem to recall, Bayard, that you yourself affirmed the truth of this on the witness stand." What would the man say?

But Bayard merely said, in a stolid way: "My brother couldn't possibly have dropped the digitalis into the grape juice while we were talking in the kitchen." Did he stress, if ever so slightly, his qualifying clause? And yet he was eying Ellery with a deep sadness, almost a deeply bitter sadness.

It was either a masterpiece of contrived expression, or the unconscious manifestation of a shocking disappointment.

All mixed up. The man's either a doubly subtle schemer or so transparent one cannot see his thoughts or visualize his motives at all.

Ellery gripped himself, and nodded. "No one else was involved—only your wife, your brother, your sister-in-law, Bayard, and yourself. Jessica, Talbot, and Emily have been exonerated on purely factual grounds. Leaving . . . *yourself*, Bayard."

Davy turned away, choking. And Linda, too, made a sound, but it was a sobbing sound. She tried to take her husband's hand, but he snatched it away.

"Bayard, you're the only person in the state—the country—the Solar System," said Ellery deliberately, "who could have poured the digitalis into the pitcher of grape juice intended for Jessica Fox. You're the only human being in the universe who could have poisoned her. And for confirmation: Did *you* have opportunity? Decidedly you did: *You were alone with the grape juice in the kitchen and on the way to the living room* after your brother left the house, Bayard."

Davy looked down at his hands surreptitiously. But Ellery saw, and he saw that they were shaking, and that Davy slipped them into the trouser pockets. And Linda saw, too, and averted her eyes, looking at the wall as if it were already part of the cell she was to occupy for the rest of her life.

"That's what it all boiled down to in court twelve years ago," said Bayard hoarsely. "I had to admit then, and I admit now, that it all sounds absolutely true—that I was the only one who *could* have poisoned the grape juice. The only thing is—" he laughed—"I didn't."

And after an instant he added, as if impulsively: "I didn't understand it then, Mr. Queen, and right now, after twelve whole years of mulling over it in a prison cell . . . I still don't understand it."

Ellery studied him with such brutal intentness that Bayard flushed and looked away. But the flush was not the flush of guilt; it was the flush of anger. And he had turned aside as if to conceal the despair he felt his eyes must betray.

At this moment Detective Howie delivered one of his rare comments.

"This is stoopid."

Ellery made no reply.

Chief Dakin remarked in a mild tone: "It ain't stupid, but it's a gosh-awful waste of time, Mr. Queen. All this was proved twelve years ago. All this was the circumstantial case against Bayard Fox. There wasn't a cranny-hole twelve years ago, and there's none today."

Ellery's lips tightened.

"I have to make sure in my own way, Dakin."

Afterwards, when Howie had taken Bayard by the arm and marched him back to the house next door, and

Emily and Talbot Fox had followed them, in a bristling silence, Captain Fox lingered.

"It was a nice try, Mr. Queen," Davy said, wryly smiling.

"Was, Davy?" Ellery shook his head. "I'm afraid everyone misunderstands the purpose of this morning's activities. I really had no great hope of uncovering anything this morning. From reading the trial transcript it was obvious Prosecutor Tom Garback and Chief of Police Dakin had done a workmanlike job twelve years ago. This morning was a sort of warm-up, Davy. Now we know, in concrete terms, as of today, where we stand. Now we can go forward."

"Go forward to what?" Davy was still smiling. Linda shook his arm anxiously.

Ellery looked at him, and under that candid stare Davy colored and looked away. "I don't know, Davy. So far, I admit, all we seem to have done was corroborate the powerful circumstances that pinned the crime on your father. But—you never can tell."

"Then you don't think it's hopeless!" Linda cried.

Ellery took her hand. "Linda, I've found that nothing is really 'hopeless' if there's any hope concealed in it. I don't know whether there is or not. I haven't made up my mind about a great many things in this case. Put it this way: I'm not satisfied.

"I'm going to keep probing. I want to go over the facts again and again and again. Only when I'm convinced beyond any possibility of logical doubt that there are no other facts in existence which can be fitted into the present structure to change its shape . . . only then will I give up and go home."

11. Fox Trail

ELLERY TELEPHONED DR. Willoughby's office.

"Could I come over to see you now, Doctor?"

"Can you make it in an hour?" asked Dr. Willoughby. "I ought to be through with my waiting list then."

"In an hour."

Ellery looked thoughtful as he hung up. Dr. Willoughby had not sounded exactly enthusiastic. He wondered again what, if anything, the physician was concealing.

He decided to purge his mind of the details—to give it a rest from its morning's intense activity. Ellery had found this regimen helpful in the past, when a certain point had been reached and all seemed over but the technical admission of failure. He did not feel half so sanguine as his talk with Davy and Linda had conveyed. The truth was, the case looked blacker than ever, and only the ghostly glow of a suspicion—it could hardly be termed a belief—of Bayard Fox's truthfulness gave it any illumination whatever. And this might be—it probably was—delusion, or wishful thinking, or the result of clever histrionics. How could he be sure Davy's father was not acting a part?

Ellery tried to shake these thoughts off as he strolled down the Hill. The afternoon was pleasant, and the great shade trees along the Hill spread peace over its dappled walks. But there was no peace within him; he could not shake the facts out of his mind.

So as Ellery walked down into the town, he went over them again. He had a baffled feeling, that soon excited him: he had missed something. Something vital. Something that was there, visible yet invisible. A something that might explain everything.

The feeling was so strong that he paused before the Professional Building, on the corner of Slocum and Washington, opposite Logan's Market, to think the whole thing through again.

But the something continued to elude him.

Annoyed with himself, he entered the Professional Building and took the wide wooden stairs two steps at a time to the first floor, where he found Dr. Willoughby's shingle.

He went in. The waiting room, with its ancient green overstuffed furniture and lumpy seats, its faded Currier & Ives prints, its tattered periodicals, was untenanted. Dr. Willoughby, in a white office coat, was seated alone in his examining room beyond, looking abstracted.

But the old physician rose at once, brightening, and came out.

"I've sent my nurse home, Mr. Queen," he said, shaking Ellery's hand, "so we've got the place to ourselves."

"You have something to tell me!"

"Well, I don't know," said the doctor slowly. "Come into my office . . . I don't know what you know and what you don't. The reason I cleared my decks here was that I'm not too proud of my 'role,' I suppose you'd call it, in Jessica Fox's case. It's worried the life out of me these twelve years."

"I see," said Ellery, although he did not. "By the way, before we get off on something else: Jessica did tell you, did she not, that all she'd had to eat or drink that morning was the single glass of grape juice Bayard poured for her?"

"That's right. When I got there I asked her what she'd had to eat, and she said: 'Nothing, Doctor. I was too excited to have breakfast. But I let Bayard make me some grape juice, and I had a full glass of it.' "

Ellery nodded. "There was no doubt at all, I take it, that the woman died of digitalis poisoning."

Dr. Willoughby looked uncomfortable, and Ellery sat up alertly. "Not afterward. Looking back on it, the symptoms were exact enough. But at the time . . . Anyway, Bayard had left Jessica in the house shortly after giving her the grape juice—he had to go somewhere—and when he got back a couple of hours later, he found her—"

"Wait." Ellery perked up again. "I'd forgotten that. I recall now that the trial records brought it out: Bayard's leaving the house after giving his wife the drink. A hurry call from his brother Talbot, wasn't it?"

"Something like that. Anyway, when Bayard returned home, about two hours later, he found Jessica vomiting. He phoned me, and I drove over immediately."

"How did you find her?"

"Wretchedly ill. Her pulse was slow. Later, it began to flutter, and on the afternoon of the following day it became very fast. She died the evening of the second day." Dr. Willoughby pushed away from his desk and began to pace the floor of his examining room with tired steps. "I can't forgive myself," he groaned. "For one whole day, Mr. Queen, I thought she'd simply had a relapse. I can't forgive myself."

"Is *that* what's been bothering you, Doctor?"

"Yes."

"Nothing else? You're not concealing something?"

"Concealing something!" Dr. Willoughby paused in utter stupefaction.

"Some fact you'd become aware of, or knew from the beginning, which you failed to tell the authorities?"

The doctor stared at him. Then he threw back his big head and laughed. "So that's what you've been thinking!" He wiped his eyes. "No, Mr. Queen. I haven't concealed a thing. What's been bothering me is that I failed to recognize digitalis poisoning in time—that I thought she'd simply had a relapse after her long illness."

He went on to say that other physicians later assured him he had not been careless, that the circumstances of the case justified his initial diagnosis of relapse; but while he was talking, Ellery reflected sourly on the death of another hope.

"Good land," Dr. Willoughby was saying heatedly, "how could I possibly have dreamed that the woman was poisoned—that Fox had deliberately planned to murder her with an overdose of her medicine? And yet —I should have. She relied on me. She'd put herself into my hands. . . ."

Ellery tried to soothe the old man's conscience.

"Why, even on the morning of the second day," the doctor said bitterly, "I wasn't suspicious. When I came to see her that morning—she was stricken on a Tuesday, and this was Wednesday morning—she seemed much stronger, and the nurse I'd got the previous evening to take care of her in the emergency said her patient had passed a not too bad night. In fact, when I dropped in Jessica was sitting up in bed, all fixed up in a bed jacket and with a ribbon in her hair, and she was writing a letter to some friend, she felt so much better; she even gave it to me to mail on my way out, along with a batch of envelopes she said her husband had written the night before—containing bills and checks, or some such household things. But that afternoon—about thirty hours after the drinking of the grape juice—she took a sudden turn, weakened rapidly, and by that time it was too late to save her."

"Is all this the usual course in digitalis poisoning?"

"Yes."

"The symptoms, then, and the autopsy findings established positively that she died of digitalis poisoning?"

"Well, the symptoms were significant—when we looked back, we realized they fitted perfectly with a diagnosis of digitalis poisoning. But we still couldn't be absolutely sure, and unfortunately digitalis goes through a process of complete absorption in the body cells and is usually impossible to detect in an autopsy. However, when Chief Dakin hunted for the bottle of tincture of digitalis in the house—I'd prescribed fifteen drops three times a day for a short time, but had ordered Jessica to discontinue the digitalis a couple of weeks before, because she was better—exactly two weeks, it was, on Memorial Day, so she hadn't taken any digitalis from May thirtieth to June fourteenth—when Dakin looked for the bottle, as I say, and found it, instead of being nearly full as it should have been—it was empty! A one-ounce bottle! Then, of course, taking the symptoms into account, we were positive."

Ellery looked dissatisfied. "It's a flabby setup," he complained. "No p.m. findings . . . You say 'positive.' How positive is positive, Dr. Willoughby?"

"Don't take my word for it," growled the old doctor, coloring. "If you read the records, you also read the testimony of half a dozen medical men besides myself—including Jonas Hefflinger, the toxicologist. They agreed unanimously that Mrs. Fox died of digitalis poisoning, basing their opinion on the hour-to-hour symptoms and the surrounding circumstances."

Ellery sat plunged in thought for some time.

Then he looked up with a glitter in his eyes. "Dr. Willoughby," he said, "is there a possibility Jessica Fox was poisoned *after* she became so ill? That her vomiting and so on *were* a reaction to simple relapse, as you first thought, but that her death the evening following was caused by an overdose of digitalis administered to her in something she ate or drank *after you took charge of her?*"

The old man smiled a glum smile. "There was a time, Mr. Queen, when I'd have been overjoyed to embrace that theory. But the facts deny it absolutely.

"In the first place, I took care of Jessica personally as soon as I was called in, neither Bayard Fox nor anyone else close to her coming near her. I spent the entire remainder of that first day—Tuesday—with her, and for Tuesday night and Wednesday, I got a trained nurse I trusted—and still trust—implicitly. Helen Zimbruski has worked with me for twenty-five years, Mr. Queen, and I've never known her to be careless on a case.

"In the second place, Jessica was given virtually nothing to eat and very little liquid after her vomiting spell; she couldn't retain. We fed her just enough to keep up her strength. Nothing passed her lips till she died that wasn't prepared by my nurse and immediately fed to the patient by her, with tested ingredients out of sterilized implements.

"No. The overdose of digitalis could only have been administered in the grape juice her husband had prepared for her the previous morning—Tuesday morning. You can take that as gospel."

Ellery rose.

"Mind if I use your phone, Doctor?" he asked.

"Help yourself."

Ellery telephoned to Chief of Police Dakin.

"Washout with Dr. Willoughby," he reported.

"I could have told you that beforehand," grunted the Chief. "So now what, Mr. Queen?"

"Dakin," said Ellery truthfully, "I'm damned if I know."

PART THREE

12.   Fox Den

SUNLESS DAY TURNED to moonless night. The bluster of the afternoon fell away, leaving Wrightsville still. It was as if everything had died in concert—sun, moon, wind, and the hopes of the Foxes.

Ellery could only sit in silence in the swelter, keeping his eye on them.

It was not pretty. Linda was trussed in an agony. The relief of giving way was denied her; she denied it to herself. She moved through the heat of the evening sluggishly, like a drifting bale in a current. Ellery perceived what an effort it cost her to move so, to keep from striking out with a shriek. This distraction of self-discipline was all for Davy, and Davy was blind to it. He had sunk into his despair, the kind of despair which, unable to rebel, can only accept. He too moved through the evening, barely pushing himself about, the embodiment of a weariness which required no outlet, since it had nothing to give vent to. Davy was an empty man this evening—emptied even of Linda.

As for the Talbot Foxes, the long years stood between them.

Talbot was mute because he was humble, Emily because she was proud. Each flick and click of her knitting needles threw off pride like sparks; she sat absorbed in her work as if content to let the steel speak for her. And it spoke a language her husband understood without difficulty, for as the woolen garment grew Talbot's humility grew with it, until at last he was an abject figure, a man held prisoner by a loquacious silence.

121

Emily and Talbot held a long conversation that night without either so much as breathing loudly.

It's because she exposed herself to him today, thought Ellery. While the secret of Talbot's relationship with dead Jessica was locked up in Emily's mind, she could play the mousy put-upon wife with equanimity; but now that he knows she has known all these years she must play herself, the woman scorned—must pay Talbot back, for he expects it; indeed, she expects it of herself.

Ellery wondered what was really going on in the brain that directed those jabbing hands.

But this was barren speculation; it advanced the cause of Davy and Linda Fox not at all. What Emily was thinking would henceforth remain with Emily. She was the kind of woman, Ellery felt sure, who does not repeat a mistake.

He turned to an inspection of Bayard Fox.

Here was the blackest enigma of them all. What was Bayard thinking? Of his prison cell, and its protecting walls? Of the possibilities for joy in the life of a free man? Or of shrewder matters? That Egyptian physiognomy told nothing. There was a touch of resignation in the relaxation of the spare old body, but that would be natural in a man whose rebellion had spent itself ten years before.

Outwardly, Bayard was the least disturbed of any.

There was no point in studying Detective Howie. That fat immensity was as primitive as a boulder. His job was to sit upon a convicted murderer; and Detective Howie sat, fatly.

When they had all gone to bed, Ellery went out to the dark porch and lay down on the slide-swing, a pillow punched under his neck and one foot dangling. The leaves of the apple and chestnut trees beyond were splashes of fixed black paint—irritatingly unnatural; there was no comfort in the stars, either, for they were sultry-looking. They made him uneasy.

The whole world seemed queer tonight.

Ellery let his mind go, as if it were a trusted horse he was riding on a treacherous night mountainside.

It clambered over dead Jessica and purple glass and the tumbled afghan and a kitchen full of frozen memories. It stumbled over six bottles of grape juice, and stumbled again. Irrelevancies and fantasies cluttered the path of his wandering.

Ellery fell asleep.

There is a neutral ground between the dark land of sleep and the realm of wakefulness where the ghostly folk of dreams fill out a little and the real world thins, until the two all but make a union.

Jessica Fox was crossing the lawn of the Talbot Fox grounds. Ellery could not see the lower part of her body, for it was cut off from his view by the porch railing; but her torso was clad in a bed jacket, she wore a ribbon in her hair, and her face was wrapped in a thick purple veil appliquéd with purple silk bunches of grapes. He could make out the conformation of her face, but not her features. He strained and strained to penetrate the veil, but could not.

He knew she was a dream he was dreaming. Yet there was the Talbot Fox porch railing, there was the walk of the Bayard Fox house dimly beyond, there was the Bayard Fox house—there, even, were the sullen stars; they were all real enough, if a little flat and wavery. The dream-Jessica was treading on real grass and making her way to the real house in which she had died in the pain of poison.

Ellery watched her undulant progress across the lawns in a disembodied fascination.

Jessica reached the lawn of her own house and moved toward one of her front windows; and this was strange, for when she reached it the window offered no impediment to her body; neither window nor wall stopped her; she melted through them.

And now Ellery could not see her—which was unlike a dream; but he could make out a sort of glow she gave forth, a luminescence, like a halo or an aura, as she moved about the living room in which she had drained a glass of grape juice twelve years before. The glow was not steady; it had a fickle quality, appearing and disappearing and appearing once more—almost as if she were a firefly trapped in a room.

The glow of Jessica blinked on and off, here and there, in the living room of her house, and Ellery lay on the swing next door, in the neutral land, watching it.

How long he watched he could not have said; there is no time in that half-world.

But for the timeless duration of that firefly phenomenon Ellery struggled within himself to step across the border into the land of consciousness. Something warned him to do so. Something drove him to do so. And as he struggled he gradually became conscious of real things: the faintest creak of the swing, the slightest sigh of a tree—there was a breeze again, he thought—the hot wetness of the pillow beneath his nape, an uncomfortable stiffness in one leg . . . the busy little tick of a watch.

And suddenly he was across.

His left hand was under his left cheek, and the wrist watch on his left wrist hung just below the level of his eyes. The radial hands stood coldly at a quarter past three.

Funny dream, Ellery thought. He straightened his leg, which had fallen asleep. Yawning, he looked over at the house next door.

For an instant—one of the few such instances in his lifetime—his heart jumped with irrational terror.

The glow of Jessica Fox was still flitting about that dark and silent room.

Ellery sat up quickly.

Ghosts there might be, and the dead may revisit their earthly domiciles; but no ghosts Ellery had ever heard of carried a flashlight on such excursions.

Someone had broken into the Bayard Fox house while he slept, someone most assuredly not Jessica Fox.

Ellery tore at the laces of his shoes, ripped his shoes off, dropped them on the swing, and sprang.

His stockinged feet made no sound as he raced across the two lawns toward the other house.

It occurred to him as he ran that the housebreaker

could not have been inside for very long. Some sound made by the grass-treading feet had half-jarred him out of sleep, perhaps as the prowler stole past the area just below the porch; in those few moments of semi-wakefulness, his eyes bewitched by sleep, Ellery had dreamed a dream of Jessica Fox. But it had been the solid prowler he had seen stealing across the lawns, not the figment of his dream. He had actually witnessed the woman—or the man—forcing one of the downstairs living-room windows of the Bayard Fox house and climbing in, although his dream-drugged eyes had transformed the figure and its entry in the magical manner of all dream-action.

There was no time for reflection. Ellery knew but one thing as he sped toward the open window: he must see the face of the man or woman who was prowling about the interior of Bayard Fox's house.

He even felt a surge of exultancy. He could not define it; it was only as if a great stroke of luck had flashed in his path, like lightning. It was as if this, in a queer way, were the very end of the Bayard Fox case.

Two strides more, and he would see the face of the person who held the flashlight.

But just as Ellery reached the window, the light went out.

He remained where he was, in a crouch, fingers touching the sill, eyes barely clearing it for a view of the dark interior. He had merely to wait where he was. In a moment the light would flash on again. It had kept up this on-and-off operation for some minutes now. There was no reason to believe it would not continue.

There!

But the leap of elation died as it was born. The light had flashed again, but this time it was not in the living room. Ellery saw its dim reflection on the slim sliver of foyer-wall visible to him from the angle made by his position at the living-room window.

The intruder had gone into the foyer.

Another flash!

But even dimmer this time.

So he was on his way to the rear of the house.

Ellery waited.

He waited and waited.

There were no further flashes, not even their reflections.

It was reasonable to assume that the intruder had entered some room at the rear of the house.

The kitchen?

It was possible. In fact, Ellery knew of no other room that might have been the housebreaker's objective. He cursed his carelessness in not having familiarized himself fully with the house during the day. Except for the kitchen, hall, and the living room he had no idea of the lower-floor layout.

It could not be the dining room. Dining rooms usually lie directly across a foyer from living rooms. But the light had come from farther down the hall. Which room could lie back there if it was not the kitchen the prowler had made for? A maid's room, possibly. Or a study.

Ellery dismissed these speculations. The question was what to do. Go in after his quarry? But then he would have to make his way across a pitch-dark room into an equally dark foyer with whose plan he was all too unfamiliar. He would probably bump into something, alarm the intruder, and the intruder might escape through the rear. Then should he remain where he was, trusting that the man or woman would quit the house by the same window used in entering it? This seemed likely, and Ellery had already settled down to waiting when it occurred to him that he was missing the whole point. *Why* had the prowler broken into the Bayard Fox house? At all?

He decided to go in.

He got through the open window without noise, froze for a moment to catch his breath, orient himself.

As he crouched there, at the living-room window, he heard a slight sound from the rear of the house.

Like the opening of a drawer.

Again!

The intruder was opening drawers, closing them, opening others.

Looking for something, then.

Looking for something!

Ellery began to grope in the general direction of the archway to the foyer. He moved stooped over, hands extended, trying to cross the living room quickly and still without sound. Halfway across the room his left knee struck the sharp edge of something low with a slight thud. He stopped at once, listening, tingling, feeling for the thing he had bumped into. It was the coffee table. . . . He waited.

No harm done. Another drawer opened and in a few seconds slid shut.

Ellery got to the archway without further incident.

Here he paused again, peering down the hall. The faintest glow came from what seemed an open doorway at the end of it, a doorway not across the line of his vision but edgewise to it.

But the kitchen was on the other side.

So the prowler was in a maid's room, or a study. And now he was not flashing the light intermittently; he kept it on as he searched through drawers.

Ellery made his way down the hall on the balls of his stockinged feet. The house had stood unheated during twelve winters, and dampness had warped the floors— he recalled how badly they had creaked during the day. So he was doubly careful, testing each board before putting his full weight upon it, inching his way down the hall toward the source of that faint light.

When he was three-quarters toward his goal, a loud sound came from the unidentified room. It was a splintery snap of a sound, like the cracking of wood. And immediately the sound of another drawer jerked open. And then a hiss, which might have been the intake of a triumphant breath.

The light vanished, leaving blackest blackness.

Ellery wasted no time bemoaning his luck. He negotiated the remaining distance in two long strides, risking a protesting board. But he reached the invisible doorway without having stepped on one. At once he raised his arms high and grasped both jambs, his body squarely in the middle of the open doorway.

Now, he thought grimly, let Mr. or Mrs. or Miss Prowler come out. The intruder can't possibly know I'm here. There's no reason for him—or her—to leave by a window of this room. The only sound I made was in the living room, and it wasn't heard, because the search continued afterward. And my breathing is inaudible, unless the creature in that room has the ears of a fox—

Ellery barely had time to complete the thought.

The front of his head seemed to rip away.

As the pain flashed through his brain and down into his body, as he felt his knees sag and his arms drop from the jambs, his falling left arm passed before his eyes. And he saw his wrist watch with the hands standing at 3:26.

Saw the time in the darkness and realized that what he could see was also visible to another.

He had forgotten that his watch had radial hands. His arm had been on the jamb, outstretched, his cuff had fallen away exposing his wrist, and the man or woman in the room had spied the luminous dial. He always wore his watch with the face turned inward.

Serves you right, his brain was saying as he went down.

A reflex caused him to twist his head far to one side. Another blow struck the side of his head, a third his shoulder.

And then he felt no further sensations, not even the foot that trampled on his hand in the dark. Nor did he hear the clatter of his assailant's escape up the hall.

Ellery opened his eyes in the middle of a firmament gone crazy with suns and comets, all different-colored and all in violent motion. For a while he had the feeling that he was floating in black space, surrounded by the galaxy.

But then he realized that he was lying across the sill of the still-unidentified room in Bayard Fox's house, in the same darkness.

He blinked the colored spots away as he struggled to sit up. Returning consciousness made him aware of his head and shoulder and hand. The top of his head was burning, his left shoulder was boiling with pain, and his left hand felt crippled.

Sitting on the floor, he shook his head slowly, trying to clear it, fumbling meanwhile for a packet of matches in his jacket pocket.

But he could not find it, so he peered blearily at his wrist watch. After a moment he was able to focus sufficiently to make out the time.

It was 3:44.

Out eighteen minutes!

Groaning, he rolled over, got to his knees, and finally, clutching at the nearer jamb, pulled himself to his feet.

No point in being careful now, he thought wryly.

The mysterious prowler had long since gone.

Should have had the electricity turned on for the investigation, he thought as he stumbled up the hall.

He blundered across the living room and dropped out the still-open window. His head was rocking with pain, as were his shoulder and hand. He plodded across the Bayard Fox lawn toward Talbot's house, fighting nausea.

It was quiet and dark and hot outside.

Nothing seemed different.

On Talbot's porch Ellery paused. Talbot's house seemed still asleep.

After a while Ellery went in.

The telephone was in the downstairs hall, near the front door, on a skimpy little table.

Ellery sat down slowly in the tiny telephone-table chair. A night-light burned on the wall, and by its yellow rays he could examine himself. His left hand was swollen and discolored; there was a trace of dried blood across the puffed knuckles. In the mirror above the table he could glimpse his forehead. At the hairline an area the size and shape of a lead sinker rose nobly. The tissue there was bloated and purplish. In one place the lump was cracked in a blood-line. At the side of his head another lump rose.

His shoulder throbbed.

But Ellery stared at his injuries in a vast excitement. They tell a story! he thought. An impossible, wonderful story.

He felt like laughing aloud.

He took the phone carefully, dialed the operator.

"Get me Chief of Police Dakin at his home," he said, his lips to the mouthpiece. "This is urgent."

"Shall I call you back, sir?"

"I'll hold on."

At the fourth buzz Dakin's voice, calmly reassuring, answered.

"This is Queen."

"What's the matter, Mr. Queen?"

"Never mind. Come right over to the Bayard Fox house."

"Sure."

"Quietly."

"Sure."

Ellery hung up. He felt his shoulder, winced, and glanced up the stairs.

The house was still.

Painfully he went upstairs, blessing the padded stair-carpeting. Along the upper hall he sought a certain door, but before he knocked he paused to listen.

Nothing.

He knocked, softly.

He heard the smothered wheeze as Detective Howie awoke, the sleepy grunt of Bayard Fox, a groaning of old bedsprings, and in a few moments Howie unlocked the door.

"Yeah?" The prosecutor's man looked startled.

"Let me in, Howie."

Ellery quietly shut the door. Howie had snapped on the bed-light, and Bayard Fox was up on an elbow, his thin white hair standing all over his head, staring.

"For heaven's sake, Mr. Queen," gasped Davy's father, "what's happened to *you?*"

"Please keep your voice down."

The detective croaked: "You look like you run into something, friend." Howie was in one-piece underwear, fatter and unlovelier than ever. He, too, was staring at Ellery's head.

"I haven't much time," snapped Ellery. "Howie, has Bayard Fox left this room tonight?"

"Huh?"

"Shut your silly mouth and concentrate, Howie. Is there any way your prisoner could have got out of this room tonight without your knowing?"

The stupid expression on the fat detective's face vanished in a savage grin. He trod heavily over to the double bed and ripped the top sheet away.

"What do *you* think?" he screeked.

I don't believe you'd be grinning, my friend, thought Ellery, if you knew the significance of your little mean triumph. Not you.

A short length of picture wire was securely twisted about Bayard Fox's left big toe.

"I'm a light sleeper," leered Detective Howie. "But when I'm on a job like this I don't take chances. No, sir. The other end winds around my ankle. Every time he moves I wake up, but then I go to sleep again."

"I could get out of it if I wanted to," said Bayard Fox with a little spate of hatred.

"Try it sometime, Fox."

"Suppose he could. It's possible," argued Ellery, his eyes bright.

"It ain't."

"But suppose it was."

"I keep the door locked."

"Doors can be unlocked."

"Not without a key. I got the key on a chain around my wrist." Detective Howie showed his bad teeth in another grin. "I mean not amatchoors like Foxy here."

"Then there's the window," objected Ellery.

"Take a look at it, friend."

Ellery crossed the room. The lower part of the window was open about six inches. Ellery tried to raise it. It would not budge. Curious, he investigated further. By an ingenious system of home-made wedges, the window had been rendered immovable.

"He could get it open," chuckled Detective Howie, "enough to wriggle out, maybe, but not without workin' on it for a long time, Queen, and not without me hearin' him . . . Makes it stuffy in here," he said slyly, "but I guess if I can stand it, he can."

"You're a careful operative," drawled Ellery.

"You said it."

"Suppose he hit you on the skull, Howie. Then it wouldn't matter how much noise he made, or how long he took getting out."

The fat lips drew back in a snarl. "Well, he didn't hit me on the skull and he better not try. . . . Say!" Howie's little eyes grew round. "*You* were hit on the skull tonight!"

"Now you're getting it," said Ellery. "Then you're prepared to swear, in court if necessary, that Bayard Fox didn't leave this room tonight?"

Detective Howie nodded, his grin gone.

"Get dressed, Howie. Put the light out. Open the door. And listen. I don't want anyone leaving this house for the next couple of hours. You might sit out in the hall, at the top of the stairs. Then nobody could slip down—or up—in the dark."

The fat man nodded again, dumbly.

"What's happened, Mr. Queen?" asked Bayard Fox in a quiet voice.

"I don't know, Bayard," said Ellery, "but I have an idea that—whatever it was—it's a very good thing for you."

It was ten minutes past four by Ellery's watch when the plain black sedan Chief Dakin ran slipped up the Hill and stopped before Bayard Fox's house.

Dakin came softly up the walk and Ellery rose from the bottom step of the small porch to greet him.

"Bring a flash, Dakin?"

"A big electric torch."

"Let's go in."

They spoke in low tones.

When they got inside, Chief Dakin unlocking the front door with the key he had appropriated during the day from Emily Fox, the Chief switched on his torch.

"Jeeps!" he exclaimed. "What happened to you?"

Ellery told him.

The Chief's long jaw kept dropping.

"But *who?*"

"I have no idea. Except that it wasn't Bayard Fox. Howie swears Bayard didn't leave his room tonight."

"Was it somebody else from the Talbot Fox house?"

"May have been."

"Or an outsider?"

"Possibly."

"Can't you remember the exact place this figure come from, Mr. Queen? You say you were half-awake—"

"Which also means half-asleep, Dakin. No. If it was someone from Talbot's house, that person may have come from the side door, gone round the house, and past the front porch where I was lying on the swing. It's even conceivable that he may have slipped out the front door past me, but that I didn't become conscious of his presence until he was down on the grass. Or, as I say, it may have been someone else entirely, coming from the Hill road and cutting across the Talbot Fox property to get to this one."

"A sneak thief, Mr. Queen?"

"I don't think so," said Ellery slowly. "No, indeed."

"You don't know what was taken?"

"I don't know that anything was taken. I haven't looked. I've been waiting out there for you. I wanted an official witness to what I saw."

"Let's take a peep at the window first."

"By all means."

They went outside again, Dakin snapping off his torch, and walked over to the window through which the housebreaker had gained entrance. Dakin swept the light over the grass below the window.

"Just tromped up. No prints," he muttered. "Can't even tell if it was a man or a female."

"And I did a bit of tromping myself, Dakin. I didn't think he'd get away. I'm getting old, Dakin, old."

"It wasn't your fault," the Chief consoled him.

He examined the side of the house from the grass to the window sill. There were several dirty streaks on the paint.

"Heels sliding."

Ellery nodded. "On the way out."

"Look like rubber to you, Mr. Queen?"

"It's hard to say."

"Do to me."

"Women wear rubber heels, too," Ellery pointed out.

Dakin swore. "Give me a boost up."

Ellery caged his hands, and Dakin stepped hard. A sword tore through Ellery's left hand, and he closed his eyes.

"Take a look at the catch while you're up there," said Ellery.

After a moment, the Chief said: "Forced. With a big heavy screwdriver, maybe. Or a heavy chisel."

"You'd relocked the windows after our session during the day?"

"Yep. I didn't close the shutters, though."

"I know that."

Dakin ran the light slowly over the window sill.

"Not a thing here," he grunted, jumping down. Ellery opened his eyes. "I thought maybe a thread or something caught on the sill. Would show if it was from a woman's dress or a man's suit. But there's nothin' I can see. Wish I had fingerprint equipment, darn it."

"I doubt very much that fingerprint equipment would do us any good, Dakin."

"Gloves?"

"Seems likely. The whole thing had a technique."

"Professional, hey?"

"No. But a technique just the same."

"Too many people read detective stories," growled Chief Dakin. "Okay, let's go in and look the damage over."

They re-entered the house by the front door.

"Living room first," murmured Ellery. "It's where my friend with the blunt instrument started."

Only two things had been touched, so far as they could determine. One was a large breakfront, a glittery mahogany piece. The lid of the secretary in the piece had been pulled down and its contents strewn over the floor. The cabinets on each side of the breakfront had also been pulled open.

The other disturbed object was a drum-table which stood against a wall, a lamp and an ashtray upon it. The small drawer had been jerked open and its contents, too, chiefly old bills, had been jumbled and scattered.

"We'd never be able to tell if he took anything," complained Dakin. "Everything's in such a mortal mess. And it's been twelve years since anybody looked into these things."

"It's reasonable to assume he didn't. Because he wasn't through. He left the living room and went down the hall to the rear of the house—to that other room there."

"He was looking for something, all righty."

"He didn't find it in here, Dakin, I'm pretty sure."

They walked down the hall from the foyer slowly, Dakin wielding the beam of the torch like a broom.

"The so-and-so was mighty careful not to drop anything," grunted the Chief.

"So-and-so's usually are, Dakin."

And there was the doorway.

"This the place where he slugged you?"

"Yes."

"Why, that's Bayard Fox's old den in there."

"Den?"

"His whatchamacallit—his study."

"Oh," said Ellery.

They went in.

It was a tiny room paneled in pickled pine, with built-in pine bookshelves and a small marble-manteled fireplace at the far side. A scarred walnut flat-top desk made the room look even tinier. Its drawers had all been pulled out and their contents dumped on top of the desk in a hopeless heap.

"He didn't have to force the locks on these desk drawers," murmured Ellery, examining them. "They weren't locked."

"Look at these smudges in the dust!"

"I've seen them. He did wear gloves, Dakin. Naked fingers would have left a distinguishable print, or part of a print, somewhere, even to the unaided eye."

"What else?" muttered Dakin, glancing around sourly.

"That secretary against the wall."

It was an old piece, an antique, of pine with a fine patina. It had three drawers below the lid. The lowest and middle drawers were pulled three-quarters open and the familiar mess had been made out of their contents. But the topmost drawer, which was open less than halfway, was empty.

"That's what I thought," said Ellery sharply, more to himself than to Dakin.

He knelt on the dusty rug, carefully scrutinizing the lock of the empty drawer.

"Look at this."

Dakin craned.

"Forced, Mr. Queen. Fresh jimmy-marks around the lock."

"Yes. Notice that the other two drawers show no marks of forcing about the locks at all. So those drawers weren't locked. But this top drawer was, and the intruder forced it with the same tool he used on the window —I heard the crackle and snap from the hall just before I reached the doorway. Incidentally, he must have hit me with the handle of that tool." His head was paining him again. In the excitement of the hunt, he had forgotten. Now, it was coming back.

"Do you suppose he found anything in that top drawer, Mr. Queen?"

"Of course, Dakin."

"But how can you be sure?"

"People don't lock empty drawers."

"Now that's a fact! But what was locked in this drawer, Mr. Queen? What was it this crook swiped tonight?"

"If we knew that, Dakin," said Ellery faintly, wincing at the throb in his head and shoulder and hand, "we might know a great deal."

"Well, all we have to do is ask Bayard Fox! This was his den."

"Yes. Let's go ask Bayard what he kept in this drawer."

13.   Fox in the Open!

THEY FOUND DETECTIVE Howie sitting on the first-floor landing with his back set against the wall and his enormous bare feet propped against the newel post. He had slipped his pants on over his underwear.

In the rays of the Chief's torch the fat man's face was moist and baleful. He looked exactly as if he had been cheated out of something.

"Anything?" Ellery whispered.

The detective shook his head, scowling.

"Where's Bayard Fox?" demanded Dakin.

"Where do you think he is?"

"Stay right here, Howie," said Ellery.

The blubberlips stretched in a snarl. "I don't have to take your orders!"

"Would you please stay right here?"

The detective glared up without answering. But he did not move. So they stepped over his legs and went quickly down the hall to the "south" room.

Bayard was lying on his back in the old-fashioned iron double bed, smoking a cigaret.

He sat up at once, tamping the butt out in an ashtray on the night-table beside his bed.

Dakin shut the door.

"What's happened, Mr. Queen? I've been lying here worried to death."

"Somebody broke into your house tonight, Bayard, and stole something."

"Broke in? Stole something?" There was no mistaking the genuineness of his incredulity.

"I have various lumps and bruises in proof," said Ellery. "Here—I'd better sit down."

"But—who, Mr. Queen?"

"I didn't see, and I don't know."

"What was stolen?"

"We don't know that either," said Chief Dakin. "We thought you could tell us, Mr. Fox."

Something like fear leaped into Bayard's eyes. "You mean you think—"

"No, no, Mr. Fox. You ain't involved; Howie cleared you. I meant maybe you can remember what was in the drawer."

"Which drawer, Mr. Dakin?"

"There's an old pine secretary in your den. Somethin' was taken out of one of the three drawers in the secretary."

"My secretary?" Bayard's lips twisted. "An antique . . . Jessica picked it up at Creecher's Barn over towards Connhaven. Not long after we were married. She . . . gave it to me. As a birthday present."

"Fine," said Dakin patiently. "But about the drawer—"

"You'd locked one of those drawers, Bayard," said Ellery. "The top one of the three."

"Locked?" Bayard frowned.

"Didn't you?"

"I—I guess I don't remember."

"Try, Bayard. It's important."

Bayard drew his white brows together, painfully. After a while he said, shaking his head: "I seem to recall that I used to keep some drawer or other for special things. . . . It's all so fuzzy."

"What kind of things, Mr. Fox?" demanded Dakin.

But Bayard shook his head again. "It's been twelve years, a long twelve years," he muttered. "I just can't remember."

"Could it have been something of value, Bayard?" asked Ellery. "Silver, or cash, or anything like that?"

"Well, we had a special silver chest, but Emily's been keeping that, and I think she's given it to Linda for Linda's and Davy's home. And I never kept cash anywhere but in my wallet, Mr. Queen—"

"Jewelry?"

"The few things Jessica had she kept in a box in our bedroom. Nothing of any importance. The only really valuable thing she had, her diamond engagement ring . . . was buried with her."

"Could it have been anything else of Jessica's?"

"I don't see how it could have been," frowned Bayard. "Jessie always used to say a man's den was his castle. That was my room, for my things."

Ellery and Chief Dakin looked at each other.

"Well, Bayard, if you should happen to remember, let me know right away."

"Of course. But what do you suppose it means, and who could have taken it—whatever it was?"

But Ellery shook his head and, followed by Dakin, left Bayard's room.

Chief Dakin relieved Detective Howie at the landing, and the fat man slap-slapped back to the bedroom looking sullen.

"You stay here, Dakin," whispered Ellery. "I'll begin with Linda upstairs."

Ellery went up to the "apartment" on the top floor. He was about to knock on the door of the bedroom Linda had until recently shared with Davy when he changed his mind and put his ear to it instead.

Linda was crying.

Ellery frowned. But then he knocked.

The crying stopped immediately.

"Yes?" Her voice was shaky.

"Ellery Queen, Linda. Might I see you?"

He heard her get out of bed. At least two minutes elapsed before Linda opened the door wide. Her face was freshly powdered and there was no trace of tears. She had thrown a negligee over her nightgown, and she looked frightened.

"What's the matter, Mr. Queen? What time is it— Oh! Your head!"

"I'll explain later, Linda." There was no one else in the room. "Would you come down to the parlor in five minutes?"

"Of course . . ."

Her twin bed was rumpled, mauled.

"In five minutes, Linda."

He went back downstairs and shrugged at Dakin on the landing and strode over to the door of the bedroom Davy was occupying. He turned the handle carefully and went in.

This was Linda's "old" bedroom, the room she had occupied from childhood until her marriage. It was a feminine, pretty room, with tester bed and frilly curtains and silk lamp shades and a kidney-shaped vanity with an organdie skirt. Davy looked uncomfortable and out of place there, even in sleep. The boy was curled up in a tangle of arms and legs, breathing noisily.

"Davy."

He awoke instantly.

He was really asleep, Ellery thought. If he'd been shamming, the waking-up process would have been elaborate and slow.

"Linda! Something—"

"No, no, Davy." Ellery sat down on the edge of the bed. A pearly cast was coming over the darkness; in it Davy's angular face floated pallidly.

"What happened to your face?"

Ellery told him.

Davy was silent. But then he said: "Here, let me fix that head of yours up. And I'll see what I can do with your hand."

"Oh, I'm fine, Davy—thanks. Tell me—do you walk in your sleep?"

"Huh?" Davy's eyes narrowed. "Say, what are you trying to make me out, a Jekyll and Hyde?"

"Now, now," grinned Ellery, "keep your head, Captain. I've got to eliminate *you*, too, you see. And I thought your recent nervous state—"

"Oh. Sorry." Davy shivered in the pearly light. "But that can't be. There's never been a trace of that."

"It was the wildest conjecture," nodded Ellery. "You heard nothing, eh, Davy?"

"Not a thing. I was absolutely pooped last night. Flopped into bed here and just went out."

"Do you have any recollection of what your father used to keep in that secretary drawer?"

"I didn't know he 'kept' anything. I wasn't allowed in Dad's den when I was a kid. Mom wouldn't let me. She said I'd only mess it up. I guess I was kind of a trial to Mom. . . . Don't forget, I was only ten or so."

"No idea what it might have been?"

"Not the remotest. I can't figure this, Mr. Queen. What's it mean?"

But Ellery merely said: "Throw something on and go downstairs, Davy."

When Ellery went back into the hall he found Chief Dakin in low-voiced conversation with Talbot Fox. Talbot's hair was disheveled, and under a shabby bathrobe he wore pajamas. There were carpet-slippers on his bare feet.

"I've just told Mr. Fox," said Dakin as Ellery joined them, "and he's just as puzzled as we are."

"It doesn't make sense, Mr. Queen." Talbot seemed excessively worried.

"It will, Talbot," murmured Ellery. "Is your wife awake?"

"Emily? I don't know."

"You don't *know*, Talbot?"

Talbot scowled down at his slippers, his hands making bulges in the pockets of his bathrobe. "I . . . slept in Davy's old room last night," he muttered.

"Oh, I see."

Talbot seemed to feel further explanation was necessary.

"Emily didn't . . . feel well."

"I'm sorry to hear that. Do you suppose she's well enough to get up and come downstairs?"

"I'll see."

Talbot shuffled up the hall to the master bedroom. Before the door he hesitated. Then, timidly, he knocked. After a few moments he knocked again.

He knocked six times before Emily unlocked her door.

"So nobody has any idea what was stolen from Bayard's secretary drawer," said Ellery cheerfully in the parlor.

They were all shivering in an unexpectedly chill dawn.

The conference had been unproductive. Emily merely compressed her lips when she was asked, as if the very question were an impertinence. Linda, of course, could not have been expected to know. And Davy had already said he did not. That left Talbot . . . and they had all looked at Talbot. It was impossible to forget that Talbot and Jessica . . . A secret relationship begot secrets. Was the secret of the locked drawer and its stolen contents somehow tied up to the Talbot-Jessica affair? The question was in all their eyes, not excluding Ellery's.

But Talbot simply said: "I haven't a Chinaman's notion of what was in that drawer. How should I have?"

And Emily sniffed, pointedly.

"This," said Chief Dakin, "is gettin' us nowhere."

"On the contrary, Dakin. It's a vastly important development. The first real ray of hope I've seen since I got going on the case."

"Hope?"

Linda uttered the word as if she had never known its meaning before.

"Well, tell us more, Mr. Queen. Don't stop there!"

Ellery shrugged. "What happened tonight? Someone broke into Bayard Fox's house, which has been shut up for a dozen years—and shunned during all that time as if it were a pest-house!—and ransacked the living room and Bayard's old den. In a locked drawer of Bayard's secretary—a drawer, so far as we can determine, locked twelve or more years ago—this unknown housebreaker found what he was looking for. For he took it with him in his flight."

Ellery sucked his lower lip, frowning.

"To conclude that our housebreaker was a professional thief would be an error. For a dozen years no one, thief or honest man, has set foot in that house. *Yet the very night of the day in which I began a reinvestigation of the case, the house is entered.* I don't believe in such striking coincidences.

"I think we may reasonably conclude this:—

"That the thief is connected with the Jessica Fox murder case.

"That the stolen object is a significant factor of the case. For twelve years, while Bayard lay in prison, a convicted murderer, while the case was a dead issue, the object locked in that drawer had no value and no importance for the thief. Today the situation is suddenly different. Today a man is on the scene, a stranger to Wrightsville, who has brought Bayard Fox back, who has entered the deserted house, who has asked old questions there . . . who has reopened the entire case. Instantly our mysterious figure springs into action. He seizes his very first opportunity to take possession of the object in that drawer. Why should he execute this hasty and dangerous maneuver? *It can only be because he's afraid I would have found that object.* But why should he be afraid of that? Well, what is it I'm trying to accomplish here? I'm trying to clear Bayard Fox of the twelve-year-old murder. *Then he knows that object—in my hands, or in the hands of the authorities—will help clear Bayard Fox.*

"Don't you see? At least until tonight, there was a clue in existence which might have cleared Bayard of the murder charge twelve years ago! Now do you see why I'm hopeful?"

They saw.

"Dakin, you and I have a real job on our hands. For the first time in the case."

Chief Dakin was looking wobbly.

"We've got to identify the dark figure of my assailant —I'm almost tempted to say the 'fox'!—who's been lurking safely in the background all these years and who's now been forced into the open by my coming to Wrightsville.

"We've got to find out who that person is, and— equally imperative, Dakin—we've got to find out what it was he lifted tonight."

Dakin nodded, swallowing. "You folks better not say anything about what happened tonight. To anybody."

They saw that, too. A new feeling of solidarity seemed to have drawn them close together. There was an excitement about them, a pleasure which they were eager to share with one another. For the first time they took Bayard to themselves, a Bayard whose thin face was transfigured by an incredulous joy.

"And now," said Ellery with a smile, "I'll have to ask you not to leave the house until Dakin and I have had a chance to look things over outside."

It was too cozy. Where was the one face, the one expression, of fear? It was not there. In dismal fact, Ellery reflected, as they left in a group, talking excitedly, the only one who seemed personally affected by the revelation was Detective Howie.

14.   The Fox and the Ledger

As SOON AS there was light enough to see by, Ellery and Chief Dakin went outside.

They examined the lawn, beginning in the area just below the Talbot Fox porch, as closely as if they were hunting lost diamonds. Not an inch of the drought-browned grass escaped their scrutiny. They worked in short circling movements, one behind the other, stooped over and silent.

But when at last they straightened, having gone over both lawns, they were empty-handed.

"If only he'd dropped something, or there'd been enough of a rain to soften up this sod," complained Dakin.

"Well, he didn't, and there wasn't," replied Ellery. "Let's try the road."

They examined the tarred road for several hundred yards down the Hill on the theory that the thief, if he were an outsider, had driven up from town and parked his car away from the Fox properties.

But this search, too, yielded nothing.

"It's going to be a toughie, Dakin," remarked Ellery as they strode back toward Bayard Fox's house.

"Maybe impossible."

"Let's tackle the interior again," said Ellery, making a face. "But this time as if we meant it."

It took them two hours to go over the ground floor of the untenanted house.

At the end all they had to show for their exertions

was a long heavy screwdriver, which Ellery nosed out from under the mahogany reception table in the foyer.

"Dropped it in his getaway after boppin' you," said Chief Dakin, handling it gingerly. "It rolled under the table."

"Do you suppose we could trace this, Dakin?"

"Not a chance. Look." Dakin pointed out the maker's name stamped on the heavy handle.

"Talbot Fox Company!" exclaimed Ellery. "Why, if—"

But the Chief was shaking his head. "I guess seventy-five per cent of Wrightsville has a couple Fox Company screwdrivers in their toolboxes," he said. "Talbot runs a retail store in connection with the Low Village shop just as a local accommodation. And the three hardware stores in town all carry a heavy line of Talbot Fox Company tools. Besides, this ain't a brand-new one, Mr. Queen. I'm afraid we wouldn't have much luck tryin' to trace it."

"We can test it for prints."

"I got no equipment, Mr. Queen."

"Well, I have. Fortunately, I brought along a small outfit from New York. Wait."

When Ellery returned, he carried a small kit.

"I'm convinced he wore gloves, Dakin, but we may as well make sure."

There were no fingerprints on the screwdriver. It had obviously been wiped clean.

"That's that," said Dakin.

"Perhaps not. I have another notion."

Dakin locked up and they walked back to the other house.

They found the family and Detective Howie at breakfast. Even the detective looked up eagerly as they came in.

But Ellery said: "Now don't let us interrupt your breakfast. We came back for a screwdriver. Talbot, may I borrow a good strong one for a few minutes?"

"Sure thing." Talbot rose. "I keep my tools in a shed on the other side of the house. I'll get one for you."

"We'll go with you."

"But won't you have breakfast first, Mr. Queen?" asked Emily. Her face was puffy and red. "And of course, Mr. Dakin, you'll—

"Thanks, Mis' Fox, but I can't."

"We have some work to do," said Ellery apologetically; and they followed Talbot out of the house.

The big man went out by the front and turned right at the foot of the porch steps, walking across the lawn parallel with the porch and then turning right again to trudge along the farther side of the house.

Ellery and Dakin looked at each other. The same thought had struck them.

But they said nothing; and when Talbot entered the large white-painted shed, they entered behind him.

It was the toolhouse and workshed of a methodical man. There were a huge workbench, an efficient-looking lathe, a variety of drills and saws and planes and chisels, and other smaller tools, all neatly racked. In one rack ten screwdrivers hung in a row, in ascending sizes.

"Will one of these do?" asked Talbot.

He indicated the largest screwdriver.

"Don't you have one that's even bigger?" asked Ellery doubtfully.

"There's one here that—" Talbot stopped, looking puzzled. "I *did* have a jumbo number."

"The one that hung in this slot?" Dakin pointed to a blank place in the rack.

"Yes. Funny, I always put my tools back after I use them. Maybe—Wait. I'll ask the family."

Talbot left quickly. When he had disappeared, Ellery and Dakin made a swift but thorough examination of the shed.

"Just as much nothin'," grunted Dakin.

Talbot came back looking more puzzled than before. "Nobody seems to have used a screwdriver," he said. "I don't understand it."

"Well, it's not important," said Ellery heartily. "It's been mislaid somewhere, no doubt. I'll use one of these others, if you don't mind."

"Help yourself, Mr. Queen." Talbot left again, frowning.

Ellery produced from his sleeve the big screwdriver he had found in Bayard Fox's foyer and dropped it into the empty space in the rack.

I completed the set.

"That's why you thought he came from around this side of the house!" exclaimed Chief Dakin.

Ellery nodded.

"He slipped into Talbot Fox's shed here first, to get some tool that would serve as a jimmy, then proceeded around the front of the house, across both lawns, to the living room window of the other house. I first became conscious of him as he passed under the porch where I was lying."

"So it could have been anybody under the sun, Mr. Queen."

"I'm afraid so. Either someone from the house, who slipped out the side door to the shed and then around to the front, or someone from outside who came up the Hill, visited the shed first, and then continued toward the other house. Anybody . . . that is, anybody but Bayard Fox."

"Anybody but Bayard Fox," muttered Chief of Police Dakin. "I swear I can't get over it, Mr. Queen. You'd think it would *be* Bayard Fox!"

And there the curious incident of the thief in the night seemed to peter out.

Chief Dakin departed to call on the Foxes' neighbors along the Hill—"drop in friendly-like, like I was on the trail of a sneak thief, and ask a few questions. You never can tell—" while Ellery bathed, shaved, tended his wounds, and then went downstairs for a belated breakfast. Davy and Linda had gone shopping in Slocum, Talbot had departed for the factory, and after Emily served Ellery his eggs and saw that the toaster and coffee pot were filled, she excused herself on the plea of housework and trudged upstairs. So Ellery found himself alone with Bayard—alone, that is, except for Detective Howie, who was drinking his fifth cup of coffee in a sulky isolation.

"Any luck with your memory, Bayard?" Ellery asked cheerfully as he buttered a piece of toast.

"I've been racking my brains, Mr. Queen, but I just can't seem to remember about that drawer."

"Well, let's see. Could you have kept, say, business records in there?"

"I don't think so," said Bayard doubtfully. "Talbot and I used to keep our records at the shop."

"Letters? Private correspondence, that you preferred not to leave lying around?"

"I didn't have any correspondence like that, Mr. Queen," replied Bayard quietly.

"Any other kind of papers?"

"I just can't recall, Mr. Queen."

Ellery said suddenly: "A gun."

Bayard looked startled, and Howie lowered the cup from his lips.

But Ellery was smiling. "Davy mentioned to me originally that you and he sometimes went camping up in the Mahoganies when he was a youngster. I thought you might have hunted. Of course, you couldn't have kept a shotgun in that drawer, but lots of people shoot at woodchucks and rabbits with revolvers—"

"I never did hunt," said Bayard.

"Oh?"

"I didn't believe in killing," said Bayard.

Detective Howie gaped at his prisoner. And then he burst into a spasm of wheezes and gurgles which, freely interpreted, might have been laughter.

Bayard flushed to the roots of his sparse white hair. He flung a bitter, shamed glance at his jailer, jumped up from the table, muttered something, and quickly went upstairs.

"Hey—" said the detective, scowling.

He ran after Bayard.

Ellery finished his breakfast in a thoughtful silence. At noon Chief Dakin telephoned. He was glum.

"No luck, Mr. Queen. Nobody saw anything, nobody heard anything, nobody found anything."

"We could hardly have expected anything else," Ellery consoled him.

"You sound mighty unconcerned!"

"Devotion, Dakin, devotion to a cause. You learn that after some few years. Remember Javert? An unlovely character, but the ideal manhunter. In fact, look at Howie."

"You look at him," growled Dakin. "I'm goin' home for a wash and somethin' to eat."

"You'll follow up on the outsider angle?"

"I'll do what I can, Mr. Queen, but after talkin' to the Hill folks, I ain't optimistic. It was dead of night, and Wrightsville's a hard-workin', hard-sleepin' town."

"Which might make the job easier, Dakin. If somebody *was* up, and *did* see our visitor, he'd be more likely to remember."

Chief Dakin grunted. "By the way, the only one I missed was Emmeline DuPré. She wasn't home. It's close by, so you might drop in on her yourself. If anybody saw somethin', it was the DuPré woman. She doesn't miss a trick, ever."

"Right, Dakin."

Ellery strolled down the Hill to Miss DuPré's house. He rang and rang, but there was no answer. For a few moments he lingered on her chaste porch, slightly irritated. It was exactly like Emmy DuPré to be missing when you wanted her. But then he shrugged and left. It was improbable that even the town snoop had seen or heard anything.

Ellery resisted the impulse to stop in at the John F. Wrights', next door to Miss DuPré's. A call now would only lead to questions about the Bayard Fox case.

He ambled down the Hill and struck out for town.

At the northeast corner of Upper Whistling and State, Ellery paused. Should he walk down State Street and drop in on Chief Dakin at Town Hall? But there could scarcely be any news yet. So Ellery crossed State Street; he would walk about High Village for a bit.

He strolled past the Upper Whistling side of the Northern State Telephone Building and crossed narrow Jezreel Lane. In the Lower Main-Upper Whistling corner "block" beyond, which is largely taken up by the sprawling building of the Five-and-Dime, there is a group of small shops facing Upper Whistling Avenue, and one of these is Miss Sally's Tea Roome. Miss Sally's Tea Roome is what upper-crust Wrightsvillians of the female sex call an *"intime"* place: it is frothy with lace curtains and shaky colonial-reproduction tables and chairs, along one wall ranges a row of booths done in lemon leatherette, the waitresses are dressed uniformly in high-waisted dun-colored dresses reaching to their shoetips and wear mobcaps, and the daily menu, hand-lettered by Miss Sally herself in Old English and peppered with "Ye Olde's," is dominated by cream sauces and sweets.

Ellery shuddered and passed on.

But it was not to be.

He heard a feminine shriek behind him: "Mr. Queen! Oh, Mr. Queen! Stop! Wait!"

An aged female was leaning out of the doorway of Miss Sally's Tea Roome, gesticulating frantically.

"Yes?" said Ellery, walking back. The woman's face, a stern, withered, withal simple one, looked familiar. Then he chuckled. "I remember. You're Miss Aikin, librarian over at the Carnegie Library on State Street."

"You remember me!" exclaimed Miss Aikin, clasping her hands to her bosom ecstatically. Then she seized his arm. "Won't you come in for a moment? Please, Mr. Queen?"

"Into the Tea Roome? Well . . . But is anything wrong, Miss Aikin?"

"You see, we don't know," whispered Miss Aikin, leading him through the crowded restaurant. Heads swiveled and eyes trailed him—elderly feminine heads largely and elderly feminine eyes—and he plowed past them leaving a wake of whispers. Damn Miss Aikin for luring him into this culinary harem! "That's why Emmeline DuPré was just trying to get you on the telephone, Mr. Queen. And while she was off at the phone I happened to look up, and there you were passing Miss Sally's! Isn't that providential?"

Ellery felt better. At least he could dispose of that loose end. Unless . . . She was trying to reach him? Then she *had* seen something! Good old Emmy DuPré!

"Where is Miss DuPré, Miss Aikin?" he asked eagerly. "I mean, where's the phone? I must talk to her."

"Oh, I'll fetch her," said Miss Aikin hastily, coloring. "Here, do sit down here, Mr. Queen, in our booth. Emmy and I purposely picked it for privacy. Of course, if we'd known that *you*—" and she was gone, disappearing through a modest little white doorway which bore the legend in baby-blue paint: LADYES.

In a moment the door burst open and Miss DuPré's mottled, ophidian features appeared. She scuttled toward the lemon-colored booth, a huge dog-eared book of some sort pressed to her flat chest. Miss Aikin scuttled after.

"Mr. Queen!" Emmeline DuPré exclaimed. "Do sit down. Do. Now please. Oh, this is fortunate! Don't ever mention miracles to me again." And she pushed him back on one of the bench-seats, pushed Miss Aikin onto the bench opposite, and crowded quickly in beside her. Ellery found himself facing the two excited spinsters across a table ghastly with the half-nibbled corpses of creamed chicken patties, Waldorf salad with *ersatz* whipped cream and maraschino cherry, and Miss Sally's famous dessert specialty, Pineapple Marshmallow Nut Mousse. "I just tried to get you at Emily Fox's, but Emily didn't know where you'd gone, and—"

"Exactly what was it you saw last night, Miss DuPré?" demanded Ellery.

Both ladies stared at him. Then at each other.

"Saw last night?" repeated Emmy DuPré. "Why, whatever can you mean, Mr. Queen? I didn't see anything last night." The bony cartilage of her nostrils quivered. "Should I have?"

Something else?

Ellery blinked. "I'm not very bright today," he said

with an apologetic smile. "I was thinking of another matter entirely. What was it you ladies wanted to tell me?"

Miss DuPré and Miss Aikin exchanged glances again.

"Well," said Miss DuPré, and her tongue flicked over her lips. "It all started with Miss Aikin's collection of autographs of famous Wrightsvillians, you see, and—"

Ellery sat spellbound as Emmeline DuPré, with an occasional timid interjection from the librarian, unfolded the saga of Shockley Wright and the elusive autograph, and how Miss Aikin had nearly found it through Myron Garback, the late proprietor of the High Village Pharmacy, when Garback recalled that in his record-book of special receipts there was a genuine Shockley Wright signature; and how Fate had then intervened—"Atropos," as Miss DuPré put it—and the precious scrawl had remained in limbo when poor Mr. Garback inconsiderately dropped dead of thrombosis that very week end when he had promised to "look it up." And finally how Garback's successor, the detestable Alvin Cain, had characteristically erected barricades against the wheels of culture by refusing to be bothered digging up the old record-book.

"At that point Miss Aikin enlisted my aid," continued Emmeline DuPré in her elegant way, "feeling that my powers of persuasion, Mr. Queen, might exceed hers." Ellery felt like saying: "Quite. Quite, old girl." But he did not. "Of course, I agreed to help out of civic duty. Miss Aikin's collection is a positive museum piece. I mean, it's *invaluable*, Mr. Queen. I mean, it will undoubtedly go down in the history of Wrightsville. No common tradesman like Alvin can—" Miss DuPré sniffed—"could be permitted to withhold the sole signature of a member of the Wright family missing from Miss Aikin's collection. Don't you agree?"

Mr. Queen agreed, cautiously.

Stand pat, old boy, he said to himself. Some sense will creep out of this heap of words yet.

"But we won!" cried Miss Aikin rapturously. "Oh, tell Mr. Queen how we won, Emmy!"

"Well, I tried and tried," said Miss DuPré grimly—
"really, I lowered myself in my own eyes, Mr. Queen;
how I coddled that swarthy vulgarian!—but not until
this morning did the creature give in. Since he virtually
ejected me from his drugstore—and not merely once,
Mr. Queen!—I've been bombarding him with letters. A
letter a day! I've waged a positive *campaign*. And this
morning he phoned me—I must say he was awfully mad
—and said all right, he'd give me the Shockley Wright
autograph, if only I'd stop bothering him, and if I'd stop
by the store this morning he'd be only too glad to—"
Miss DuPré's skinny neck lengthened—"I believe his
exact words were 'get you out of my hair.' "

"At which Miss DuPré hurried down to High Village," said Miss Aikin breathlessly, "and the next *I*
knew about it, she appeared at the Library with Myron
Garback's old record-book under her arm, and I went
out with her to an early luncheon so we could look up
Shockley Wright's signature and . . . oh, I'm so grateful to you, Emmy, I shan't ever be able to pay you
back!"

"Nonsense, Dolores," said Miss DuPré gruffly, although she was pleased. "It was my duty to posterity."

And after Miss Aikin cleared some dishes away, Miss
DuPré laid the large, worn tome she was still clutching
to her down on the table between them.

Ellery saw now that it was not a book, as he had at
first thought, but a ledger.

Shockley Wright's signature . . .

He was puzzled and alert. He had never even heard
of Shockley Wright, through the John F. Wrights or
anyone else in or out of Wrightsville. He could not imagine why the Misses DuPré and Aikin should think the
tale of the Wright clan's black sheep and Miss Aikin's
Javert-like hunt for a specimen of his handwriting would
interest the man who had come to Wrightsville expressly
to settle the guilt or innocence of Bayard Fox.

With trembling hands Miss Aikin leaned over her
friend and opened the ledger.

"You see, Mr. Queen," she explained, "Shockley

Wright once came into Mr. Garback's drugstore to renew a prescription, and because the medicine had dope
in it or something, Mr. Garback made Shockley *sign* for
the renewal in this book. That's how Providence works
its wonders! . . . There! Isn't it a *dream?"*

The "dream" was an almost illegible scrawl on a long
page full of other signatures, all precisely dated and
bearing notations in a uniformly copperplate handwriting, presumably the hand of the late Myron Garback
himself. As for the precious autograph of Shockley
Wright, its author must have been in an especially *bra-
vura* mood when he signed for the renewal of his
prescription . . . away back, Ellery noted, in 1928.

"So when we found the Shockley Wright," Miss Aikin
babbled on, "we naturally kept searching through the
record-book—you never can tell, and a ledger like this
is such a *fountain* of autographs!—and as a matter of
fact I found two or three specimens of other famous
Wrightsvillians far superior to those I already have in
my collection—"

"The fact is," interrupted Emmeline DuPré, "we've
found something else."

She lowered her head and narrowed her eyes and
sprayed Miss Sally's Tea Roome with a glance that very
nearly hissed.

"Something else," said Ellery.

His pulse told him that he might now dismiss the matter of the prodigal Wright from his mind. He had been
summoned in a matter far more important.

"Something else?" he repeated. "What?"

"The year 1932," whispered Miss DuPré, with the air
of an Underground heroine plotting liberation under the
noses of the Gestapo.

"The year 1932," said Ellery, blinking.

"To be exact," whispered Miss Aikin. "June 5, 1932."

"June 5, 1932?" Ellery sat up very straight.

"You see, Miss Aikin—I mean, Dolores?" said
Emmy DuPré triumphantly. "I told you so!"

"You were so right, Emmeline," said Miss Aikin
adoringly.

"What about June 5, 1932?" snapped Ellery.

Miss DuPré riffled through the ledger with a maddening smile. But finally she found a page, about one-third through, and the horny nail of her predacious forefinger immediately stabbed at a line of writing.

"There," she announced, "it is, Mr. Queen!"

Ellery seized the book and read the following, in the prevalent copperplate script: "Renewal prescription #32541. June 5, 1932." And after that, in an altogether different handwriting, the name "Bayard Fox."

"It struck me *instantly,*" Emmeline DuPré was hissing. "I followed the trial very closely, you know. That date in Myron Garback's ledger was only a week or so *prior* to the murder of Jessica Fox! And *I* don't recall anything's coming out at Bayard Fox's trial about a medicine renewal just before the murder, Mr. Queen!"

"So Emmy said to me," Miss Aikin said, her eyes behind the severe spectacles round as a child's, "that it was *very* significant, and that you would *certainly* be interested, because you were looking into the whole case, Mr. Queen—"

"Yes, yes," said Ellery. "I certainly am, ladies. You were quite right to call this to my attention. Er—Miss Aikin. I'm going to appropriate this ledger—"

"Oh, no!" shrieked Miss Aikin. "Not again! My Shockley Wright—"

"Lower your voice!" Miss DuPré poked her friend sharply in the side.

"But Emmeline, you didn't say Mr. Queen would take—"

"How should I know he'd want the old book permanently?" mumbled Miss DuPré. But her eyes were glittering.

"As if you didn't, Emmy DuPré! Oh, I might have known I'd lose out somehow if I got mixed up with you! You don't have a reputation in Wrightsville for nothing!"

"I like that!" snapped Emmy DuPré. "After I went and got you your old Shockley Wright! That's gratitude, isn't it, Dolores Aikin? I've a good mind to—"

"Ladies, ladies," said Mr. Queen hurriedly. "Miss Aikin, you may remove the pages right now that contain the signatures you want for your collection. As long as you leave this page intact."

"Oh, *thank* you!" It took the librarian two minutes to locate the page on which the rare Shockley Wright autograph appeared, her hands shook so. Finally she tore the page out, and two others. "Thank you, Mr. Queen!" she beamed.

"Don't mention it. And I mean—don't mention it. That goes for you, too, Miss DuPré."

Ellery sat studying Bayard Fox's signature in the ledger for some time after Miss Aikin and Emmeline DuPré left Miss Sally's Tea Roome, Miss Aikin clutching her autographs and trying to placate Miss DuPré, and Miss DuPré stalking on ahead with chin high, implacable.

At last Ellery rose.

"Sir?"

One of Miss Sally's mobcapped damsels was offering him a slip of chartreuse paper.

"What's this?"

In Miss Aikin's case it had undoubtedly been excitement. But there was no mistaking the case of Miss DuPré, who never forgot anything.

In passing, she had stuck him with the check for the Creamed-chicken Patties, the Waldorf Salad *Garni,* and the Pineapple Marshmallow Nut Mousses.

15. Fox at Bay

ALVIN CAIN WHISKED out from behind the fumed-oak parapet of his prescription department.

"One teaspoonful every four hours, Mrs. Gonzoli," he said briskly, wrapping the medicine bottle in the distinctive candy-striped wrapping paper of the High Village Pharmacy. "Kapeesh?"

"Four hou'," repeated the Italian woman.

"And that doesn't mean every time your old *Signor* feels like a snort. Eighty-five cents. *Viva Italia!* Next, please . . . Oh."

"Hullo, Alvin," said Chief of Police Dakin.

"'Lo, *Chef*."

"Afternoon, Mr. Cain."

"And Mr. Queen. Still doing the snooperoo, huh?"

"Still doing the snooperoo," said Ellery, looking around.

"Say!" Cain's shrewd eyes fixed upon the ledger under Ellery's arm. "Isn't that my ledger?"

"It is."

"Well, I'll be—How'd *you* get it?" Cain demanded hotly. "I'll bet that DuPré bag—I might have known a favor to that damned old creep would be a sure way to get into trouble!"

"No trouble, Alvin," said Chief Dakin. "We just dropped in to check up a point. How far back does your prescription file go?"

"All the way—to when Garback opened this store. Why?"

"We'd like to take a look at the original prescription for your number 32541."

158

"Come on back."

They followed the pharmacist into his stock room. It was surprisingly clean and orderly.

"What number was that again?"

"Thirty-two five forty-one."

"Any idea what year it would be?"

"You might try 1932," said Ellery.

Cain turned to the wall. A row of long steel needle files hung there, thousands of prescriptions jammed onto a file.

"What's up?" the pharmacist asked curiously as he ran his eye over the bunches of prescriptions.

"We found a record in here," said Dakin patiently, "that may have somethin' to do with the Fox case. So we want to check the original prescription, Alvin."

"Oh. Sure."

Cain took down one of the files and began to run through the tightly packed papers. "Thirty-two five forty-one? . . . ought to be along in here somewhere . . . 32822 . . . 32654 . . . 32550 . . . along here . . . yep."

He held the prescription exposed. It bore the printed name MILO WILLOUGHBY M.D., and the address "PRO-FESSIONAL BUILDING, WRIGHTSVILLE." The date, in Dr. Willoughby's pinched handwriting, was May 23, 1932. Ellery could make out the name "Mrs. B. Fox" and something-"ox," but the rest was gibberish to him.

"What's this prescription say, Cain? I never have understood how pharmacists can decipher the hen-scratches on most doctors' prescriptions."

"Tincture of digitalis, 1 ounce," said Alvin Cain.

"The original prescription that Doc Willoughby wrote for Jessica Fox's digitalis!" exclaimed Chief Dakin.

"What's the rest of this scrawl?" asked Ellery.

"It says '15 drops three times daily.'"

"It's the original prescription, all right, Dakin," said Ellery, frowning. "Cain, do you happen to recall a renewal of this prescription? In early June of that same year? In fact, on June fifth?"

"What d'ye think I am, a mental giant?" laughed

Cain. "This pharmacy's handled I don't know how many thousands of prescriptions and renewals. And that was over twelve years ago."

"But it concerns the Fox murder case," said Ellery. "Everyone's had such a wonderful memory about the Fox murder case, Cain."

The pharmacist stared at him. "You kidding?"

"No indeed."

"Well, I don't remember. Twelve years!"

"Take a look at this note in Garback's record-book." Ellery set the big ledger down on Cain's worktable and opened it to the page which bore the copperplate-hand notation and the Bayard Fox signature.

"Here?" The pharmacist was puzzled.

"Who wrote this line, Alvin?" asked the Chief.

"About 'Renewal prescription #32541, June 5, 1932'? It's Myron Garback's writing."

Ellery and Dakin exchanged glances.

"The old poop owned this store at that time," Cain went on, "and I was just a lowly clerk here. Ah, them were the days—no headaches and all of twenty-eight per! I guess Foxy must have breezed in for a renewal and Garback made him sign for it."

"Oh, then you recognize this 'Bayard Fox,' " asked Ellery quickly, "as being Bayard Fox's signature?"

"Say, what are you trying to pull, Queen?" asked Alvin Cain angrily. "I don't recognize anything. I wouldn't know Bayard Fox's signature from a hole in the head. It says 'Bayard Fox' and it's not in Garback's handwriting, so I take it for granted Bayard Fox signed it. Anything more I can do for you gents? I hear a customer out there."

"We'll take that prescription, Alvin," said Chief Dakin mildly. "Go ahead and serve your customer. I'll fish it off this hook myself."

Dakin was abstracted as he drove Ellery out of town and back up the Hill. It was as if he were trying to catch up with something which was just beyond a bend of his brain. He kept glancing at Myron Garback's record-book in Ellery's lap, worriedly.

Ellery merely stared ahead.

Linda and Davy were seated on the top step of the porch.

"Mr. Queen!" cried Linda. "Well?"

" 'Well,' Linda? 'Well' what?"

"Well—anything," Linda laughed.

"There's something, Linda—but I doubt if it's going to be a great comfort."

Linda stopped laughing.

"But what you said during the night—" began Davy blankly.

"Oh, that. No news on that yet. Eh, Dakin?"

"No." Dakin pursed his lips. "I guess it's hopeless, Davy. We ain't found a trace of the one who broke into the house last night."

"You will—I'm sure you will, if you keep looking hard enough," said Linda eagerly. She touched the ledger under Ellery's arm with a timid finger. "What's this, Mr. Queen?"

"It's an old record-book Myron Garback used to keep," said Ellery. "Davy, where's your father?"

"In the parlor. With Three-Chins."

Ellery and Dakin hurried into the house. Linda and Davy looked at each other, and then just as hurriedly followed.

Bayard was sitting back at one end of Emily's settee, a checkerboard on the middle seat beside him. At the other end squatted Detective Howie, in a dark red rage, glaring at the board.

"Take me," chuckled Bayard. "Take me, Howie, and you're licked."

Howie's paw flicked out to slap the board from beneath, so that it leaped like a wounded thing from the settee. The pieces flew in all directions.

"I'll take you, you s.o.b.," he choked. His little eyes were flaming with hate. "I'll take you and I'll lose to you, but I won't lose in the end, you s.o.b."

Bayard calmly retrieved the fallen checkers. He

straightened the board and began to set a new game up.

"That makes eleven games," he smiled. "Come on, Howie, I'll play you another."

Howie slapped the board again. This time Bayard did not smile, nor did he attempt to go after the checkers.

"You got the right name, Fox," panted the detective. "Yeah, you're smart, all right. But just the same you're jail-bait, Foxy. And you're going to stay jail-bait. I'll—" Then Howie saw Ellery in the doorway, and his complexion turned yellowish.

"Hello," said Ellery.

Howie started to hoist his great body, then sank back. "Well, look who's here," he snarled. "The master mind from New York. The genius who's gonna whitewash the wife poisoner. How you doing, genius?"

"Is this life of idleness getting you, Howie?" murmered Ellery, stepping into the room. Dakin lingered in the doorway, the ledger behind his back. "Oh, Bayard."

Bayard was staring from him to Dakin and Linda and Davy in the doorway. "Yes, Mr. Queen." He sounded anxious.

Ellery handed him a sheet of blank notepaper and a fountain pen.

"Write your name," he said.

"Now he's gonna play games," sneered the fat man. From the doorway Davy said: "Linda, let go of me!"

"No, Davy!"

"He's got it coming to him, Lin!"

Detective Howie, grasping the arm of the settee, had half-risen, his great calves taut.

"I won't take any more of his poison! The way he talks to Dad—and now he's started on Ellery Queen—"

"Davy," said Chief Dakin gently. He put his big hand on Davy's arm.

"Write your name, Bayard," said Ellery again.

"But Mr. Queen, why—"

"Please."

Bayard took the pen and notepaper, placed the paper on the checkerboard, and slowly signed his name.

Ellery took the sheet and glanced briefly at it. He nodded at Dakin. Dakin came into the room with the ledger, opened it, and placed the signature Bayard had just written near the signature in the ledger.

"They don't look *exactly* the same, Mr. Queen," Dakin muttered.

"No two specimens of a person's handwriting ever are the same, Dakin," frowned Ellery. "A million samples will show a million variations . . . But the base-characteristics remain. There's no doubt this name in the ledger is in the handwriting of Bayard Fox."

Dakin said softly: "Mr. Fox, will you take a look at this signature?"

Bayard's glance followed the route of the Chief's forefinger to the line on the ledger.

"Is this your John Hancock?"

"But Mr. Dakin," began Bayard, "I don't begin to see—"

"Is this your signature, Mr. Fox?"

"Yes, but—"

Dakin rapped: "That's all we want to know."

Ellery sank into the big tapestried armchair with a sigh. "Come in here, Linda. You, too, Davy."

Linda and Davy obeyed in perplexity.

"Briefly, the situation's this," said Ellery wearily. "On June 5, 1932, Bayard Fox entered the High Village Pharmacy and asked Pharmacist Myron Garback for a renewal of a prescription numbered 32541. Garback renewed the prescription but had Bayard sign for it in this old-fashioned record-book, whose authenticity is unquestionable: Garback himself mention its existence to Miss Aikin, the librarian, only a day or so before he dropped dead, and there are thousands of people in Wrightsville who will vouch for the genuineness of it . . . because they wrote their names in it.

"The drug Bayard wanted a renewal of, and for which he signed, turns out to have been the drug called for by Dr. Milo Willoughby's original prescription—the tincture of digitalis for Jessica Fox's weakened heart."

Bayard's hands were semaphoring their protest. He was pale and he kept moistening his lips.

But before he could speak, Davy said, "I don't get it, Mr. Queen. What's the point?"

And Linda nodded in the same bewilderment.

"The point," sighed Ellery, "arises out of a simple matter of chronology. Dr. Willoughby's original prescription is dated May twenty-third. On Decoration Day —May thirtieth, according to the doctor's own testimony and Jessica's corroboration—Willoughby ordered her, and Jessica obeyed the order, to stop taking the prescribed digitalis. Yet according to the notation in this ledger, *Bayard Fox renewed the prescription on June fifth*—five days after Jessica *discontinued* taking the digitalis!"

They saw it now.

"Why did Bayard renew that prescription? *What did he want with a fresh one-ounce bottle of digitalis—when his wife was no longer taking digitalis on her doctor's orders?*"

Bayard shrank.

"I suppose," said Chief Dakin heavily, "you busted the first bottle, Fox, or maybe you thought there wasn't enough left in it, so you wanted some more digitalis to make *sure* she'd kick off when you—"

"*No!*"

Bayard sprang to his feet. His skinny neck resembled a picket fence.

Linda ran out of the parlor. Davy looked after her, swallowing. And then his jaws crunched and he strode out, too.

"Davy—" cried Bayard hoarsely.

But his son neither paused nor looked back.

"If this evidence had come out twelve years ago at the trial," said the Chief of Police quietly, "you wouldn't be servin' a life sentence now, Fox—you'd have fried."

Bayard sank back onto the settee. He seemed dazed.

Oh, thought Ellery, if I could only make up my mind about this man.

Bayard whispered: "There's some mistake somewhere. I never went to Garback's drugstore for a renewal of that digitalis prescription."

Dakin regarded him almost with admiration. But then he shrugged and turned away.

"Mr. Dakin—Mr. Queen, you'll listen to me! I swear to you—I'll swear on anything—tell me what to swear on—I swear this isn't true. I *didn't* get a second bottle of digitalis from Garback. Or from anyone else! You've got to listen, Mr. Queen—I didn't!"

"And your signature in this ledger showing receipt of the renewal?" asked Ellery, closing his eyes.

"It's a lie!"

"But you just identified it yourself."

"I didn't know what it meant—what this was all about!"

"Sure you didn't," said Dakin dryly. "You forgot about signing in Garback's ledger, Fox—twelve years is a long time to remember every detail of your crime. If you'd remembered, or if we'd told you first off what it meant, you'd have said it *wasn't* your signature. D'ye think we're fools?"

"Listen. Listen," said Davy's father. "You said 'Is this your signature?' and I said 'Yes.' Because it is. I mean —it *looks* like my signature. But I tell you I never wrote that signature! I've never *seen* this ledger before!"

Ellery opened his eyes. "Then what's your explanation, Bayard?" he asked sharply.

"I haven't any, Mr. Queen. I can't give you one. All I know is I didn't sign this ledger and I didn't renew that prescription."

Dakin glanced at Ellery, shaking his head. "I guess that's that, Mr. Queen." He picked up his hat.

"And about time, too," said a screeky voice.

Detective Howie wore three fat grins now.

"Do I take this wife poisoner back to the Pen now, or do I wait till mornin', Mr. Queen? You're the doctor." Howie sounded positively jovial.

Ellery grimaced. "Go away, Howie. I want to think."

The detective guffawed. "Come on, Foxy!" he roared. "Your genius wants to think."

He hustled Bayard out of the parlor.

Chief Dakin hesitated for a moment, looking down at Ellery. Then he said, in an uneasy way: "Well. I'll be at my office if you want me, Mr. Queen."

"Right, Dakin. 'By."

But Chief Dakin did not go. Instead, he said encouragingly: "Don't feel too bad about this, Mr. Queen. After all, it was in the cards."

"Yes, yes, Dakin. Good-by now."

"Well . . ." Dakin, shaking his head, went out softly.

16.   The Fox and the Judge

IT SEEMED TO Ellery that only a few minutes had elapsed, but when the door slammed upstairs and Linda's smothered shout broke in on his senses he found his muscles stiff and the parlor filled with late-afternoon shadows.

He sat up straight in the tapestried chair, listening. The door-slam had been brutal and Linda's cry a formless utterance, the very voice of despair. Ellery ran out into the hall.

He found Emily Fox there, looking up the stairs anxiously.

"Wasn't that Linda, Mrs. Fox?"

"Yes." Emily called up: "Linny! What's wrong?" There was no reply.

"Linda—"

"Just a moment, Mrs. Fox," snapped Ellery.

In the silence they heard, faintly, a wild weak sobbing.

Ellery took the stairs three at a time, Emily panting

behind him. Linda was not on the first floor. They ran up another flight.

She was stretched out on the top-floor landing.

Emily dropped to her knees.

"Lin baby. Lin. Dearest—"

"It's Davy," sobbed Linda. "Mother, he's packing."

Emily grew pale. She put her chubby arms about Linda, pulling the girl up to her breast. Linda clung, like a child.

Ellery went to the door of the "apartment" bedroom and knocked.

Davy's voice said hoarsely: "I tell you no, Linny. No!"

Ellery went in, shutting the door behind him.

Captain Fox was in full uniform. He was packing a duffel bag and a valise, which were spread out on the twin bed he had not slept in since the night of the lightning storm. When he saw who it was, he reddened.

"Hi," he said.

"Davy, why are you packing?"

Davy looked him in the eye. "I should think that would be obvious to you . . . of all people."

"You're going away?"

"Naturally."

Ellery leaned against the door and lit a cigaret. "You have it a little twisted, Captain. I should say—'*Un*naturally.' "

Davy stopped packing. "Are you kidding?"

"Not at all."

"But I don't get it. You ought to be packing, too!"

"Why?"

"Well . . . you're through, aren't you?"

"What makes you think that, Davy?"

"Well . . . the evidence you just turned up—that prescription renewal—"

"What about it, Davy?"

"What about it!" Davy's nose wrinkled with pure astonishment. "Maybe I'm missing today," he complained. "What about it? You told us yourself what about it— this afternoon!"

"You mean that the development today makes your father look like your mother's murderer?"

"Well, sure!"

"But that's been the pattern all along, Davy," said Ellery dryly. "Nothing's really changed, you know. I see no reason why finding another indication of your father's guilt should make us all quit cold."

Davy could only stare at him.

"It isn't as if turning up this fresh evidence made Bayard break down and admit it's been true all along. On the contrary. He's more vehement than ever in his denials."

Davy sank onto his bed to clasp his hands between his knees and kick at the hooked rug between his bed and Linda's. "I don't know what you expect me to say," he muttered. "How much blind faith am I supposed to have?"

"At least as much as Linda. She's out there in the hall crying her eyes out because the man who tried to strangle her wants to leave her."

Davy scowled ferociously.

"Mind you," continued Ellery, examining a smoke ring very critically, "I'm not saying I believe Bayard, Davy. And I don't deny the importance of a corroborative bit of evidence. But I'm still dissatisfied."

"Takes an awful lot to satisfy you, seems to me," mumbled Davy.

Ellery ground his cigaret out in an ashtray on Davy's highboy. "Well," he said, "there's still a point or two."

"Huh?"

"The most immediate being: Who broke into the house next door last night, and what was it he stole?" Ellery frowned. "Davy, no investigator worth beans would quit on a case with a tag end like that left hanging. The fact is, your father simply couldn't have been the housebreaker-thief last night, on the positive testimony of our fat friend Howie, who of all people on this planet is least likely to want to cover Bayard Fox up. Bayard being eliminated, the field is left wide-open. . . . Before I give up, I want to know what was taken from your father's secretary last night. And I want to know who took it. And also why. Don't you?"

"I—I guess I do," muttered Captain Fox. "I guess I didn't think."

"I guess you didn't," smiled Ellery. "Now suppose you go on out there and put your arms around your wife and tell her what a damned fool you are . . . you bloody hero."

Davy flushed scarlet. "Socko," he said. "Watch me crawl."

Adjusting his khaki tie in Linda's vanity mirror, he swallowed a few times, and then he went to the door like a small boy bound on order for the woodshed.

Emily was waiting for Ellery in the downstairs hall.

"Thanks very much, Mr. Queen," she said quietly.

"Oh, he couldn't have been permitted to leave now, Mrs. Fox." Ellery was abstracted. "Tell me—I meant to ask you when Linda cried out upstairs and broke my chain of thought. What's happened to the lawyer who defended Bayard at the trial?"

"Mr. Moodus? I don't know, Mr. Queen. Mr. Moodus went away after the trial and—"

"Wasn't Moodus a local man?"

"Oh, no. He was a Boston lawyer. Judge Eli Martin recommended him to Bayard as a very good trial man, I seem to recall."

"Really? I didn't know old Judge Martin'd been involved."

"He wasn't, Mr. Queen. It was just a friendly gesture. The Judge was always very fond of 'the Fox boys,' as he used to call Talbot and Bayard. He watched them grow up in Wrightsville."

"Judge Martin, eh?" Ellery smiled. "Well, thanks, Mrs. Fox. I think I'll take a little walk."

"Ought to be horsewhipped," said Judge Eli Martin severely. "In town for the Lord knows how long and didn't look me up!"

"Guilty, guilty," sighed Ellery. "But Judge, I've been a little busy."

"So I hear." Wrightsville's eminent jurist was as gaunt

and little and dry-mannered as ever, and his eyes were just as deceptively sleepy as Ellery remembered them from the days when he defended Jim Haight, stepping down from the Bench to do so. "So I hear."

"Shut up in this museum piece," grinned Ellery, "I wonder that you hear anything, Judge."

Judge Martin looked around, chuckling. "It *is* on the Blackstone side. But I've had this fusty old retreat in the County Lawyers' Block for forty-five years, and I wouldn't change it for all the marble in the newfangled County Court House. . . . When are you going to give up, Mr. Queen?"

"Give up?"

"Phil Hendrix tells me you're having a time of it."

"How would Phil Hendrix know?" retorted Ellery.

"Detective Howie," said Judge Eli dryly. "Well, well, what is it, young sir? How can I help you? You didn't drop into my office at five-thirty just to hold my feeble hand."

Ellery laughed. "All right, Judge. What do you know about the Jessica Fox murder case?"

Judge Martin rather deliberately opened the lowest drawer of his battered walnut desk, reached far in, came up with a black and bowlegged Italian stogie, lit it, puffed long and vigorously, and finally sat back. "Have to hide my smokes from Miss Finegold," he grunted. "That's my secretary. Finey and Doc Willoughby are in a conspiracy to lengthen my life by five years. . . . Why, I don't know what you mean. 'Know' about it?"

"You know exactly what I mean," drawled Ellery. "Well . . ."

"I take it you haven't any undisclosed facts in that secret drawer of yours—or have you?"

"Heavens, no."

"How familiar were you with the proceedings?"

"I followed it fairly closely at the time."

"And your sympathies?"

"In my business," remarked Judge Martin to his stogie, "if you have any such, you sit on 'em till they smother to death."

"Then you did have some."

"Perhaps."

"For the victim or the defendant?"

Judge Martin tapped ashes into his wastebasket. "Young fellow, you're not going to pump me on *that*. Where my sympathies lay is irrelevant—purely emotional, you understand. No basis in fact, no evidential value, no standing in court."

"What did you think of the verdict?" persisted Ellery.

"My personal opinion?" Judge Eli squinted at him through the acrid smoke. "I don't like the kind of evidence they convicted Bayard on. As a judge, I mean. I prefer something substantial when you're trying a man for his life and liberty—like fingerprints."

"But from a sheerly logical point of view—"

"Oh, certainly." The Judge waved his cigar.

Ellery sucked the knuckle of his right thumb, frowning. "It's true," he admitted. "I haven't got very far. . . . How well did you know Bayard Fox, Judge?" he asked suddenly.

"Very well."

"Did you consider Bayard the killing type?"

"Is there one?" retorted the Judge.

Ellery grimaced. "You see the sort of thing I'm reduced to."

"But why are you trying so hard?"

"Because I'm not convinced Bayard Fox committed that crime. Among other reasons."

"You think he didn't?" asked Judge Martin slowly.

"I didn't say that. I just don't know one way or the other. The circumstances say he did. The man himself says he didn't. I mean—not merely his mouth. The whole man. His eyes. The tone of his voice. The way he moves his hands."

"People earn their living that way," the Judge growled.

"Oh, yes. That's part of my problem."

"Very interesting," murmured Judge Eli. "I may as well tell you . . . I've felt the same way for twelve years."

Ellery nodded. "I gathered as much."

"Let me tell you something I wasn't going to." Judge Martin put his high-topped shoes on the desk and puffed at the ceiling with its intricate plaster curlicues around the modernized old chandelier. "About six months or so before Jessica Fox's death, she invited Clarice and me to her home for dinner. There were just the four of us—Jessica and Bayard, and my wife and I. Davy was only a sprout of eight or nine, so he'd been given his dinner beforehand and sent to bed.

"It was a very pleasant dinner and Clarice and I had a nice time. I liked their home, because it was just that —not an institution, like so many of the houses on the Hill. And the thing that made it a home was—strangely enough—not Jessica, but Bayard."

The Judge frowned.

"Bayard was at peace there—that was it. He liked his home. He was proud of it. And proud of Jessica. More than proud. He was deeply in love with her. You could see it in the way his eyes followed her every gesture and movement. They followed her like the eyes of a dog. Like my old Pete, who died last year."

The Judge sighed.

"And then after dinner. It was one of those times when Jessica was minus a maid—she was the kind of woman who has maid troubles all the time—so she cleared the table, and Clarice helped her. I admired that in Jessica—she didn't indulge in the fussy little formalities that make Hill dinners such a trial.

"Bayard and I went into his study for cigars and brandy while the women were busy. As we sat there, Bayard said to me: 'As long as you're here, Judge, I wonder if you'd mind looking something over for me.' I said of course I didn't mind, and he showed me a will. He'd typed the will out himself, he said—he'd always neglected making one before—and he'd signed it and had it witnessed, but he wanted to make sure it was a sound legal instrument. As it happened, it was—a perfectly good will, and I told him so.

"But my point is the way Bayard acted that night. In his will he'd left everything to Jessica—everything he owned, down to the last collar button. The language of the will—his own language—was almost embarrassing, it was so full of endearing terms. And the way he talked to me about his wife in the study—well," said the Judge queerly, "if that man wasn't head over heels in love with that woman, I don't know a thing about human nature. And I'd have sworn it wasn't the kind of love that makes a man kill. I'd have said it was the love that's unselfish and sacrifices itself—that would hurt itself before it hurt its object—the real kind of love." And the Judge fell silent.

"But that was long before Bayard found out about another man," Ellery pointed out. "Feelings change. People change."

The Judge squinted at him, his brows together. "I knew I shouldn't have said anything," he grunted at last. "It's—" he waved the cigar—"it's unjuridical."

Ellery rose. "Well," he said, "I'm much obliged."

"Come visit Clarice and me before you leave Wrightsville, Mr. Queen," said Judge Martin, rising too.

"Thanks, I'll try, but don't count on it. Please give Mrs. Martin my very best."

"She'll hate you if you don't give her a chance to throw a dinner—and what's more, make the rest of my life miserable." The Judge shook Ellery's hand warmly. "If there's anything I can do—say, with Phil Hendrix, if Phil gets difficult—"

"Thanks, Judge." Ellery went slowly to the door. There he paused, frowning. "This will you mentioned," he said. "Could it possibly have had anything to do with—?"

The Judge smiled sadly. "Not a thing, Mr. Queen. There was nothing in it that had the remotest connection with the events of Jessica's subsequent illness and death. All it said was that it left everything to Jessica. There were no other bequests, no conditions—not a word in it could have had any significance as far as the murder case was concerned. For all I know, Bayard never even looked at that will again after that night. When I handed it back to him, he locked it in a drawer of his secretary and we went back to join the women—" The Judge put his frail hand quickly on Ellery's arm. "Why, what's the matter, Mr. Queen?" he exclaimed.

"Did you say," asked Ellery hoarsely, "did you say *Bayard locked the will in a drawer of his secretary?* Is that what you just said, Judge Martin?"

"Why, yes." The old gentleman looked blank. "What's so startling about that? It was an empty drawer, and he put the will in it and locked it with a key from his key ring. Why?"

Ellery breathed in deeply. "An empty drawer. Do you happen to recall which drawer, Judge?"

"The top drawer, I think."

"The top drawer," repeated Ellery. "You're sure of that?"

"As sure as I can be after so many years. But—"

"Tell me, Judge. The will was a simple document—"

"Typed on an ordinary sheet of white paper."

"It bore the date—"

"December something, 1931."

"Who were the witnesses?"

"Amos Bluefield, the Town Clerk, and Mark Doodle, who used to run the cigar stand at the Hollis—Mark was a notary, too. You remember old Amos—I think he died while you were here a few years ago on the Haight case."

Ellery's eyes were snapping. "Yes, indeed," he said. "Judge, may I use your phone?"

"Without letting me in on it? Well, well, go ahead."

Ellery grinned and telephoned Chief of Police Dakin's office. "Dakin, I've found out what was in that locked drawer of Bayard's."

"You have! What?"

"Bayard's will. Dated 1931."

"His *will?* I didn't know he ever had a will."

"Well, he made one out, but Jessica's death and what happened to him afterward apparently drove it out of his mind. It's understandable."

"It is? Not to me! Why in tunket should somebody

swipe a will thirteen years old that—Who was the beneficiary?"

"Jessica."

"His wife? Then why was it swiped? Twelve years after she died and was buried!"

"I can supply the answer to that question," said Ellery grimly, "now."

Dakin was astonished. "I s'pose you'll tell me you
know who stole it, too."

"Certainly, Dakin."

"Huh?"

"Once you know all the facts, it's simple enough."

Dakin sounded both eager and fearful. "Who? Who
was it, Mr. Queen?"

"I'll meet you in Prosecutor Hendrix's office in fifteen
minutes."

17. All For The Love of a Fox

ELLERY FOUND PROSECUTOR Hendrix pacing the floor
of his office at the County Courthouse. Chief of Police
Dakin was hunched in a chair with his big hands between his knees, looking uncomfortable.

"Oh, Queen." Hendrix hurried forward. "Now what's
all this?"

"I've told Phil everything that's happened, Mr.
Queen," said Dakin, rising hastily.

"You seem worried, Mr. Hendrix," remarked Ellery.

"Worried? Certainly not. Why should I be? It wasn't
my case. I mean—" The Prosecutor spread his hands.
"See here. If there's been a mistake—a miscarriage of
justice—go easy, will you, old boy?"

"May I sit down?"

"Sorry! Here, Queen, here."

"I'm afraid," said Ellery, crossing his legs, "that friend Dakin's been premature. Did you tell Hendrix I'd cracked the case, Dakin?"

"Well, sure. Didn't you just say on the phone—"

"I said I knew why Bayard's will was stolen last night, and who stole it."

"But—"

Ellery shook his head. "Let's go back," he said. "I've now established beyond a doubt the facts about that locked drawer. I've checked them. After phoning you, Dakin, I phoned Bayard at his brother's house. When I mentioned the word 'will,' Bayard suddenly remembered. And he confirms Judge Eli Martin's account. He'd locked the will in the top drawer of his secretary, a drawer otherwise empty, and he was positive he hadn't opened the drawer again. We have no reason to doubt that statement. Wills are made out and put away. Bayard made his out and put it away. I think we can reasonably conclude that Bayard's will lay in that locked secretary drawer for twelve and a half years."

"And then all of a sudden somebody comes along lookin' for it," cried Chief Dakin.

"Not necessarily."

Prosecutor Hendrix demanded: "Now what do you mean by that, Queen?"

"I mean that the fact that the housebreaker *took* the will doesn't prove he broke into the house to *look* for the will. As a matter of fact, the most cursory consideration of the data at our disposal shows that, on the contrary, the prowler didn't want the will *as a will* at all."

The two men looked bewildered.

"For what conceivable use could that will have been to anyone—anyone on earth?" Ellery went on. "It was Bayard's will, disposing of his estate in the event of his death and naming his wife sole legatee. But look at this peculiar pair of circumstances: The wife is dead, and has been dead for twelve years!—she predeceased the testator, as you lawyers say, Hendrix. What does that do to the will?"

"Makes it obsolete, of course."

"What does a testator usually do when his will becomes obsolete by virtue of the beneficiary's prior death and the will moreover has not provided for a—what do you call it, Hendrix?—a contingent beneficiary?"

"Why, if testator doesn't want to die intestate, he'll make out a new will naming a new, living beneficiary."

"Exactly. Did testator do that? The fact is—our second circumstance—he's done better than that. *He disposed of his estate before his death—gave up all title to it during his lifetime.* Bayard Fox, shortly after he went to prison, signed legal papers turning his whole estate over to his son, in trust until Davy should come of age.

"So today—last night, when that 1931 will was stolen —the will was not only obsolete as a legal instrument, it was also *meaningless.* The whole question of Bayard's estate was a settled and dead issue years and years ago.

"Consequently I say: The thief could not have stolen the will for its significance as a will—it has none. Therefore he stole it for a different reason entirely."

Dakin was shaking his head. "I can't even imagine a different reason, Mr. Queen."

"And yet, Dakin, a different reason must exist, since the thief did steal that document. Well, let's see. If the will was not stolen as a will, what *could* it have been stolen for? For the paper it was typed on?"

Hendrix laughed. "You're not serious."

"No, because Judge Martin told me the paper was the most ordinary type. If not for the paper, then for what?"

"The date?" asked the Prosecutor doubtfully.

"But the date, too, is obviously meaningless. It was dated December something, 1931—months before the people and the events resolved themselves into the tragedy. But what else appears in every will?"

"The witnesses' names?" suggested Chief Dakin.

"But Judge Martin told me—and Bayard confirmed this over the phone just now—that the witnesses were Amos Bluefield, Wrightsville Town Clerk at the time, and Mark Doodle, a notary. Why should the thief have wanted those witnesses' names? For some obscure reason to discover who the witnesses had been? But then he'd merely have had to look at the will, he wouldn't have taken the will away with him. Then did he want a sample of the witnesses' names, their autographs? He'd scarcely have to resort to housebreaking and theft if that was his purpose. There must be thousands of documents extant bearing the name of the Town Clerk, and of course a notary's name would appear in hundreds of very ordinary papers. So the witnesses can't have any signficance in the theft. What's left?"

"The only other thing on a will," shrugged Hendrix, "is the name of the testator, but that certainly can't be—"

"Why can't it be?" asked Ellery.

"The name Bayard Fox?" ejaculated the Prosecutor.

"It's not just a name, Mr. Hendrix," said Ellery gently. *"It's a signature."*

"Signature?"

"Bayard Fox's signature?" said Dakin blankly.

Ellery nodded. "Bayard Fox's signature. What's more, Bayard Fox's indisputably authentic signature. If there's one place a man would be careful to have a good, clear, unimpeachable specimen of his signature, it would be in his will."

And there was silence.

"I don't understand, Queen," said the Prosecutor finally.

"Me neither," groaned Dakin.

"But it's so simple!" cried Ellery, leaping from his chair. "Doesn't Bayard Fox's signature have a significance in this case? Dakin, you ought to be able to answer that! Because we found Bayard Fox's signature in a certain place today, everyone's given up!"

"The Bayard Fox signature in Garback's record-book of prescription renewals!" said the Chief slowly.

"Of course. *Now* re-examine the facts. Last night, after twelve years, someone broke into Bayard Fox's house and stole an obsolete document whose only possible value to the thief, as we've just seen, was the authentic signature Bayard Fox signed to it twelve and a half years ago. *That was last night.* And what happens *this morn-*

ing? A piece of new evidence comes to light, the crux of which is a Bayard Fox signature! Coincidence, would you say, Mr. Hendrix?"

"The thief wanted a specimen of Fox's signature," gasped the Prosecutor, "in order to *forge* a Bayard Fox signature in Garback's old record-book!"

"Yes, Mr. Hendrix. If you'll have that entry in Garback's ledger examined by an expert, I'm sure he'll find that a previous, authentic entry in that space was eradicated and the Bayard Fox prescription-renewal entry cleverly written in over it. A palimpsest, by thunder! I never thought I'd find *that* in Wrightsville!"

"Then the note about the prescription number in Garback's handwriting," muttered Hendrix, "must be a forgery, too."

"Undoubtedly. For that the thief needed to look no farther than the ledger itself—it contains hundreds and hundreds of samples of Garback's writing. But a sample of Bayard Fox's signature was another matter. He decided the old residence of Bayard Fox, which had remained untouched since the murder, would be a likely place to find one. So he broke in and ransacked it, starting with the breakfront and drum-table in the living room, being unsuccessful, and hunting further. In the study he tackled the desk. Unsuccessful there, too, he tackled the secretary. And then he came across a locked drawer. He could scarcely have resisted forcing it to see if the drawer might not contain what he was looking for. And he was lucky—he found an old will."

" 'He'—'he'!" exclaimed Chief Dakin. "Who's 'he,' Mr. Queen? You said you knew."

Ellery stared at the lank Police Chief. "But don't you see that, Dakin?" he asked incredulously. "That's the clearest part of it! How did that ledger of Garback's, with the forged Bayard Fox signature, come to light?"

"Miss Aikin and Emmy DuPré were lookin' through it—"

"How did Miss Aikin and the DuPré woman come to *be* looking through it?"

"Why, Miss Aikin's been tryin' for years to get hold

of the ledger so she could snag Shockley Wright's autograph for her collection," said the Chief blankly. "And when Alvin Cain gave it to Emmy DuPré this morning —" His mouth remained open.

"Exactly," said Ellery dryly. "Alvin Cain gave it to Emmy DuPré this morning—the morning after the theft of the authentic signature! After years of refusing to be bothered turning the ledger over to Miss Aikin, or more recently to Emmeline DuPré, this morning Alvin Cain suddenly does so! In fact, this morning Alvin Cain was so obliging as to *phone* Emmy DuPré that he'd give her the ledger if she'd stop in for it . . . when he's been evicting her from his drugstore merely for asking!

"I don't think there's any doubt about it, gentlemen. It was Alvin Cain who broke into the house last night, stole the will, and banged me on the head. It was Alvin Cain who spent the rest of the night forging that entry in the ledger. And he knew there was an excellent chance two snoopy old ladies like Dolores Aikin—always on the hunt for autographs—and Emmy DuPré—always on the hunt for anything—would come upon the forged entry and call it to my attention. And I don't doubt that, if they hadn't done so, Alvin Cain was prepared to 'run across' the entry himself."

Prosecutor Hendrix took his hat from the clothestree. "Come on," he said.

They found Alvin Cain in his pharmacy exchanging pleasantries with a young lady of high-school age who was giggling over a chocolate ice-cream soda.

Cain paled slightly when he saw Dakin, Prosecutor Hendrix, and Ellery.

"With you in a minute, boys!" he called gaily.

"No hurry, Alvin," drawled the Chief of Police.

The three men sat down at one of the tiny triangular service tables near the soda fountain. They said nothing, merely looking at the pharmacist.

Cain's pallor deepened. He winked at the girl and started busily for his prescription department.

"You'll find Officer Charley Brady out there by your back door, Alvin," called Chief Dakin gently. "That is, in case you wanted some company for a walk, or something."

Cain looked foolish. He turned on his heel and went slowly back to the fountain. He said to the girl, quite without humor or charm: "Come on, girl friend, there's no nourishment in bubbles. Shake your bobby-socks."

The girl stared at him. Then she threw fifteen cents on the counter and stalked out.

At once Chief Dakin rose from the little table, went to the front door, and latched it.

"What is this, *Chef?*" grinned the pharmacist. "A holdup? I don't close till eleven."

Dakin drew the dark heavy door-blind and snapped off the lights at the front of the store.

"Just so we won't be interrupted," he explained. "Now come over here to the table, Alvin, and sit down so we can have a nice, friendly little talk."

The short man in the starched and spotless ecru linen jacket came over reluctantly. He looked smaller and squatter suddenly, as if he were drawing himself in around his center. He sat down in a gingerly way, on the very edge of the tiny chair, looking from one to another of those set faces with a half-expectant, rather silly smile.

"What do we do now," he joked, "cut for dealer?"

"All right, Cain," said Prosecutor Hendrix abruptly. "Why'd you forge Bayard Fox's signature and fake that prescription-renewal entry in Myron Garback's old ledger?"

Alvin blinked. He kept blinking.

"Forged? Fake? What—what are you batting about, Mr. Hendrix?" he stammered.

"I owe you a little something," remarked Ellery pleasantly. Cain's glance darted at him, and away. "For that crack on my skull, Cain. Remember? Also, my shoulder still aches, and you can see the deplorable condition of my hand for yourself. But I'm perfectly willing to trade. Open up, and I won't knock you stupid."

Alvin Cain, Wrightsville's fashion-plate, raconteur, and Casanova, kicked over the small table, hurled his chair at the three men, and rushed for the latched front door.

Prosecutor Hendrix went down, but Ellery caught the chair and Chief Dakin, who had staggered back against a showcase full of cosmetics, drew a snubby automatic and fired one shot at the wildly scampering pharmacist.

Cain stopped short, lost his balance, and fell.

He lay still.

"Dakin, you hit him!" cried the Prosecutor, scrambling to his feet.

"Naw," said Dakin. "I purposely shot wide. The bullet's in the doorjamb." He was white with anger. He strode over to where Cain was lying, grasped the man by the back of the collar, and yanked. "Yellow," he said. "These blowhards are all the same. You goin' to talk, Cain?"

All the muscles of the man's face were out of control. His lips flapped and his jaws twitched, and his eyes rolled in his head.

"I'll talk," he babbled. "I'll talk. Just don't shoot. I'll talk."

"Tell the pretty story to the Foxes," drawled Ellery.

They were all in Prosecutor Hendrix's office—Hendrix, Dakin, Ellery, Alvin Cain, the Talbot and the Davy Foxes, Bayard Fox, and Detective Howie. The pharmacist, his linen jacket streaked with the oily grime of his drugstore floor, his thinning curly hair on end, his shoes scuffed, cowered in a chair with his hands over his face, motionless.

"Well, Cain," said Ellery. "Tell it."

Cain blubbered without uncovering his face. "I didn't mean any harm. Fox is guilty as hell anyway. I didn't commit any crime. I didn't—"

"I might," said Ellery amiably, "turn you over to Captain Fox. He used to dream you were a Jap, Cain, and you know what our hero did to the Japs."

Cain's hands dropped quickly.

Davy went over to the chair and stood before it. "Stand up, Cain."

The pharmacist shrank, looking up terrified. "No! Don't let him—"

"Stand up," said Davy through his teeth, "or—"

"He'll talk, Davy," said Ellery. "He's already talked, but you're all entitled to hear it, and telling his cute yarn to you folks may help wash some of the spots off his grimy little soul."

"I'm waiting, Cain," said Davy.

Cain began to talk, fast. "I knew what Queen was trying to do here—Dakin told me over the phone when he said I'd be needed for questioning. Yesterday I . . . got to thinking. Maybe this Queen would get old man Fox off. The odds were against it, because everybody knows Fox poisoned Mrs. Fox—"

The silence cut in as deeply as an interruption.

"I mean," stammered the pharmacist, "he was convicted, wasn't he? Sent up? And nobody ever questioned his being guilty till this snooper Queen showed up. . . ."

And now Bayard Fox asked slowly: "What difference is it to you, Cain, if I'm cleared or sent back to prison?"

Cain licked his lips, glancing at Ellery almost as if for help.

Seeing none there, he muttered: "Dakin'd said it was being done, most of it, for Davy Fox. He was going to —to leave Linda if Queen couldn't get you off, Fox. I guess I . . . wanted to make sure Queen didn't get you off."

Linda was staring at the cowed pharmacist with complete incredulity. "You mean you did all this to . . ."

Cain flushed. He looked down at the Prosecutor's floor and cracked his knuckles in an agony of nervousness.

"Let me get this," said Captain Fox calmly. "Cain, you tried to frame an additional piece of evidence against my father so Mr. Queen would say my father was really guilty and I'd walk out on Linda?"

Cain grasped the arms of the chair.

"I'd leave Linda . . . *so you could have her?*"

Cain blabbered: "Now Davy—now listen, Davy—"

Davy rushed at him. Cain got out of the chair like a cat and darted behind the massed backs of Ellery, Chief Dakin, and Prosecutor Hendrix. He crouched there, clinging to Ellery's coat-tails. Ellery caught Davy's arm, and Linda sprang forward to cling to him.

"No, Davy! You can't believe I'd *want* him! Davy, don't! He isn't worth it! Please, Davy!"

"So he *was* making a play for you while I was in China," panted Davy. "Linda, let go! Mr. Queen, let go of me! I want to teach him a lesson he won't—"

Dakin and Hendrix jumped in, and they got him out —Linda and Emily and Talbot pleading with him, and Bayard following with a look of intense concern, as if his only stake in these events was the well-being of his son.

Detective Howie, bewildered, brought up the rear.

Chief Dakin and the Prosecutor and Ellery were seated in Hendrix's office a little later, Alvin Cain having been packed off to the top-floor County Jail for booking and detention.

"But can we hold him?" frowned Dakin. "After all, Phil, he tried to frame a man for a crime the man was convicted of and's been servin' sentence for for a dozen years! That's a peculiar situation, Phil."

"Don't worry," said Prosecutor Hendrix with a grim smile. "We've got enough on Mr. Alvin Cain to keep him busy for some time. He committed forcible entry— that's burglary. If Mr. Queen wants to press another charge, we can get the fellow for assault. And I'm not sure he isn't guilty on a technical count of forgery."

"And all he did it for was to split up the Davy Foxes." Dakin shook his head. "Most ridiculous thing I ever heard of. However, Mr. Queen, 'pears to me you're back just about where you started from."

"Eh?" Ellery looked up.

"On the Bayard Fox case, I mean."

"Dakin's right," said Prosecutor Hendrix. "We know Cain's motive, and we know what he did. So we know

Bayard was telling the truth when he denied having renewed the digitalis prescription on June 5, 1932. But where does that leave you? As Dakin says, right where you started, without a thing changed: With the whole case against Fox exactly as it stood twelve years ago—the case on which he was convicted of poisoning that grape juice."

"Can't see it any other way, Mr. Queen," nodded Dakin.

Ellery regarded them with a curious half-smile. He seemed about to make a crisp remark, but apparently he changed his mind, for he shook his head slightly and gnawed at one of his swollen knuckles.

Then he looked up. "By the way, whatever happened to the original pitcher and tumbler? The ones Bayard actually used in the preparation and serving of the grape juice twelve years ago?"

"They were exhibits in the trial," replied Chief Dakin. "You back on *that* tack, for tripe's sake?"

"I've been going over the facts again."

"Man, you're a hound."

"You don't mean to say you're still going to work on this case?" asked Hendrix, astonished.

"Oh, yes, Mr. Hendrix."

"But I thought with the washout of this last development you'd see the handwriting on the wall and—"

"It's only been a couple of days," said Ellery humbly. "And you promised me a couple of weeks."

"Naturally I'll keep my promise, Queen, but I tell you this is a sheer waste of—"

"Time. I know, Mr. Hendrix. But I have plenty of time, and we haven't annoyed you very much, have we? To get back to the pitcher and tumbler—"

"They can't be any use to you, Mr. Queen," said Chief Dakin. "By the time I'd laid hands on 'em twelve years ago, they'd both been washed. Remember, there was no suspicion of murder till Mrs. Fox died a whole day and a half later."

"But what happened to them, Dakin?" Ellery persisted.

"The usual. After the conviction, they were turned over to the Property Clerk at the Police Department. I think—Wait a minute."

Chief Dakin picked up one of the Prosecutor's phones and called his office.

"Uh-huh." He hung up. "I thought so. The Property Clerk returned 'em to the Fox house wrapped up in a cardboard box after the trial, Mr. Queen."

"Thanks, Dakin." Ellery rose. "I believe," he said mildly, "I'll amble on back and see what happened to that box."

PART FOUR

18.   The Fox and the Pitcher

DINNER THAT NIGHT was horrid. Except for Detective Howie, who ate with the slow greediness of the fat, they scarcely touched Emily's food; and there was no conversation at all. They seemed to be waiting upon Ellery's pleasure, as if he held the key to their mood. But Ellery nibbled away in silence. So they were all relieved when Chief Dakin dropped in during the dessert.

"Find what you were lookin' for, Mr. Queen? I happened to be passing on my way home, so I thought—"

"I had an idea you would, Dakin," grunted Ellery. "So I've been waiting for you." He turned to the Talbot Foxes. "Chief Dakin tells me that the Property Clerk of the Police Department returned the original pitcher and tumbler used in the preparation of the grape juice shortly after the end of the trial twelve years ago. Do you happen to remember what you did with them?"

"I don't recall any pitcher or tumbler being returned," Emily said doubtfully. For the first time in over a day she addressed her husband. "Do you, Talbot?"

Talbot brightened. "You're talking to me again, Emily!"

"Why, I never stopped," said Emily, reddening. "Anyway, do you, Tal?"

The big man's chest expanded perceptibly. "Well, now," he said, beaming, "let's see. Pitcher and glass . . . No, I can't say I do."

"They were delivered in a cardboard box," explained Chief Dakin. "Wrapped in brown paper, and sealed."

"Brown paper . . ." Emily frowned. "Why, Talbot, you remember!"

187

Talbot looked puzzled. "I don't seem to, dear."

"Well, I do. I didn't know what was in the package or I'd have recalled right off." Emily became positively voluble, and Linda, holding Davy's slack hand, smiled a little. At least *someone's* straightening out her troubles, her smile seemed to say. "The package was put in Bayard's house before we locked the house up."

"It was?"

"Mercy, Talbot, you put it there yourself!"

"I did?" Talbot was embarrassed. "Funny, Emily, I don't seem to recollect a thing about it."

"You never did have much of a memory," sniffed his wife. "Mr. Queen, that package is next door. When we took Davy to live with us—"her voice softened—"we decided to get him everything new. Clothes, toys, books, everything."

"I remember that, Aunt Emily," said Davy suddenly. "I remember it was like Christmas."

"I remember that, too," said Talbot. "I put all Davy's kid things—the things he'd been using up to that time —up in the attic in the other house, for storage."

"Well, I'm sure you'll find that cardboard box up there, Talbot, too," said Emily.

Chief Dakin glanced at Ellery.

Ellery pushed back from the dinner table. "Do you suppose we could desert the dishes for a while, Mrs. Fox?" he smiled. "I'm rather anxious to inspect the contents of that box, and I think we all ought to be there when it's opened."

So back they went, in the soft Wrightsville evening, to the house of Bayard Fox. It looked unreal in the waves of the swimming moon, a dark house growing out of dark rank vegetation, and all as if suspended—an unknown world at the bottom of an alien sea.

The night and death are brothers; and this was where both had dwelt for a dozen years.

The group carried flashlights, silent.

The smell of must was so strong in the attic that Ellery and Dakin hastened to open the fanlights.

Every board groaned underfoot; each rafter was laced with swaying webs; and the moon peered through cracks in the roof.

"Goodness," said Linda with a shaky laugh. "It's like a set for a Boris Karloff movie, Davy."

"The old attic," said Davy softly. "Remember, Dad?" And Bayard smiled back: "I remember, son."

"All my toys," Davy said, looking around. "Every last one of 'em! Here's my football!" He stooped to pick up a sodden pulp of pigskin, long since deflated. The skin was scuffed and tattered. He stroked it with an embarrassed forefinger.

"Your catcher's mitt, Davy."

"That League ball I snagged when Linny and I sneaked over to Exhibition Park and got our hides walloped for staying away at the baseball game till dark!"

"It was a double-header," giggled Linda. "And oh, gosh, I couldn't sit down the whole next day, Daddy Tal was so mad."

"Here's my chem set, that I used to do experiments with!"

"And look, son," exclaimed Bayard, "your Erector construction set. Remember that bridge you and I built?"

"We worked on it for a week!" Davy stood wide-legged in the glimmer-streaked darkness, his teeth showing white and his blue eyes dancing.

Talbot retrieved a loose-leaf album with battered corners from beneath a mound of broken toys. "Say, Davy," he said, "isn't this your old stamp album?"

"By gosh, it is!"

"Ought to take it over to John F. Wright. He's a collector. Maybe there's something valuable in here."

"Aw, they were just kid stamps, Uncle Tal. In terrible condition. They're not worth anything."

"They are to me!" cried Linda, and she took it from her foster-father. "I'll save it," she said softly, "for— some other little boy."

And Emily said: "Your *marbles,* Davy. Mercy, there must be hundreds of them in this old flour sack."

"And my 'tickets'!"

Ellery let them exclaim and rummage as he went quietly about among them, nodding and smiling and his eyes very sharp.

Suddenly he pounced.

They stopped chattering to look at him with something like apprehension.

"This solves *one* mystery," said Ellery, standing up.

He had found beneath the splintered wooden lid of the boy's chemistry set a bottle of 100 aspirins.

"The missing aspirins," chuckled Dakin. He looked at Ellery almost with pity.

"Never even opened," muttered Ellery. "This case is one let-down after another. Ah! Is this the package the Police Property clerk returned?"

Under a heap of dog-eared books he had found a square box, wrapped in the plain brown paper, tied with string and the string pressed to the wrapping with wax seals.

"That's the one!" cried Emily.

"Now I remember," her husband said foolishly.

"Yes, it bears the Police Department seal and rubber stamp. Would you mind concentrating your lights on this?" Ellery said.

They surrounded him as he tore the rotten string and ripped the brown paper away. Beneath the paper there was an ordinary white cardboard box. Inside the box, carefully wadded with newspapers bearing the date "1932," were a big wide-mouthed purple-glass pitcher, covered with incised grape designs, and a purple tumbler identical with those in the kitchen cabinet downstairs.

As Ellery held the pitcher and glass up to the light, turning them over and over, their spirits fell again, as if the purple objects drew to themselves all the sparkle the group had found in the attic, leaving the place—and them—in black emptiness.

"What is it, Mr. Queen?" asked Chief Dakin. He had seen a flash in Ellery's silver eyes.

"I'm not sure, Dakin," murmured Ellery. "Let's go

downstairs to the kitchen. . . . No, there's no water in the house, is there?"

"I had the water turned off twelve years ago, Mr. Queen," said Talbot Fox. "Same time as the electricity and gas."

"I must have some sort of liquid." Ellery clutched the pitcher and tumbler as if he were afraid someone might try to take them from him. "We had better get back to your house, Mr. and Mrs. Fox. Immediately!"

"It occurred to me, Dakin," Ellery explained as he studied the interior of the purple pitcher under a strong light in Emily Fox's kitchen, "that even though the original pitcher had been washed, as you told me this evening, something might still be salvaged. If the grape juice had stood in the pitcher for some hours, and if the washing had been a hasty rinse, particularly under cold water, there might still be some evidence left inside the pitcher."

"Evidence?" Chief Dakin's tough forehead split into brown wrinkles. "What kind of evidence, for the Lord's sake?"

Ellery said, "Come here."

They crowded around.

"Unfortunately, the glass is practically opaque, so you can't see the line very clearly through it. But look directly inside."

His finger tip accused the faintest, thinnest dark line rimming the inner circumference of the pitcher in a perfect circle.

"Sediment," Ellery said. "The grape juice stood undisturbed for a long time, and where its surface touched the pitcher wall a sediment formed and eventually caked. It caked so hard that when the grape juice was poured out and the pitcher rinsed, the sediment line was not washed away. It remained. And here it is."

"What does it mean, Mr. Queen?" Linda asked eagerly.

Ellery smiled. "Well, Linda, by the position of the water-line on a jetty you'd be able to calculate how high the tide had been. In the same way, by this sediment line, we can tell exactly how much grape juice was left in this pitcher twelve years ago after the fatal drink was poured. Let's make a test. Linda, may I borrow your engagement ring for a moment?"

"My engagement ring?" frowned Linda. "You mean —take it off my finger, Mr. Queen?"

"Please."

"But that's supposed to be bad luck!"

"In this case," replied Ellery with a smile, "it might be very good luck."

Linda took her diamond ring off quickly. Ellery held the pitcher up to the powerful light: the sediment line was barely discernible as a faint hair of shadow through the deeply purple glass. Using the diamond of Linda's ring, Ellery scratched a careful line on the outer surface of the pitcher to mark the precise position of the sediment line inside. Then he handed the ring back to Linda, who slipped it on very hurriedly indeed.

"Merely for convenience," Ellery explained. "Now let's see. We know Bayard prepared exactly one quart of dilute grape juice, or four glassfuls. Let's use this purple tumbler as a measuring cup, since it was a glass identical with this that Bayard used twelve years ago in measuring out the equal parts of grape juice and water, and it was actually this glass from which Jessica drank."

He went to Emily's spotless sink and, turning on the cold-water tap, filled the purple glass to the brim and emptied it into the pitcher. He did this four times.

"Now," he continued, turning to them again, "four of these half-pint glasses make one quart, so there's exactly a quart of liquid in the pitcher, as there was when Bayard first prepared the grape juice. Look at the sediment line."

The water level inside the pitcher was considerably higher than the guideline Ellery had scratched on the outside.

"Well, sure," said Davy. "The sediment formed *after* Mom's one glass of grape juice had been removed from the pitcher. You just put in a whole quart, but there was a quart minus one glassful when the sediment line caked."

"Quite right, Davy. Then you would say," Ellery asked, "that if I poured out into this glass all the water now showing above the sediment line, the excess water would make exactly one glassful?"

"Of course. It must."

"That's right," said Dakin. "One glassful—the amount Davy's ma drank."

Ellery canted the pitcher and filled the purple glass to the brim.

Then he held the pitcher up to the light.

The water-line and the sediment line did not coincide. The water level was still higher than the scratch-mark.

"Do you find that strange?" murmured Ellery. "Well, let's keep pouring water out of the pitcher till the water-line and the sediment line do meet."

He did so, slowly, to make sure the water level did not sink below the scratch. And when, under the light, water level and guide-line coincided, Ellery held up the purple glass into which he had poured off the excess liquid.

It was filled to the brim.

"One *more* glass," gasped Dakin. *"Another glassful!"*

"I don't understand," said Emily, bewildered.

"It's simple enough, Mrs. Fox," said Ellery briskly. "For twelve years Wrightsville has believed that only one glass of grape juice was poured from the purple pitcher that morning, the glassful Bayard poured for Jessica.

"This demonstration proves that *two* glasses of grape juice were poured that morning!"

"But we were so sure Jessie drank only one," said Bayard, dazed. "Why, she told that to Dr. Willoughby herself after she felt so sick. Why should Jessie have lied about a thing like that?"

"Exactly. *Then who drank the other glassful?"*

For the first time since coming to Wrightsville, Ellery's voice rang with the old authority.

"Because someone did. Was it you, Bayard?" And

Ellery added in a quiet tone, "If you've never told the truth before in your life, Bayard, tell it now. Did you drink that second glassful of grape juice that morning?"

"No!"

"You, Talbot? Before you left the kitchen after your talk with Bayard? Or at any time before Bayard emptied this pitcher and rinsed it so carelessly?"

Talbot shook his head emphatically.

Ellery turned to Bayard again: "You poured Jessica a glass of grape juice and you then left the house. You returned after an absence of two hours and found Jessica violently ill. Those are the facts. Was she alone when you got back home, Bayard?"

"Yes, Mr. Queen."

"What did you do? Try to recall everything."

"Immediately ran to the phone and called Dr. Willoughby. He said he'd rush right over."

"And then?"

"I tried to make Jessica comfortable, help her some way. She was being sick to her stomach, and I held her head. I don't know what else I did. Marked time, I suppose, till the doctor came. He was over in a matter of minutes."

"And during this interval the pitcher of grape juice stood on the coffee table in plain sight."

"Yes."

"You touched it."

"I did not!"

"Did Jessica?"

"No. She was too busy retching, vomiting, holding on to me. She was crying and scared—"

"Did Dr. Willoughby touch the pitcher when he arrived?"

"He didn't even glance at it. He hurried Jessica upstairs to the bedroom and went to work on her there."

"You're positive Dr. Willoughby didn't touch the pitcher of grape juice."

"I'm positive."

"Did you go upstairs with Dr. Willoughby and your wife?"

"No—the doctor told me to stay downstairs, that I'd only be in his way. He said he'd call me up if he needed me. So I stayed where I was."

"In the living room?"

"Yes."

"With the pitcher of grape juice—still untouched."

"Yes."

"What did you do then?"

"The living room was in a mess. I was upset about my wife . . . I tried to occupy myself by cleaning up after her. It took me . . . well, a long time."

"Yes? Go on."

"When the mess was all cleaned up—I just sat there. In the living room. Waiting."

"And you still hadn't touched the pitcher of grape juice, Bayard?"

"That's right."

"Precisely when did you empty and rinse the pitcher?"

"I guess I must have sat there most of the afternoon, Mr. Queen, Dr. Willoughby was still working on Jessie upstairs. I'd say it was around five o'clock before I remembered I hadn't removed the pitcher of grape juice."

"And during all that interval—of waiting in the living room—no one touched the pitcher?"

"No one could have—no one else was there. Just myself, and I didn't go near it till five o'clock."

"Then what did you do? At five o'clock?"

"I remembered that the pitcher and glass were still there, so I got up, took them out to the kitchen, emptied the pitcher into the sink, rinsed it once under the cold water—and the glass, too—and put them both on the drainboard."

"Which is just where I found 'em two mornings later," exploded Chief Dakin. "The fact that he emptied and rinsed the pitcher was a big strike against him, Mr. Queen, at the trial, if you'll remember the transcript. Tom Garback convinced the Jury he'd done that to get rid of the evidence—the poisoned grape juice left in the pitcher."

"I told Mr. Garback, I told the Jury," said Bayard wearily, "that I was upset, I was cleaning up. Lord, I didn't know anything about poison! I thought what Dr. Willoughby thought—that the exertion and excitement of Jessie's coming downstairs had made her sick all over again."

Ellery had been fingering his lower lip.

Now he looked up and said: "We've struck a really new clue after twelve years, people. And it's so important it may change the complexion of the entire case."

19. Fox and Company

THEY ALL BEGAN to ask questions at once, pressing around him. Ellery shook his head impatiently.

"Just let me follow through, please. Bayard, you'd left Jessica alone in the house that morning, directly after she drank her glass of grape juice?"

"Yes, Mr. Queen."

"How did you come to leave?"

"The phone rang just as Jessie finished drinking. She lay back on the sofa and I went out into the hall to answer the phone. It was my brother, calling from the shop."

"Calling about what, Bayard?"

"Talbot said that if it was possible he wanted me to come down to the factory for a while. One of our biggest customers was in town and he'd asked to deal with me personally in connection with an order."

"That's right, Mr. Queen," Talbot said. "This buyer had dropped into town unexpectedly. It was an important account, and I thought I'd better let Bay know about it before trying to handle him myself."

Bayard nodded. "We couldn't afford to antagonize the man," he said. "I told Talbot I'd be right down if I could. I hung up and went back to ask Jessie if she thought I could leave her for an hour or so, and told her why. Jessie said: 'Don't be silly, Bayard. Of course I'll be fine. You go on downtown.' I suggested she call Emily over to stay with her, but Jessie said Emily'd mentioned going down to an Eastern Star meeting or luncheon or something. I was a little worried, because Jessie hadn't been left alone for months. Even Davy wasn't coming home for lunch, because I'd given him a lunch box to take to school and Emily'd given Linda hers so they wouldn't be whooping through the house at a time when Jessie'd be excited enough as it was.

"Anyway, I finally went when Jessie promised she wouldn't move from the sofa till I got back, and that if she felt sick or anything she'd phone me right away at the shop."

"You went to the factory. Then?"

"Our business with this buyer took longer than Talbot and I expected. At the end of an hour I wasn't near through with him."

"So you phoned your wife?"

"Yes. I was worried about her. But she still felt fine —at least, that's what she told me over the phone—and she talked me into staying and finishing with Mr.—who was that buyer again, Tal?"

"Mr. Quimby of the U.S.-Canadian Processing Company, Bay. As a matter of fact, Quimby's still doing business with me—with us." Talbot flushed.

"He is, eh?" said Bayard quietly. "Well, anyway, I stayed and finished up with Mr. Quimby, then I drove back home, leaving Tal at the shop to see Quimby off."

"He was going on to Montreal," nodded Talbot.

"And that was when you found your wife so ill, Bayard?" asked Ellery.

"Yes. I'd been gone just two hours, Mr. Queen. Jessie

was alone, in the living room, on the sofa, the way I'd left her, and she was just as sick as she could be."

"The times involved," said Ellery crisply. "You left the house to go to the shop at what time?"

"Eleven o'clock."

"You phoned your wife at noon?"

"Yes."

"Then you got back to the house at one."

"That's right."

"Let's see what we have." Ellery scowled. "Jessica was alone in the house for two hours, between eleven and one.

"Now we know two glasses of grape juice were drunk, the first by Jessica just before Bayard left—just before eleven. The other glassful, then, must have been drunk between eleven, when Bayard left, and one, when he returned." Ellery turned to Dakin. "Dakin, I think you'll agree with me that *someone came to Bayard Fox's house during his two-hour absence, that Jessica offered this visitor a glass of grape juice from the pitcher on the coffee table, that the visitor drank it, and that the visitor left before Bayard's return.*"*

---

* I have been asked an interesting question relative to the two glasses of grape juice, the answer to which—while not directly relevant to the issues of induction that were involved—nevertheless will bear exposition, if only for the benefit of those who fret over the finer points.

The question is: Since the two glasses of grape juice were drawn from the pitcher *at different times,* why weren't *two* sediment lines found in the pitcher? What happened to the sediment line which must have formed in the interval between the pouring of Jessica's glassful and that of the visitor's?

It is a fair question, and the answer eluded me for some time. But then I saw what must have happened, and a jog to Bayard Fox's memory confirmed my theory.

The "lost" sediment line, having resulted from the *first* glassful, was therefore the *higher* of the two lines inside the pitcher; that is, it was the line nearer to the pitcher's mouth. In rinsing the pitcher, Bayard must have used his fingers—carelessly, but he used them. *He inserted his hand a short way into the pitcher and ran his fingers around the inside.* This had the effect of wiping away the upper of the two sediment lines, leaving the lower intact. Had Bayard been thorough, had he swabbed the interior of the pitcher to the bottom, past the *lower* sediment line, that line too would have been wiped away . . . and there would be no solution of the twelve-year-old mystery.

—E. Q.

Chief Dakin did not reply at once. He rubbed his lowslung jaw, scratched his head, pulled his nose. Then he muttered: "Sure looks like it, Mr. Queen."

Detective Howie's mouth was widely open.

"But who?" cried Linda.

"Nothing like that came out in the trial," said Emily Fox, confusedly.

"It's sure a queer one," said her husband. "I can't imagine who—"

"Aside from who," cried Davy, "why didn't that visitor—whoever it was!—come forward at the trial? This is the first anybody's ever heard of such a person!"

"Yes, that's peculiar," nodded Ellery. "Dakin, tell me —did anybody else in Wrightsville come down with digitalis poisoning during the time Jessica did?"

"None that a careful checkup showed, Mr. Queen. We went into that when we knew Mrs. Fox had died of digitalis. No one was reported sick with the same symptoms, and no one—this we're certain of—died of it except Jessie Fox."

Ellery's eyes sparkled. "Let's see it through. Was it the visitor who put that overdose of digitalis into the pitcher of grape juice? Impossible." Their faces fell. "Jessica drank her glassful—the only glassful she did drink by her own testimony—before Bayard left the house. She was poisoned by that grape juice. So when the visitor appeared and Jessica offered him—or her—a glassful from the same pitcher, that glassful must also have contained poisoned grape juice. It's inconceivable that the visitor would have drained a glassful of a liquid he'd poisoned with his own hands. Conclusion: The visitor is innocent."

Davy and Linda exchanged the grimmest of glances.

"Now, I think, we have sufficient facts upon which to base a conclusion about that visitor," continued Ellery, ignoring the gloom that had come over the family. "He drank a glassful or part of a glassful—he may have poured some out—of poisoned grape juice. No one in Wrightsville, Dakin says, died of digitalis poisoning but Jessica Fox. The visitor failed to come forward at the trial. . . . The visitor, I say, was a stranger—*not a resident of Wrightsville or environs at all.*"

"A tramp!" exclaimed Linda.

"Hardly, Linda," said Ellery. "Can you see your sick aunt inviting a vagrant into her living room and offering him a drink when she was alone in the house? No, it begins to appear like someone she knew but who didn't live in town. . . . Tell me, Dakin," he said abruptly. "Is there a train that stops in Wrightsville between eleven A.M. and one P.M.?"

"The local to Montreal stops at one o'clock every day, Mr. Queen."

"No good. Bayard returned at one to find Jessica alone. The visitor couldn't have *come* at one—he'd already come and gone by that time. No other train stops between eleven and one during the day, or stopped twelve years ago? We'll have to follow that trail back and see if we can't—"

"Wait!" said Captain Fox. "There's a train about noon—the train that let me off when I came home a few months ago!"

"The Atlantic Stater," nodded Emily. "The express from New York to Montreal."

"But the Atlantic Stater doesn't usually stop in Wrightsville," objected Chief Dakin. "Mostly it goes right on through."

"Just a minute," said Talbot Fox slowly. "Just a minute. That day twelve years ago the Atlantic State Express *did* stop in Wrightsville."

"It did?" Ellery said quickly. "And how can you remember a detail like that, Talbot?"

"Because of Mr. Quimby. Bay," Talbot said, turning to his brother, "remember when you left the shop to scoot back to Jessica, Quimby was saying he'd have to be hustling right on to Montreal?"

"Yes?" Bayard said doubtfully.

"Well, after you left I drove Quimby down to the Station. He asked Gabby Warrum about trains, and Gabby said—I distinctly remember—that it was too bad he hadn't come an hour earlier, *because the Atlantic Sta-*

ter'd stopped at noon. I remember because of the fuss old Quimby kicked up. He was hopping because he'd not only missed the Stater but the one-o'clock local to Montreal as well—we'd been just too late to catch it— so he had to wait four hours for the regular five-twelve local-express, and I waited with him."

"The Atlantic Stater stopped that day," breathed Emily.

"And it never stops in Wrightsville," said Linda, *"except to let a passenger off!"*

"Yes," said Ellery quietly, "it's a reasonable theory from the facts that someone traveling from New York to Montreal may have dropped off in Wrightsville, at noon, visited Jessica for a half-hour or so, and then caught the Montreal local at one P.M.—all while you, Bayard, were at the shop."

"Theories," sneered a voice. They all looked around. But it was only Detective Howie.

"Oh, shut up," growled Chief of Police Dakin. "To think all this new stuff could come out after a dozen years!" He looked ashamed. "If it's true," he muttered, "then we pulled an awful boner—I mean, Tom Garback and me. I thought we'd investigated everything. How could we have missed a big thing like a stranger gettin' off a train in a town like Wrightsville?"

"I can't imagine, Dakin," said Ellery sympathetically. "For a flying visit like that, the stranger would certainly have taken a cab from the Station, and the least check—"

"Cab!" shouted the Chief. "If that doesn't beat hob. Because that's it. The cab!"

"Cab?" Ellery looked interested.

"Back in '32 there was only one cab operatin' out of the Station—run by old Whitey Pedersen. Whitey was an institution around here; he'd started hackin' in the horse-and-buggy days. Well, Jessica Fox was poisoned on a Tuesday, so that was the day this stranger may have got off the train. But Mrs. Fox didn't die till Wednesday night and we didn't really suspect murder and start an investigation till Thursday mornin'. Well, Thursday mornin' of that week was when Whitey Pedersen had an accident—ran right off the road, to avoid one of the Low Village kids who was playin' in the middle of the street, and smacked into Pete's Diner! They had to pull Whitey out of a mess of hamburgers."

"Pedersen died?"

"On the spot."

"Then that's it," agreed Ellery. "If the cab driver knew anything, his death before your murder investigation got fairly under way kept him from telling about Jessica's visitor. And apparently Pedersen was the only one who did know, or you'd have hit some trail."

"I s'pose Gabby Warrum, the stationmaster, was in his dinky and didn't see this stranger get off," Dakin nodded glumly. "Pedersen picked the stranger up, drove him to the Bayard Fox house, stranger says I've got to catch the one o'clock, so Whitey picks him back up and drives him to the Station in time to catch the Montreal local. There's always a mob takin' that one, so the stranger on the return trip was lost in the crowd. That's it," he said, shaking his head.

"What stranger?" jeered Detective Howie. "This fancy baloney. Theories. It's a pipe-dream."

"You keep your mouth shut and your eyes open, Howie," growled the Chief, "because you're goin' to have to report what you see and hear to Hendrix, and I'll be there to see you give it to him straight. Go on, Mr. Queen."

"Well, we've conjured up a stranger getting off the New York-Montreal express," frowned Ellery, "for a half-hour visit to Bayard's wife. Bayard, that suggests a relative—"

Bayard shook his head. "Jessica had one brother, Mr. Queen, that's all. And he was—still is I imagine—a Commander in the U.S. Navy. He was on maneuvers in the Pacific all the time this happened." The Talbot Foxes nodded.

"Then a friend," suggested Ellery. "It would have to be a close friend to have gone to all that trouble for a mere half-hour visit."

"Friend?" Bayard sucked his lower lip. "Jessica did have one good friend. . . . What was that woman's name again?"

"Woman?" Emily Fox grew excited. "Bayard. You don't mean the Bonnaire woman—that singer?"

"Bonnaire, that's it!" cried Bayard, his face clearing. "Gabrielle Bonnaire, Mr. Queen, of—" And then his eyes widened. "Of *Montreal!*"

Ellery smiled. His work produced small satisfactions sometimes.

"She's French-Canadian, Mr. Queen," Emily raced on. "Jessica and Gabrielle had gone to school in Maine together, and they were *intimate* friends. Why, Jessie used to write Miss Bonnaire at least once a week— didn't she, Bayard? She used to say it was lots of fun chasing Gabrielle around the globe."

"Yes, Emily. That's right."

"Gabrielle Bonnaire," Ellery said thoughtfully. "The contralto."

"Oh, she's famous—or was," babbled Emily. "When she wasn't giving a New York concert, she was on tour. She sang all over the world." Emily paused, to frown. "Come to think of it, I wonder what became of her. I haven't heard or read about her in years and years. And she never sent flowers, or even a note of condolence. You'd think . . . her best friend . . . it's sort of funny, isn't it, Mr. Queen?"

"Very," said Ellery dryly. "Mrs. Fox, do you mind if I use your telephone to make a long-distance call or two?"

When Ellery returned to the kitchen, he was smiling again, but grimly this time.

"Howie," he said, "your cynicism got the better of your judgment. It's not a theory at all."

The fat detective looked blank.

"You don't mean to say," said Chief Dakin slowly, "that it *was*—"

"Yes, Dakin. I've just located Gabrielle Bonnaire in Montreal. It was the Bonnaire woman who visited Jessica Fox that day twelve years ago, all right, and I've persuaded her to come to Wrightsville.

"She'll be here tomorrow evening."

20.   The Hopeful Fox

EVERYONE HAD GONE upstairs, leaving Ellery alone on the porch. He had evaded their questions, and they left him with noticeable dissatisfaction. But there was no point in talking, and there was nothing to explain; it all depended on the woman who was coming from Montreal. It was obvious that none of them foresaw the possibilities. Even Chief Dakin, with a distinctly odd look at Ellery, had said good night and left, clumping down the walk as if to accent his sense of injury.

Ellery sprawled in the darkness smoking a cigaret and turning certain matters over in his mind. The occasional grunt of a Hill-climbing car only emphasized his feeling of aloneness; it did not disturb him. From where he sat, the sky to the southwest had a bonfire look—the red neon lights of High Village. Elsewhere there were stars in profusion. The same lights and the same cold stars, Ellery thought, had been visible to Jessica Fox from very nearly the same observation point.

He wondered what her thoughts had been before her long illness—married to quiet Bayard Fox, perched it must have seemed for eternity on the barren eyrie of Wrightsville, and a handsome and virile brother-in-law next door whose own restlessness, no doubt, matched hers and drew them together in a communion of dissatisfaction.

Ellery did not doubt the force of that communion.

Wrightsville can be cramping to those who yearn for long horizons. He thought that Jessica's unflagging correspondence with the worldly Gabrielle Bonnaire during uneventful years of marriage and domesticity in the small town beckoned to an end more vital than feminine friendship. To Bayard Fox's wife, imprisoned in Wrightsville, Gabrielle Bonnaire must have personified the glittering Outside. Gabrielle was Paris, and London, and Buenos Aires, and Rome, and Cairo, and all the rich far places which Wrightsville sees only at the Bijou. By maintaining the postal friendship with the singer, Jessica Fox achieved a superiority of experience over her fellow-Wrightsvillians which must have satisfied, however imperfectly, her cosmopolitan cravings. . . .

Ellery was jarred from his thoughts by an outrageous bang.

It was the screen door.

"'Oh, Howie. I thought you'd gone to bed."

The fat man loomed against the stars, blotting out the house next door.

"I've got to go out for a while," said the detective in his unpleasant voice.

"Go out? You don't mean you're actually leaving your prisoner unguarded, Howie! What's come over you —an attack of faith?"

"Fox'll be all right till I get back."

Ellery thought he smelled a sneer in those nasal tones, and he was puzzled.

"You're not afraid Bayard'll escape, Howie?"

"Nope." The fat man plodded down the porch steps.

"But where are you bound for?" Ellery called after him.

"Home."

"Home?" Ellery realized that he had never pictured Detective Howie in the conventional garments of life. And yet it was true—the man lived in Wrightsville; he must have a home. Somehow he could not visualize Detective Howie's home.

"Will you be gone long?"

The thin voice winged back. "An hour, maybe two.

My wife's got some fresh laundry for me. I ain't had a change since I came on this case."

And Howie's bloated shadow disappeared.

So the fat man had a wife who washed his socks and ironed his underwear! Was he father to children, too?

"This case," Ellery thought with a chuckle, "is certainly full of surprises."

He was about to toss his last cigaret away and get out of the slide-swing to stretch and yawn before turning in, when he heard a rush of feet and the screen door flew open again.

"Mr. Queen?"

It was Linda, and in the starshine her face was marbled and old with contortion.

"Linda. What's the matter?"

"Davy. Upstairs. I've had to lock him in. Please—" And she was gone.

Ellery raced after her into the house.

Davy? Again?

Ellery reached the first-floor landing to find Linda at her husband's door, a key in her hand.

"Let's not make any more noise than we can help," she whispered. "Daddy Tal and Mother are asleep, and I don't see any point in adding to their worries."

Ellery took the key from her.

Davy was perched on the edge of the tester bed, calmly enough. His hands, however, were deep in the pockets of his tunic.

"You shouldn't have done that, Linny," he said. "The guy deserves it. You know he does."

Linda looked scared. "Mr. Queen, Davy was going to . . . to kill that detective!"

"I was going to teach the hog a lesson."

Ellery said: "Howie?" and recalled the sneer in the fat man's voice. "What's the matter, Davy?"

"He can't do that to my father. Jailbird or no jailbird. This is a house, with people in it, not a damned prison! My dad's a broken man. Anyone with two eyes can see that. He wouldn't pull anything. Howie's got no right, Mr. Queen!"

"What's the fellow done, Davy?"

The hero of Wrightsville began to cry.

Linda said, "Davy. Davy." Ellery regarded them both with a great tenderness. Then he said, "Wait here for me," and he went out, being careful to lock Davy's door behind him.

He strode down the hall to the door of the south room. He tried the knob; the door was not locked. Frowning, he knocked lightly.

After a moment, Bayard's voice, sounding very strange, said: "Come in."

Ellery went in, shutting the door behind him.

The room was dark, and for a few seconds he saw nothing. Then as his eyes accommodated themselves to the darkness he made out Bayard's frail figure on the old-fashioned iron double bed, outstretched and relaxed.

In fact, Bayard's arms were over his head, grasping the low headrail in an attitude of utter restfulness.

Ellery was puzzled.

"Are you all right, Bayard?"

"Oh, Mr. Queen. It's so dark in here—I'm fine."

"Then what—"

"I'm just fine, Mr. Queen."

"Mind if I switch the light on?"

Bayard laughed.

Completely baffled, Ellery pressed the light-button.

Davy's father was manacled to the iron headrail by both wrists.

After a long time Ellery trusted his voice.

"Howie?"

"Yes."

"What had you done, Bayard?"

"Not a thing."

"You didn't attempt anything silly—like trying to make a break for it?"

Bayard laughed again. "Lord, no. I'd already gone to bed. I usually sleep this way, with my arms over my head. I thought Howie was undressing. But the next thing I knew he was snapping handcuffs to my wrists and attaching the other ends to the bedrail."

"Did he offer an explanation?"

"He said he had to go home for a while, and he wasn't taking any chances on my trying to escape. He called me a lot of dirty names." Bayard paused. "He could have locked me in. He didn't have to do this, Mr. Queen."

"No," said Ellery dryly. Then he said: "Take it easy, Bayard. I'll be back in a few minutes."

Ellery went downstairs to the telephone and dialed Operator.

"Get me Prosecutor Philip Hendrix's residence," he said.

When Ellery returned, Davy and Linda were with him.

"Detective Howie," Ellery told Bayard grimly, "will be back here in a few minutes. With the handcuff keys, I might add. It's pretty hard to get cuffs off without the keys, and then there's a certain amount of poetic justice to be served. He put them on—let him take them off."

"Thanks, Mr. Queen," said Bayard with a feeble smile. "And son—"

"I almost made a fool of myself again," Davy muttered. "I'm sorry, Dad. But I saw red when I came in to say good night to you and found you trussed to the bed like a damned turkey."

"I'm beginning to like having a son," said Bayard.

Davy looked embarrassed. "Is this ever going to get anywhere, Mr. Queen? Is it?"

"Just have patience, Davy."

"But what does all this business about Gabrielle Bonnaire mean? Will it get Dad off? Will it settle—"

"We'll just have to wait and see, Davy."

Davy looked at Ellery, aroused by something in those even tones. Whatever it was he read on Ellery's face, it made him go over to the bed and grin down at his father.

"We'll work this deal out yet, Dad."

"Of course, son."

"How about you two getting some sleep?" Ellery suggested mildly. "I'll wait up with Bayard for Mr. Howie."

"Just keep him out of my way," said Davy. "Come on, Linny—no wench ever held her husband by toting two valises around under her eyes. It's bed for you. I'll tuck you in."

"Davy, will you?"

He kissed her, and she clung to him for a little while. Then they said good night and went out.

Ellery and Bayard were silent for some time.

At last Ellery said: "Smoke?"

"It would be sort of clumsy, Mr. Queen."

"I'll provide the service."

"Well . . . thanks."

Ellery put a cigaret between Bayard's lips and held a match to its tip. Bayard strained, puffing. Then his head fell back and he released the smoke slowly.

"It's just that . . . he treats me—It's the indignity."

"I know, Bayard." Ellery put the cigaret to Bayard's lips again.

"Mr. Queen, you've gone through a lot of trouble—because of my boy, haven't you?"

"And Linda." Ellery removed the cigaret.

"Thanks. . . . I know you're not sure about me. I mean about whether . . . I did it or not."

"Do you?"

"I don't blame you. The facts make a liar out of me, even in my own eyes."

"Some of the facts, Bayard."

Bayard's white brows drew close together.

"The returns aren't all in," said Ellery. "For instance, we uncovered a new fact tonight."

"Yes, I've been thinking about that. . . . I'd like to tell you something, Mr. Queen."

Ellery nodded, putting the cigaret to Bayard's lips again.

"Something happened to me tonight. After Howie manacled me to the bed and left me here alone."

"What was that?"

"Up to then—I'll admit it—I hadn't any hope of anything. Maybe I was . . . afraid of hope." Ellery nodded again. "When you explained to me on the drive over from the Penitentiary what this all meant to my son, I was only too glad to co-operate, but not for my sake, as I said that day—only for his."

"You said you weren't sure you wanted to be set free."

"Yes." Bayard closed his eyes. "After tonight—I'm not sure I don't."

"You've had a taste of freedom."

"Well . . ." Bayard opened his eyes, smiling wryly. "Not what you'd call real freedom. At least I didn't think of it that way. I'm in a house, and there aren't any bars on the windows, but there's Howie always behind me, eating with me, sleeping in the same bed . . . It hasn't been so much different from the prison as you'd think, Mr. Queen."

"I hadn't thought of it in quite those terms, but I see what you mean. And tonight, Bayard?"

"Tonight opened my eyes. When Howie snapped those handcuffs on me—he did something to me, Mr. Queen. For the first time I wanted to get away. For the first time I was scared. Scared of going back. All of a sudden I realized I wanted my freedom terribly. It was all I could do to keep from losing my head and—making a scene." And then Davy's father was straining at the steel about his wrists. "Is there any hope?" cried Bayard. "Mr. Queen, tell me there's some hope!"

Ellery studied him for a long moment before he replied.

"Yes," he said finally, "there's hope."

The sunken eyes glittered—not a flash this time, but a steady outpouring of flame.

"The clue to Gabrielle Bonnaire," said Ellery, "may very well prove to have been the break in the case. What the singer has to tell us tomorrow evening is—I think—of crucial importance."

Bayard licked his lips. "I knew you'd hit something big tonight, but I don't see—"

"Don't you?" Ellery smiled. "You don't grasp the significance of what Miss Bonnaire will have to say to us?"

"But how can I? I mean, not knowing what she'll—"

Ellery put the cigaret to Bayard's lips once more.

"I may be wrong—there may be a dozen alternate explanations which will advance us nowhere. Let's wait, Bayard. You've waited twelve years—you can wait one day more, I'm sure."

When Detective Howie slowly opened the door Ellery rose and extended his hand, palm up.

Without a word the fat man placed in it the keys to the handcuffs.

His jowls hung gelatinously and there was fear in his little eyes. The handkerchief about his neck was soaked.

"I take it, Mr. Detective," murmured Ellery, stooping over Bayard's wrists, "that you've heard a thing or two from your boss."

The fat man mumbled something.

"Well, Howie," said Ellery from the doorway. "I think you'll be rid of this annoying case very, very soon. Good night."

21.   The Innocent Fox

THE WOMAN CHIEF Dakin awkwardly assisted from his sedan the following evening was deep-chested and tall and dressed in black; and as she approached the porch with Dakin the tensely waiting group saw that she was almost grotesquely ugly. But it was the sort of ugliness artists paint; and indeed Gabrielle Bonnaire in her heyday had sat for eminent portrait painters all over the civilized world. She carried her ugliness as if it were beauty.

"A woman of distinction," was Ellery's first thought.

The introductions were not too embarrassing, for it turned out that Gabrielle Bonnaire had never met any of her dead friend's family. She was aloof with Bayard, gracious with Linda, and upon Davy's trim figure in his uniform she bestowed a glance of feminine approval.

"And these," she said in a throaty voice, "these are the Talbot Foxes?"

Emily was nervous. "Jessie used to talk about you so much, Miss Bonnaire."

"Jessica was my friend, Mrs. Fox."

The singer mentioned Jessica's name without emotion, as if she had laid away in a secret drawer long, long since her ties to the dead woman. Indeed, studying her, it struck Ellery that the nobly ugly face had suffered ravages far more devastating than the death of a friend, and that in standing up to them she had learned to steel herself against emotional self-indulgence of any sort.

Her English was precise and a little careful, as if at times she had to rummage through her mind for a word once known but long unused.

"Well, I am here," she said simply, seating herself in the chair Chief Dakin held for her. "I suppose, Mr. Queen, the letter I told you about—" She fumbled in her bag.

"There's no hurry, Miss Bonnaire," said Ellery with a smile. "Seeing you now, after all these years, it doesn't take much imagination to see myself again at Carnegie Hall, listening to you sing Bach's *Komm', süsser Tod.*"

"You remember?" Her beautiful eyes flashed. Then she sighed. "I must not indulge myself in memories," she said with a smile. "That is bad for an old woman."

"Old?" cried Linda. "Why Miss Bonnaire—"

"You are sweet, my dear, but what I have seen—" the volatile features hardened—"it makes people old. Particularly it makes women old."

Prosecutor Hendrix, who had been pacing the porch for an hour before the singer's arrival, coughed and glanced at Ellery. They had arranged that it was to be Ellery's show, but Hendrix was obviously impatient for the questioning to begin.

Chief Dakin could not contain himself at all. "What I

want to know, Miss Bonnaire," he demanded, "is why in thunderation you didn't come in with your story twelve years ago—while Mr. Fox was on trial."

"The gentlemen of Wrightsville's law-and-order portfolios," said Ellery, "are not unnaturally eager to have that question answered, Miss Bonnaire."

"Oh, but I could not," said Gabrielle quickly. "For one thing, I was on another continent. For another—I did not learn of Jessica's murder until months after her husband was sent to prison for it."

She employed the words "murder" and "prison" with ease, as if they were words common to her thoughts, if not to her vocabulary . . . in whatever language.

"Suppose you tell us the whole story, Miss Bonnaire, as it comes back to you."

The tale the dark woman unfolded then, on Talbot Fox's porch, was told in quiet tones, without dramatic gestures or even perceptible feeling. Listening to her, Ellery gathered the impression of colossal weariness— weariness so great it was part of nature, a habitual moment-to-moment taste of death.

Gabrielle Bonnaire had sung in New York that week twelve years ago—the final concert of a triumphant American tour. She had known of Jessica's illness but her engagements had prevented her from visiting her friend. Now, feeling exhausted herself from the long tour and eager to get to her home near Montreal, she nevertheless acted on impulse and had the Atlantic State Express drop her off in Wrightsville.

"Tired as I was," said Gabrielle, "I could not have passed through with a clear conscience. Jessica and I had been dear friends and had conducted a faithful correspondence for many years.

"I dropped off the express, being told that I could continue my journey home by taking the local train one hour later. At least that would give me a half-hour with her, I thought. The taxicab took me directly from the Station to Jessica's house—" her black eyes glanced over at the silent, lightless house next door, and away

—"and called for me in time to catch the local. I was with Jessica perhaps thirty-five minutes.

"She was happy to see me, although I thought she had something very troubling on her mind.

"As for me, I was overjoyed to find her convalescing from the pneumonia."

Gabrielle had promptly invited Jessica to visit with her. "Every woman can use a change of scene," she had said to her friend with a smile, "and you've just got over a serious malady. At *Mon Ciel* you may do absolutely nothing, Jessica—play the *grande dame, ma chérie,* and get well very fast. We shall be quite alone, you and I. And you may remain for as long as you can bear my company. What do you say? Come home with me now —or tomorrow!"

But Jessica had smiled faintly and thanked Gabrielle and said she could not—not just now, much as she would love to. Gabrielle had not pressed her, for Jessica had seemed distressed and abstracted; and after a few minutes more of nostalgic conversation and many embraces, Gabrielle had left to catch the one o'clock local and continue her homeward journey.

She had reached her Montreal house that night to find her manager waiting for her.

"It was maddening," she sighed. "The beast had flown up from New York to anticipate me, and he greeted me at *Mon Ciel* with an armful of tickets and contracts. An unexpected opportunity had arisen for me, he said, for a grand tour of South America and Europe. It was a chance I had hoped for for many years. I tried to plead my fatigue, but he was inexorable.

"In short, I had no time even to unpack. He flew me back that very night to New York and set me on a plane for Florida. In Miami I changed planes and was on my way to South America. I had no time to breathe. And so I did not know that during my flight to another continent Jessica had died. And later, singing in South America, I knew nothing of her husband's arrest. By the time the trial was over, I was in Europe."

The singer paused to stare into the darkness.

"The letter," said Ellery gently.

She started "Oh, yes, the letter. It caught up with me months after I had left Montreal so hastily. Jessica had addressed it to me at *Mon Ciel,* naturally, knowing nothing of my tour. It was forwarded by a stupid servant to the wrong address in South America, and it kept following me throughout South America and Europe—it did not catch up with me until I was singing in Prague. Even then I knew nothing of Jessica's death. I intended to reply to her letter at once, to explain my unexpected departure; but I was so busy in those days, and a whole week passed. In that week I learned the news."

"How?" asked Prosecutor Hendrix crossly.

"By chance I picked up a copy of the *Paris Herald* and there I read of the little *cause célèbre* of Wrightsville—how Bayard Fox had 'just' been convicted of the murder of his wife, Jessica Fox. It was a small item, undetailed—it did not give the dates, or even the method of the crime, merely a few lines. So I made no connection between my visit to Wrightsville and Jessica's death. And knowing that Jessica was dead and buried, I was so heartsick that I canceled the remainder of my Prague appearance. I did not sing again until Vienna. The Opera House."

Her eyes brooded over the past.

"Of course, I did not write; to whom should I write? And after that . . . But I kept Jessica's letter. I have kept it through all these years, through everything that has happened . . . as a memory of my friend."

She took a stained and creased linen envelope from her bag and handed it to Ellery. He turned on another porch light and examined it avidly. Over his shoulders, Prosecutor Hendrix and Chief Dakin examined it, too.

"After that," murmured Gabrielle Bonnaire, "the deluge."

"What do you mean, Miss Bonnaire?" asked Linda, torn between the letter and the fascinating woman.

The singer shrugged. "It is not pretty for a nice young girl like you to hear. Let it be."

"The Nazis?" asked Captain Fox.

Her dark eyes swept over him. "I came recently to my home in Canada, Captain Fox, fresh from a German concentration camp. They do not like the arts, those Germans, except for paintings of fat women. . . . I was one of the fortunate ones. I escaped. I have been in Montreal only a short time. It is so peaceful there."

"But you'll go back to the concert stage, won't you, Miss Bonnaire?" asked Linda. "When you've rested?"

Gabrielle smiled. "To play the piano, perhaps?"

"Piano? I don't understand—"

"The Nazi surgeons performed a slight operation on my throat," said the singer. "They thought it was a big joke."

Prosecutor Hendrix cleared his throat. "Well, we're . . . awfully grateful, Miss Bonnaire. Making this special trip, I mean—" She did not reply. He turned to Ellery abruptly and said: "Let's get on with this, Queen."

But Ellery was looking at the singer. "I'm sorry, Miss Bonnaire. If you'd told me—"

"It does not matter, Mr. Queen. Please do not think of me."

"Thank you," he said in a low voice. He tapped the envelope, addressing the others. "This is the letter Dr. Willoughby said Jessica was writing when he called to see her the day after the grape juice episode—the morning of the day she died. She gave it to the doctor to mail, you'll recall, along with some other letters—bills and things. I imagine Willoughby didn't even glance at the envelope—simply dropped all the letters into the nearest mailbox."

"It's the letter, all right," said Chief Dakin. "Her date on it and the postmark agree."

Ellery nodded. "Let me read it to you," he said to the silent group. "We all ought to know what Jessica Fox wrote to her best friend on the very morning of the day she died."

He read quickly:—

Dearest Gabrielle!!—

I suppose you won't expect to be hearing from me so soon after your visit, but I simply must write. In the first place, only a few minutes after your taxi left yesterday I got terribly sick again—a relapse, Dr. Willoughby says—he feels badly about having let me get out of bed so "soon" after the pneumonia, though heaven knows I spent lifetimes in that bed upstairs! It's unquestionably caused by the excitement of my getting up—and something else I haven't told *anyone* about. You know what worry and aggravation will do to one. . . .

Gabrielle darling, I've thought it over and I've changed my mind. Would you think me perfectly awful if I accepted your sweet invitation to come visit you at *Mon Ciel* after I turned you down yesterday? I'd like to spend a few weeks with you, if you'll have me. I can arrange it easily enough—Davy stops school soon and he's going to camp for the summer, so I won't have him to worry about, and as for Bayard—well, my husband is part of my "problem" and besides he's been saying I ought to get away somewhere for a rest, where I won't have the house and family to worry me. . . .

Oh darling I've had the most terrible problem! When I spoke to you yesterday, I hadn't made up my mind what to do—that's why I refused your invitation. But getting sick so suddenly after you left—I had lots of time to think hard last night—and somehow I saw things in a clearer light, and I knew there was only one thing I could do about it—my "problem," I mean. But before I do it, I do want you to hear what I've decided, and why, and see if out of your stock of worldly wisdom—you know how I admire you as a *woman,* Gabrielle!—you don't agree that I'm doing the only thing possible. I suppose this is weak of me, and I suppose if you say I've decided the wrong way I'll *still* do it, but . . . O Gabrielle, I do hope you'll give me the advice I want to hear!

My doctor's just come in and he'll mail this for me

on his way back to his office, so you ought to get it to-morrow. Could you write, or better, wire me that I may come? Gabrielle, I'm *counting* on you.

All my love,
JESSICA

"Of course," said Gabrielle Bonnaire to the darkness beyond the porch, "I had no idea what her problem was. I have often thought about it."

"She'd decided," said Emily Fox.

Emily glanced from her husband to her brother-in-law, and back to her husband, and then straight out at the invisible Hill road.

Gabrielle Bonnaire followed the direction of Emily's glances. And then she looked sad, and wise.

"It doesn't matter, Emily," said Talbot huskily. "Not now it doesn't, Emily—"

"I'm all right, Talbot."

"We'll never know how Jessica decided," Talbot mumbled, "and maybe that's best."

And Bayard nodded and said: "Yes, maybe it is, Tal."

And after a moment Emily nodded, too.

But Ellery was on his feet, his lean face turned towards the ravaged face of Gabrielle Bonnaire.

"Miss Bonnaire, only fate kept you from settling this case twelve years ago," he said swiftly. "Now you're here, and very serious matters hang on your answers. We've deduced that during your visit to Jessica—your thirty-five-minute visit—you drank some grape juice from a purple-glass pitcher which was standing on the coffee table before Jessica's sofa. Tell me—is that true? *Did you drink some of the grape juice from that pitcher?*"

Gabrielle Bonnaire stared. "Oh, yes."

Prosecutor Hendrix choked.

"Could you give us the details?" murmured Ellery. His eyes were dancing.

Gabrielle nodded. "As we sat there talking, Jessica asked me if I wouldn't have some grape juice—she indicated the purple pitcher and said her husband had prepared it for her just before leaving the house. She had had one glass, she said, and it had stimulated her. I said yes, I would, and Jessica began to rise from the sofa. 'I'll get you a clean glass, Gabrielle,' she said.

"But I forced her back on the sofa. 'You will do nothing of the sort,' I said. 'Where are your glasses kept?' Jessica laughed and told me how to find her kitchen. I went there and took a purple glass of the same set from the cabinet and brought it back to the living room. Jessica poured some of the grape juice for me—"

"Out of the pitcher," Ellery interjected quickly.

"But yes, Mr. Queen."

"And you drank it? How much of it?"

The singer shrugged. "She had poured a full glass. I drank it all."

They were staring at her as if she were a ghost.

"But why didn't we find that glass?" muttered Dakin.

"The one I drank from?" Gabrielle Bonnaire laughed. "Why, just before I left the house I returned to the kitchen for a drink of water. I took my glass with me, rinsed it at the sink, drank some water, and then—" she shrugged—"a woman is always domestic, no?—I washed the glass and wiped it and put it back into the cabinet."

Ellery drew a long breath. And now he said: "Miss Bonnaire, you drank a full glass of grape juice from that pitcher. *Did it make you ill?*"

"Ill?" Her eyes widened.

"Yes, Miss Bonnaire. You went immediately to the Station and caught the one-o'clock. Were you ill on the train—en route to Montreal?"

"But no."

"Were you sick to your stomach when you got home?"

"No . . ."

"Did you experience any peculiarity in your heart action, Miss Bonnaire?"

"My heart? But certainly not!"

"Were you, in fact, otherwise than in perfect health

for, say, forty-eight hours after you drank the grape juice Jessica had poured for you from the purple pitcher?"

"Certainly not, Mr. Queen. Why should I have been?"

"Because," cried Ellery, "a man went to prison for life through the contents of that pitcher." He strode over to where Davy was sitting close to Linda. Davy stared up at him, paper-cheeked. "Listen to me, Davy," said Ellery. "I want you to understand clearly, and exactly, what I say now. Have you followed the facts so far?"

"Yes. Sure I have, Mr. Queen."

"Your mother drank her glassful *before* Miss Bonnaire's arrival—she told that to Miss Bonnaire, and it agrees with your father's testimony. Or, to put it conversely, Miss Bonnaire drank *her* glassful *after your mother drank hers*. But Miss Bonnaire's drink came from the same pitcher, Davy—*it was part of the same grape juice.*"

Davy jumped up. "But Miss Bonnaire says she didn't get sick from her drink, Mr. Queen!"

"Correct, Davy. Miss Bonnaire experienced no ill effects of any kind after sampling the contents of that pitcher. *Davy, the contents of that pitcher were therefore not poisoned.* Do you follow that? Do you?"

"Do I!" shouted Davy.

"The grape juice in the pitcher could not have contained digitalis—or any other toxic substance—as Miss Bonnaire's testimony on the state of her health after drinking establishes. Yet the State convicted your father of your mother's murder on the ground that the drug must have been administered to her *through that pitcher of grape juice,* and the further ground that your father was the only person who could possibly have put the drug *into* that pitcher. You see that?"

"See it!" Davy choked. "Dad, they were wrong. Garback, Dakin, the Jury, the Judge—Dad, they were all wrong! The grape juice in the pitcher wasn't poisoned —*so you never poisoned it!* You're innocent—the way you've claimed all these years! You're not a killer at all!"

And Captain Fox ran to his father to pound the frail shoulders, jumping up and down on the porch like a wild man.

Bayard sat numbly under his son's blows, staring at Ellery.

Linda was crying and laughing, hugging Emily and Talbot, who seemed dazed.

And Detective Howie was sitting there with his lips parted, like a caught fish.

He, too, was staring at Ellery.

"I'll be damned," he said. "He cracked it. He cracked it!"

22.   The Guilty Fox

GABRIELLE BONNAIRE REPEATED her statement officially that night before a stenographer in the Prosecutor's office.

When she had signed it, she said: "I will gladly make the statement again in person, either in a court or to other authorities. Please call upon me at any time."

Chief Dakin gave her a police escort to Upham House, where she was to spend the night.

"It's staggering," grumbled Prosecutor Hendrix to Ellery when the ugly woman had left. "It puts us in a miserable spot. Fox can certainly insist on a new trial, Queen—the Bonnaire woman's testimony kicks the old circumstantial case into the middle of the next county. And he's bound to get off. Twelve years in prison!"

"Maybe it would be a lot easier on everybody," suggested Chief of Police Dakin, "if you placed the facts before the Governor, Phil, and got Mr. Fox a pardon and some sort of public exoneration."

"Yes, yes. And a lot less embarrassing. The Governor'll do it on my recommendation. Particularly since the prisoner is the father of the big Wrightsville hero." Hendrix glanced shamefacedly at Bayard. "But of course—just a pardon—"

"I don't want to embarrass anybody, Mr. Hendrix," Bayard said slowly. "Or go through another trial." He shuddered a little. "I'll agree to a pardon."

"Well." The Prosecutor was relieved. "That makes it cosier all around. Mighty handsome of you, Fox—Mr. Fox. Of course, you're still in the custody of my office, and don't forget it. But under the circumstances—" He waved handsomely. "Go on home, Mr. Fox, and God bless you."

"Without Howie," said Ellery Queen.

Hendrix colored. "Oh, yes, yes, of course. Without Howie."

Ellery was tucking shirts into his suitcase the next morning when there was a light tap on his door.

"Come in," he called.

It was Bayard Fox.

"Oh. Morning, Bayard. I was just packing."

Bayard shut the door. "Yes, Davy told me you were leaving today, Mr. Queen."

"Dakin's driving me over to Slocum to catch the one-five express to New York."

"Mr. Queen." Bayard hesitated. "I tried to see you last night, after that business in the Prosecutor's office, but you'd disappeared—"

"I've got to get back to New York, but I couldn't leave without spending a little time with some friends of mine here. The Wrights and the Bradfords. I had a few hours with them, anyway. Didn't get back till three in the morning."

"Well, I—" Bayard hesitated again.

"Now see here," said Ellery grumpily, "if you're trying to thank me, and all that—"

"Thanks."

Ellery looked at him. And after a moment, in silence, he gripped the hand Bayard was holding out.

Then Davy's father sat down in a rocker and took out his handkerchief to blow his nose mightily, while Ellery returned to his suitcase.

"Any plans?" asked Ellery.

"Plans?" Bayard looked out the window at the lawn, and the Hill, and Wrightsville. "Well, just to walk around the town. Chew the fat with old Phinny Baker at the *Record*. Drop into Al Brown's for an ice-cream soda. Go over to the shop—"

"You're going back into the business when all the legal details are settled?"

"Tal wants me to."

"You may find it tough, Bayard," murmured Ellery. "After twelve years . . . away."

Bayard stuck his chin out, flushing. "This is my town," he said.

"Good man," Ellery chuckled. And then he said: "But you didn't drop in here just for chit-chat."

"No."

Ellery looked at him again.

"Who murdered my wife?" asked Bayard. He asked it very quietly.

Before Ellery could answer, there was another knock on the door. Ellery opened it and grinned.

"Well, well. The whole Fox tribe."

It was Linda and Davy, and Talbot and Emily. Their faces were solemn.

It was Captain Fox who acted as spokesman.

"Mr. Queen, we don't have to tell you—"

"Exactly. But come in anyway." They came in, gravely, and Bayard rose to stand beside his son. "How do you feel now, Captain?"

"Swell."

"The itchy shakes?"

"Gone with the wind."

"You ought to spend the rest of your life kissing the hem of Linda's dress. The one with the deepest hem."

"I'm going to."

And Linda threw her arms around Ellery and kissed him. "I'm so gosh-darned delirious I . . . Now Davy, don't look jealous!"

"Who's looking jealous? Kiss him again, Linny!"

So they all laughed, but their laughter died very suddenly, and then they were silent.

Ellery surveyed them critically.

Talbot scuffed the rug. "Mr. Queen," he muttered, "it's imposing on you after all you've done, and all that . . . but Davy and Linny and Emily and I—we've been talking things over—"

"And you want to know who poisoned Jessica, if Bayard didn't."

"Yes!" They flashed that at him in unison.

"The answer," said Ellery, "is—no one."

Five pairs of eyes reflected shock.

"It's very simple," said Ellery. "Jessica didn't have anything but that single glass of grape juice the morning she took sick. We've already shown that the liquid in the pitcher was not poisoned. Yet it was by drinking the juice poured into her glass *from* the pitcher that Jessica was poisoned. There's only one possible explanation: it was the *glass* that was poisoned, the glass Jessica drank from. *The digitalis had been dropped into that glass while it was empty.*

"Who handled that glass? Think back. It was Jessica who took it down from the kitchen shelf after the one Bayard had brought her smashed in the living room. It was Jessica who carried that glass from the kitchen back to the living room where the pitcher of grape juice had been left. It was Jessica who held out that glass to Bayard to be filled, and who drank from it. *Jessica throughout.* Therefore—Jessica is the only one who could have dropped the digitalis into the glass."

"Jessica," whispered Emily. "Herself!"

"But she couldn't have," said Bayard Fox, frowning.

"Didn't I tell you and the Court she couldn't have? I'd have seen it if she had, Mr. Queen. She couldn't have dropped *anything* into it without my seeing! I was with her all the time."

Ellery shook his head. "You're mistaken, Bayard. Logic says the poison *must* have been dropped into the glass, now that the pitcher's been eliminated; logic says the only person who could have dropped poison into the glass was Jessica herself; therefore logically she did so."

"But how? When?"

"Possibly when you threw the pieces of the broken glass into the kitchen garbage pail. Possibly at the moment she reached for the glass in the kitchen cabinet. I don't know. But the facts say she did it, right under your eyes."

"Then—" Davy's eyes were awed—"My mother committed suicide, Mr. Queen?"

"The only possible solution."

"But why?" cried Linda.

"Linda, Davy's mother was faced with an impossible dilemma. If she left Bayard to marry Talbot, it meant the breaking up of two homes, scandal, losing her young son. If she remained with her husband, it meant living out the rest of her life secretly pining for another man. She'd been very ill. She was in a weakened state physically and emotionally. Suicide must have seemed to her the way out. Don't blame her too much, Davy," said Ellery gently. "Or you, Bayard. Or you, Talbot. Or, most of all, you, Emily. My advise to you all is—forget the whole thing. That's what Jessica would want you to do, after the misery and tragedy and injustice her hysterical act caused."

When they had left his room, Ellery lit another cigaret and blew a long, long streamer of smoke.

That's that, he thought. The hardest part of a hard business. And he made for his suitcase again.

But he did not reach it. A very soft knock on his door stopped him where he was.

The knocker did not wait for Ellery's invitation. The

door was opened without sound, quickly, and it was closed the same way.

It was Bayard Fox again.

But this time the frail man set his back against Ellery's door and said, very grimly: "Now suppose you tell me the *truth*, Mr. Queen.

"Because it won't wash," Bayard went on steadily. He spoke in low tones, as if he did not wish anyone to overhear. "Jessie didn't commit suicide, and you know it."

Ellery blinked.

"I understand why you pinned it on my wife just now. You had to satisfy Davy—yes, and Linda, and Talbot and Emily. And they are satisfied—they're all chattering away downstairs making plans and being very happy. But Jessie was my wife, Mr. Queen. I knew her better than anybody. It doesn't wash."

"I'm afraid," said Ellery carefully, "I don't quite grasp what's bothering you, Bayard."

"The letter she wrote to Gabrielle Bonnaire the day she died," said Bayard doggedly. "What did she tell her friend—the day after you claim she tried to poison herself? She wrote that she'd had a 'relapse.' She said her sudden attack of sickness was caused by 'excitement' and worry and aggravation. *She asked Miss Bonnaire to let her come to Montreal for a visit of several weeks.* Does that sound like a woman who'd just taken poison? And not only that! In the letter she wrote that she'd definitely made up her mind what to do. Of course she meant as between my brother Talbot and me."

"Not necessarily," said Ellery. "She might have meant suicide by what she 'had to do.'"

"So she wants to visit Gabrielle for 'advice'?" cried Bayard. "Advice? Advice as to committing suicide? Whoever heard of suicides asking for advice, Mr. Queen! No, sir! When Jessie wrote that letter to her friend she had no more idea of suicide than I have right now. Suicide was the furthest thing from her mind, and you know it."

"Suppose," said Ellery slowly, "in a moment of weakness she *had* taken poison the day before, Bayard, but afterward regretted it. That often happens with would-be suicides. So that, finding herself still alive the following day and apparently saved from the consequences of her own impulsive act, Jessica saw how foolish she had been and wrote the letter to Gabrielle Bonnaire as if she had never attempted suicide at all. As a matter of fact, that's the explanation I gave to Hendrix and Dakin last night. And it satisfied them."

"Well, it doesn't satisfy me," said Bayard Fox stubbornly. "Because if *that's* your answer, then I ask you again: When did she get a chance to drop the poison into the tumbler? I tell you she didn't, Mr. Queen! She didn't drop *anything* into that tumbler. Your solution is wrong—every bit of it. My wife didn't commit suicide and she didn't try to commit suicide. She was murdered, and I want to know who murdered her."

Ellery looked at Bayard for a long time.

Then he sighed, took the frail man by the arm, led him to a chair, and retraced his steps to lock the bedroom door.

Bayard sat waiting on the edge of the chair.

Ellery turned around and said: "Of course you're right, Bayard. Your wife did not commit suicide."

"Who did it?" demanded Davy's father.

"Don't *you* know?"

"Don't *I* know?" Bayard grew angry. "You mean you still think *I* poisoned her? Don't tell me you went through all that stuff about Jessie's committing suicide just to save Davy and Linda from knowing that I *was* guilty!"

"No, Bayard, you didn't poison your wife."

"Then who in God's name did, Mr. Queen? The digitalis must have been in the glass she drank from, as you've proved. If Jessie didn't commit suicide, then she didn't drop the poison into her glass. And yet she was the only one who touched the glass. That's what I can't understand, Mr. Queen. How do you explain it?"

Ellery sat down on the bed. "I was hoping I wouldn't have to explain at all, Bayard. . . . You're sure you want me to tell you?"

"I can't rest till I know, Mr. Queen."

Ellery sighed. "Well, the poison must have been in the glass, and only your wife handled it—from the moment she took it off the shelf. Yet she didn't drop the poison in. The gimmick is concealed right there. Let's go back a bit. Where had Jessica got that glass?"

"From the kitchen cabinet."

"It was one of a set in that cabinet."

"Yes."

"Jessica opened the cabinet door, reached up, and did —what?"

"Why, took down one of the purple glasses."

"*One* of the purple glasses—exactly. *A random selection.* No one in the world could have predicted which glass Jessica would select. In fact, no one in the world knew Jessica would break a glass and have to take another at all. She happened to pick that one—and in the glass when she took it from the shelf must have been the poison. So we have two facts: *The poison was in the glass before Jessica picked it out, and no human being could have known she would pick that glass.* The final conclusion, then, is that your wife was poisoned *by accident*, Bayard." Bayard blinked and blinked again. And again.

"Accident?" he repeated. "But . . . I mean, why didn't she *see* the poison? The grape juice wasn't poured in till after we walked back to the living room!"

"Remember," sighed Ellery, "the glass of that set is deep purple, Bayard—practically opaque. And any shadow of the digitalis at the bottom of the glass would seem to have been cast by the cut-glass grape pattern which covered the outer surface. The only way Jessica could have noticed the poison would have been if she'd looked *down into* the glass. Even then the drug, which is dark green in color, would be virtually invisible against the dark purple of the glass. As it was, she didn't happen to look. Since the glass stood on the shelf in the cabinet among other glassware, she naturally assumed it was clean and it was empty."

Bayard groaned:"And as it happened, I didn't look

either. I poured the grape juice right over the digitalis like a fool!"

"It was a combination of unfortunate circumstances, Bayard."

"But—you say it was an accident. How could digitalis —almost an ounce of it!—have got into one of the purple iced-drink glasses . . . by *accident*?"

"The crucial question." Ellery frowned at the cherry tree outside one of the two bedroom windows. "I got the answer to that question when we solved—" he smiled— "what we might call 'The Mystery of the Missing Aspirins.' "

Bayard looked blank.

"You recall that first bottle of 100 aspirin tablets, which Alvin Cain delivered the day before the poisoning, and which disappeared?" Bayard nodded. "Where did we ultimately find that missing bottle of aspirins?"

"In the attic, among the rubbish."

"Or more precisely," said Ellery, "in Davy's boyhood chemistry set. But where had you put the bottle of aspirins when it was orginally delivered, Bayard?"

"In the bathroom medicine chest."

"In other words, your son Davy had raided the medicine chest for 'chemicals'—that is, what his ten-year-old mind considered chemicals. Can't you see a boy of ten —a bright, quick, high-spirited, inquisitive boy like Davy—dissolving milk of magnesia tablets, or stomach pills, or aspirins in a chemistry-set test tube, or a house glass, mixing it with other 'chemicals,' and thinking he has performed a momentous experiment in research chemistry?"

"Well, it's true that Davy went through quite a phase with that chemical set of his," said Bayard, bewildered. "Most kids do. But what of it, Mr. Queen?"

"Nothing so far as the aspirin is concerned. But the incident has enormous significance in another direction, Bayard. For if Davy sneaked a bottle of aspirins for his 'experiments,' *then he must have sneaked other things, too.*"

"Other things?" said Bayard faintly. "You mean—"

"I mean," said Ellery through his teeth, "that a one-ounce bottle of tincture of digitalis stood in that same upstairs medicine chest, a nearly full bottle. It was no longer being used—your wife had stopped taking her three-times-daily dose of fifteen drops some time before. So Davy figured its absence wouldn't be noticed.

"Davy took that bottle of digitalis, Bayard, and during one of his world-shaking ten-year-old boy's experiments, he also took one of the purple glasses, poured the entire contents of the digitalis bottle into the glass, performed some meaningless monkeyshines with it . . . and when he returned the glass to the kitchen cabinet—perhaps under pressure, when you were near by and might discover what he'd been up to—*he simply forgot to pour its deadly contents out.*

"He set that purple glass, Bayard, with its contents of digitalis, back on the shelf of the cabinet with the purple pitcher and the rest of the glasses, and promptly forgot about it, as children will. And that glass with the digitalis in it simply stood on the shelf, perhaps for days—remember, Jessica wasn't able to do her own housework; you were doing it for her, and no man is as thorough as a woman in these matters—the glass stood on the shelf waiting for someone to pick it up and use it. Pure chance dictated your avoiding that glass and taking down two clean ones in the course of preparing the pitcher of grape juice—one for measuring, the other for Jessica which she dropped and smashed. Pure chance dictated that when Jessica broke the second glass, she should return to the kitchen with you and, with her own hands, take down the third glass with its deadly contents.

"In one sense, Bayard, pure chance murdered your wife.

"But in another, we must conclude that Davy, a ten-year-old boy, killed his mother . . . *and never knew it.*"

"Davy," said Bayard. "Davy."

"Obviously," said Ellery with a scowl, "the child didn't mean any harm. He had no idea of what he was doing; and when his mother became ill, and then died, no doubt details were kept from him—the hush-hush policy towards a child which would be natural under the circumstances; in fact, Davy said as much—so that he did not connect her death with his own careless act. And years later, when he did get to know the details, he had long since forgotten his 'experiment' with the stolen digitalis and his hurried restoration of the purple glass— with its poisonous contents—to its usual place in the kitchen cabinet."

"Davy made her die," muttered Bayard. "Davy."

"Now you see," said Ellery with a shrug, "why I tried to keep the truth a secret, Bayard. You know what happened to Davy when he thought he was the son of a murderer. Suppose he were now told that *he's* the murderer! In his emotionally disturbed state, Davy wouldn't be able to rationalize away his personal responsibility. It wouldn't do much good to tell him that, while he caused his mother's death in effect, morally he was innocent, since the whole affair was an accident."

"No," said Bayard, getting up slowly. "No, it wouldn't. He mustn't ever know, Mr. Queen. He mustn't ever find out."

"Nor must Linda."

"Or anyone else."

"That's right. If it got to him, the boy's life would be ruined—and so would Linda's. The world would say it was an accident, but that wouldn't save Davy's sanity."

Bayard turned aside as if seeking something beyond the walls and the windows. And suddenly Ellery saw that frailty may have strength, too.

"That sort of gives me a real job for what's left of my life, doesn't it?" said Bayard. He was smiling. "Keeping my boy from ever knowing."

"It's a tremendous responsibility."

"I guess that's what fathers are for, Mr. Queen."

When Bayard had left the room, Ellery resumed his packing; but all at once it became tiresome, and he lit a cigaret and went over to a window to stare out.

Jessica Fox buried in Twin Hill Cemetery . . . Alvin

Cain pacing the floor of his cell in the loftiest part of the County Courthouse building . . . Talbot and Emily mending the torn fabric of their lives . . . Davy and Linda and the life that was beginning . . . an emancipated Bayard facing Wrightsville with the strength of his secret to bolster him . . .

It all seemed orderly now, somehow, and just right.

Ellery was about to return to his valise when he spied a figure scurrying up the Hill toward the Talbot and Bayard Fox properties—a female, juiceless figure with a destination.

Emmeline DuPré.

Ellery grinned as he ducked behind the curtain.

You're wasting your valuable time, Emmy my girl, he thought with a chuckle. This is one secret you—and Wrightsville—won't ever smell out.